THE ONE HUNDRED YEARS OF LENNI AND MARGOT

www.**penguin**.co.uk

THE ONE HUNDRED YEARS OF LENNI AND MARGOT

Marianne Cronin

doubleday

TRANSWORLD PUBLISHERS
Penguin Random House, One Embassy Gardens, 8 Viaduct Gardens,
London SW11 7BW
www.penguin.co.uk

Transworld is part of the Penguin Random House group of companies
whose addresses can be found at global.penguinrandomhouse.com

Penguin
Random House
UK

First published in Great Britain in 2020 by Doubleday
an imprint of Transworld Publishers

Lyrics from 'How Deep Is The Ocean' on p. 81 written by Irving Berlin.
Lyrics from 'Starry Eyed' on p. 168 written by Earl Shuman and Mort Garson.
Lyrics from 'I Fought The Law' on p.191 written by Sonny Curtis.
Poetry extract on p.268 from 'The Old Astronomer to His Pupil' by Sarah Williams.

Every effort has been made to obtain the necessary permissions with
reference to copyright material, both illustrative and quoted. We apologize
for any omissions in this respect and will be pleased to make the
appropriate acknowledgements in any future edition.

A CIP catalogue record for this book is available from the British Library.

ISBNs 9780857527196 (hb)
9780857527202 (tpb)

Typeset in 11/15.5 pt Sabon Next LT Pro
by Integra Software Services Pvt. Ltd, Pondicherry

Printed and bound in Great Britain by Clays Ltd, Elcograf S.p.A.

Penguin Random House is committed to a sustainable
future for our business, our readers and our planet. This book
is made from Forest Stewardship Council® certified paper.

1 3 5 7 9 10 8 6 4 2

PART ONE

Lenni

WHEN PEOPLE SAY 'terminal', I think of the airport.

I picture a wide check-in area with a high ceiling and glass walls, the staff in matching uniforms waiting to take my name and flight information, waiting to ask me if I packed my bags myself, if I'm travelling alone.

I imagine the blank faces of passengers checking screens, families hugging one another with promises that this won't be the last time. And I picture myself among them, my suitcase wheeling behind me so effortlessly on the highly polished floor that I might be floating as I check the screen for my destination.

I have to drag myself out of there and remember that that is not the type of terminal meant for me.

They've started to say 'life-limiting' instead now. 'Children and young people with life-limiting conditions . . .'

The nurse says it gently as she explains that the hospital has started to offer a counselling service for young patients whose conditions are 'terminal'. She falters, flushing red. 'Sorry, I meant *life-limiting*.' Would I like to sign up? I could have the counsellor come to my bed, or I could go to the special counselling room for teenagers. They have a TV in there now. The options seem endless, but the term is not new to me. I have spent many days at the airport. Years.

And still, I have not flown away.

I pause, watching the upside-down rubber watch pinned to her breast pocket. It swings as she breathes.

'Would you like me to put your name down? The counsellor, Dawn, she really is lovely.'

'Thank you, but no. I have my own form of therapy going on right now.'

She frowns and tilts her head to the side. 'You do?'

Lenni and the Priest

I WENT TO meet God because it's one of the only things I can do here. People say that when you die, it's because God is calling you back to him, so I thought I'd get the introduction over and done with ahead of time. Also, I'd heard that the staff are legally obliged to let you go to the hospital chapel if you have religious beliefs, and I wasn't going to pass up the opportunity to see a room I'd not yet been in *and* meet the Almighty in one go.

A nurse I'd never seen before, who had cherry red hair, linked her arm through mine and walked me down the corridors of the dead and the dying. I devoured every new sight, every new smell, every pair of mismatched pyjamas that passed me.

I suppose you could say that my relationship with God is complicated. As far as I understand it, he's like a cosmic wishing well. I've asked for stuff a couple of times, and some of those times he's come up with the goods. Other times there's been silence. Or, as I have begun to think lately, maybe all the times I *thought* God was being silent, he was quietly depositing more nonsense into my body, a kind of secret 'F-you' for daring to challenge him, only to be discovered many years later. Buried treasure for me to find.

When we reached the chapel doors, I was unimpressed. I'd expected an elegant Gothic archway, but instead I came up

5

against a pair of heavy wooden doors with square frosted windows. I wondered why God would need his windows frosted. What's he up to in there?

Into the silence behind the doors the new nurse and I stumbled.

'Well,' he said, 'hello!'

He must have been about sixty, wearing a black shirt and trousers and a white dog collar. And he looked like he couldn't have been happier than he was at that moment.

I saluted. 'Your honour.'

'This is Lenni . . . Peters?' The new nurse turned to me for clarification.

'Pettersson.'

She let go of my arm and added gently, 'She's from the *May Ward.*'

It was the kindest way for her to say it. I suppose she felt she ought to warn him, because he looked as excited as a child on Christmas morning receiving a train set wrapped in a big bow, when in reality, the gift she was presenting him with was broken. He could get attached if he wanted, but the wheels were already coming off and the whole thing wasn't likely to see another Christmas.

I took my drip tube, which was attached to my drip wheelie thing, and walked towards him.

'I'll be back in an hour,' the new nurse told me, and then she said something else, but I wasn't listening. Instead, I was staring up, where the light shone in and the glow of every shade of pink and purple imaginable was striking my irises.

'Do you like the window?' he asked.

6

A cross of brown glass behind the altar was illuminating the whole chapel. Radiating from around the cross were jagged pieces of glass in violet, plum, fuchsia and rose.

The whole window seemed like it was on fire. The light scattered over the carpet and the pews and across our bodies.

He waited patiently beside me, until I was ready to turn to him.

'It's nice to meet you, Lenni,' he said. 'I'm Arthur.' He shook my hand, and to his credit he didn't wince when his fingers touched the part where the drip burrows into my skin.

'Would you like to sit?' he asked, gesturing to the rows of empty pews. 'It's very nice to meet you.'

'You said.'

'Did I? Sorry.'

I wheeled my drip behind me and as I reached the pew, I tied my dressing gown more tightly around my waist. 'Can you tell God I'm sorry about my pyjamas?' I asked as I sat.

'You just told him. He's always listening,' Father Arthur said as he sat beside me. I looked up at the cross.

'So tell me, Lenni, what brings you to the chapel today?'

'I'm thinking about buying a second-hand BMW.'

He didn't know what to do with that, so he picked up the Bible from the pew beside him, thumbed through it without looking at the pages, and put it down again.

'I see you ... er, you like the window.'

I nodded.

There was a pause.

'Do you get a lunch break?'

'Sorry?'

'It's just, I was wondering whether you have to lock up the chapel and go to the canteen with everyone else, or if you can have your break in here?'

'I, um—'

'Only, it seems a bit cheeky to clock out for lunch if your whole day is basically clocked out.'

'Clocked out?'

'Well, sitting in an empty church is hardly a nose-to-the-grindstone job, is it?'

'It's not always this quiet, Lenni.'

I looked at him to check I hadn't hurt his feelings, but I couldn't tell.

'We have Mass on Saturdays and Sundays, we have Bible readings for the children on Wednesday afternoons, and I get more visitors than you might imagine. Hospitals are scary places; it's nice to be in a space where there are no doctors or nurses.'

I went back to studying the stained glass window.

'So, Lenni, is there a reason for your visit today?'

'Hospitals are scary places,' I said. 'It's nice to be in a space where there aren't any doctors or nurses.'

I think I heard him laugh.

'Would you like to be left alone?' he asked, but he didn't sound hurt.

'Not particularly.'

'Would you like to talk about anything specific?'

'Not particularly.'

Father Arthur sighed. 'Would you like to know about my lunch break?'

'Yes, please.'

'I take it at one until twenty past. I have egg and cress on white bread cut into small triangles, made for me by my housekeeper. I have a study through that door' – he pointed – 'and I take fifteen minutes to eat my sandwich and five to drink my tea. Then I come back out. But the chapel is always open, even when I'm in my study.'

'Do they pay you for that?'

'Nobody pays me.'

'Then how do you afford all the egg and cress sandwiches?'

Father Arthur laughed.

We sat in silence for a while and then he started talking again. For a priest, he wasn't that comfortable with silence. I'd have thought the quiet would give God an opportunity to make himself known. But Father Arthur didn't seem to like it, so he and I talked about his housekeeper, Mrs Hill, and how she always sends him a postcard whenever she goes on holiday and then, when she returns, how she fishes them out of his 'in-tray' and sticks them on the fridge. We talked about how the bulbs are changed for the light behind the stained glass window (there's a secret passageway around the back). We talked about pyjamas. And despite how tired he looked, when the new nurse came to collect me, he told me that he hoped I would come back.

I think, however, he was surprised when I arrived the next afternoon in a fresh pair of pyjamas and now free of my IV. The head nurse, Jacky, wasn't thrilled about the idea of me going back a second day in a row, but I held her gaze and said in a small voice, 'It would mean a lot to me.' And who can say no to a dying child?

When Jacky called for a nurse to walk me down the corridors, it was the new nurse who turned up. The one with the cherry red hair, which clashed with her blue uniform like there was no tomorrow. She'd only been on the May Ward a matter of days and she was nervous, especially around the airport children, and desperate for someone to assure her she was doing a good job. As we made our way along the corridor towards the chapel, I commented on how excellent her chaperoning skills were. I think she liked that.

The chapel was empty again except for Father Arthur, who was sitting in a pew, wearing long white robes over his black suit and reading. Not the Bible, but an A4-sized book with cheap binding and a glossy laminated cover. When New Nurse opened the door and I followed gratefully through, Arthur didn't turn round right away. New Nurse let the door close behind us, and at the sound of the heavy thud he turned, put his glasses on and smiled.

'Pastor, um . . . Reverend?' New Nurse stumbled. 'She, um, Lenni asked if she could spend an hour here. Is that okay?'

Arthur closed the book in his lap.

'Certainly,' he said.

'Thank you, um, Vicar . . . ?' New Nurse said.

'Father,' I whispered. She grimaced, her face reddening – which clashed with her hair – and then she left without another word.

Father Arthur and I settled into the same pew. The colours in the stained glass were just as lovely as the day before.

'It's empty again today,' I said. It echoed.

Father Arthur said nothing.

'Did it used to be busy? You know, back when people were more religious?'

'It *is* busy,' he said.

I turned to him. 'We're the only ones here.'

Clearly, he was in denial.

'It's okay if you don't want to talk about it,' I said. 'It must be embarrassing. I mean, it's like you're throwing a party and nobody's turned up.'

'It is?'

'Yes. I mean, here you are, in your best white party dress with lovely grapes and things sewn onto it, and—'

'These are vestments. It's not a dress.'

'Vestments, then. Here you are, in your *party vestments*, you've got the table laid ready for lunch . . .'

'That's an altar, Lenni. And it's not lunch, it's the Eucharist. The bread of Christ.'

'What, he won't share?'

Father Arthur gave me a look.

'It's for the Sunday service. I don't eat the holy bread for lunch, and I don't eat my lunch at the altar.'

'Of course, because you have egg and cress in your office.'

'I do,' he said, glowing a little because I had remembered something about him.

'So, you've got everything ready for the party. There's music' – I pointed to the sad CD/cassette tape combo in the corner, beside which some CDs were neatly piled – 'and there's plenty of seating for everyone.' I pointed to the rows of empty pews. 'But nobody comes.'

'To my party?'

'Exactly. All day, every day, you are throwing a Jesus party and nobody's coming. It must feel horrible.'

'That's . . . um . . . Well, that's one way of thinking about it.'

'Sorry if I'm making it worse.'

'You're not making anything worse, but really, this isn't a party, Lenni. This is a place of worship.'

'Yes. No, I know that, but what I mean is that I get where you're coming from. I had a party once, when I was eight and I'd just moved to Glasgow from Sweden. My mum invited all the kids in my class, but hardly anyone came. Although, at that point my mum's English was patchy, so there's every chance they all went to the wrong place, holding presents and balloons and waiting for the party to start. At least that's what I told myself at the time.'

I paused.

'Go on,' he offered.

'So, when I was sitting there on the dining-room chairs that my mum had arranged into a circle, waiting for someone to turn up, I felt horrible.'

'I'm sorry to hear that,' he said.

'So, that's what I'm saying to you. I know how much it hurts when nobody comes to your party. I just wanted to say I'm sorry. I just don't think you should deny it. You can't fix a problem until you've faced it head on.'

'But it *is* busy, Lenni. It's busy because you are here. It is busy with the spirit of the *Lord*.'

I gave him a look.

He shuffled in the pew. 'And besides, a little solitude isn't to be laughed at. This may be a place of worship, but it's also a place of peace.' He glanced up at the stained glass. 'I like to be able to talk to patients one-to-one; it means I can pay them my full attention, and don't take this the wrong way, Lenni, but I think you might be a person the Lord would like me to pay my full attention to.'

I laughed at that.

'I thought about you at lunch time,' I said. 'Did you have egg and cress again today?'

'I did.'

'And?'

'Lovely, as always.'

'And Mrs . . . ?'

'Hill, Mrs Hill.'

'Did you tell Mrs Hill about our conversation?'

'I didn't. Everything you say here is confidential. That's why people like coming so much. They can speak their minds and not worry who will find out later.'

'So this is confession then?'

'No, although if you wish to go to confession, I would gladly help you arrange it.'

'If it isn't confession, then what is it?'

'It's whatever you want it to be. This chapel is here to be whatever you need it to be.'

I took in the empty rows of pews, the electronic piano draped in a beige dust cover, the noticeboard with a picture of Jesus pinned to it. What would I want this place to be if it could be anything?

'I would like it to be a place of answers.'

'It can be.'

'Can it? Can religion ever really answer a question?'

'Lenni, the Bible teaches us that Christ can guide you to the answer to *every* question.'

'But can it answer an actual question? Honestly? Can you answer me a question without telling me that life is a mystery, or that everything is God's plan, or that the answers I seek will come with time?'

'Why don't you tell me your question, and we will work together to see how God can help us find an answer?'

I leant back in the pew and it creaked. The echo reverberated around the room.

'Why am I dying?'

Lenni and the Question

I DIDN'T LOOK at Father Arthur when I asked him the question; instead I looked at the cross. I heard him breathe out slowly. I kept thinking he was going to answer, but he just carried on breathing. I considered that perhaps he didn't know I was dying. But, I rationalized, the nurse had told him I came from the May Ward, and nobody on the May Ward is looking forward to a long and happy life.

'Lenni,' he said gently after a while, 'that question is bigger than all other questions.' He leant back and the pew creaked again. 'You know, it's funny, I get asked *why* more often than I get asked anything else. *Why* is always the hard one. I can do the *how* and the *what* and the *who*, but the *why*, that's the one I can't even pretend to know. When I first started doing this job, I used to try to answer it.'

'But you don't any more?'

'I don't think that answer is in my jurisdiction. It is only for Him to answer.' He pointed to the altar as though God might be crouching behind it, just out of sight, listening.

I gestured towards him, in a 'see, I told you so' kind of way.

'But that doesn't mean there is no answer,' he said quickly. 'It is just that the answer is with God.'

'Father Arthur ...'

'Yes, Lenni?'

15

'That's the biggest pile of crap I have ever heard. I'm dying here! And I have come to one of God's designated spokespeople with a really important question, and you refer me back to him? I tried him already, but I didn't get an answer.'

'Lenni, answers don't always come in the form of words. They can come in a variety of forms.'

'Well then, why did you say that this was a place of answers? Why not be honest and say to me, "Okay, well the biblical theories aren't watertight and we can't give you answers, but we do have a nice stained glass window"?'

'If you got an answer, what do you think it might be like?'

'Maybe God would tell me he's having me killed because I'm restless and annoying. Or maybe the real God is Vishnu, and he's hella pissed that I've never even tried to pray to him but kept wasting my time with your Christian God. Or maybe there is no God and there never was, and the whole universe is being controlled by a turtle who's massively out of his depth.'

'Would that make you feel any better?'

'Probably not.'

'Have you ever been asked a question you couldn't answer?' Father Arthur asked.

I had to admit, I was impressed at how calm he was. He really knew how to turn a question around. I was obviously not his first 'why am I dying' rant. Which, in a way, made me feel worse.

I shook my head.

'It's horrible, you know,' he continued, 'to have to tell people I don't have the answer they want. But that doesn't mean this isn't a place of answers – it's just that they might not be the answers you expect.'

'Tell me then, Father Arthur, shoot from the hip. What is the answer? Why am I dying?'

Arthur's soft eyes fixed on mine. 'Lenni, I—'

'No, just tell me. Please. Why am I dying?'

And just when I thought he was going to tell me that an honest answer was in breach of church protocol, he ran his hand over the grey stubble on his chin and said, 'Because you are.'

I must have frowned, or he must have regretted being tricked into saying something truthful, because he couldn't look at me. 'The answer I have, the only one I have,' he said, 'is that you are dying because you are dying. Not because of God's deciding to punish you and not because He is neglecting you, but simply because you are. It is a part of your story as much as you are.'

After a long pause, Arthur turned to me. 'Think of it this way. Why are you alive?'

'Because my parents had sex.'

'I didn't ask *how* you came to be alive, I asked *why*. Why do you exist at all? Why are you alive? What is your life for?'

'I don't know.'

'I think the same is true of dying. We can't know why you are dying in the same way that we can't know why you are living. Living and dying are both complete mysteries, and you can't know either until you have done both.'

'That's poetic. And ironic.' I rubbed at the spot on my hand where the cannula had been digging in the day before.

It had left behind an ache. 'Were you reading religious stuff when I came in?'

Arthur held up the book beside him. It was yellow with wire binding, tatty edges and bold letters – *The AA Road Atlas of Great Britain*.

'Were you looking for your flock?' I asked.

When New Nurse came to get me, I thought Arthur might fall to the ground and kiss her feet or run through the newly opened door screaming, but instead he waited patiently as I made my way to the door, handed me a pamphlet and said he hoped I would come again.

I don't know whether it was the impertinence of his refusal to shout at me, his reluctance to admit I was annoying him or the fact that the chapel was so nice and cool, but as I took his pamphlet, I knew that I would be back.

I left it for seven days. I thought I would give him long enough to presume that I probably wasn't coming back. Then, just as he settled into his lonely life inside his empty chapel, bam! There I was, tottering slowly towards him, my best pink pyjamas on and my next round of challenges to Christianity loaded and ready to fire.

This time, he must have spotted me coming down the corridor through those frosted windows, because he was holding the door open for me and saying, 'Hello, Lenni, I wondered when I'd be seeing you,' and just generally ruining my dramatic re-entrance for everyone.

'I was playing hard to get,' I told him.

He smiled at New Nurse. 'How long do I have the pleasure of Lenni's company today?'

'An hour,' – she smiled – 'Reverend.'

He didn't correct her, but instead held the door open as I rattled down the aisle. I chose a front-row seat this time, to get a better chance of God noticing me.

'May I?' Father Arthur asked and I nodded. He sat beside me.

'So, Lenni, how are you this morning?'

'Oh, not too bad, thank you. And yourself?'

'You aren't going to comment on how empty the chapel is?' He gestured around the room.

'Nope. I figure that the day when someone other than us is in here will be the day worth commenting on. I don't want to make you feel bad about what you do.'

'That's very kind of you.'

'Maybe you need someone to work on your PR?' I asked.

'My PR?'

'Yeah, you know, the marketing: posters and adverts and stuff. We need to get the word out. That way the pews will fill up and you might make a profit.'

'A profit?'

'Yeah, right now you can't possibly be breaking even.'

'I don't charge people to come to church, Lenni.'

'I know, but think how impressed God would be if you had a nice buzzing church and started making some money for him at the same time.'

He gave me an odd smile. I took in the smell of recently blown out candles, which made me feel that a birthday cake must have been lurking somewhere.

'Can I tell you a story?' I asked.

'Of course.' He clasped his hands together.

'When I was at school, I used to tag along with this group of girls on nights out in Glasgow. There was this really expensive night club that nobody could ever afford to go in. It never had a queue outside, but you could tell just from the black velvet ropes and the silver-painted doors that it would be special. It had two bouncers either side of the doors, despite the fact nobody ever seemed to go in and nobody seemed to come out. All we knew was that it cost seventy pounds to get in. We told ourselves it was too expensive, but any time we passed that club, we got more curious. We had to know why it was so expensive and what was on the other side. So we made a pact, saved up, and we took our fake IDs and we got in. And do you know what?'

'What?' he asked.

'It was a strip club.'

Father Arthur raised his eyebrows and then self-consciously lowered them, as though he were worried I might mistake his startled look for one of intrigue, or arousal.

'I'm not sure I understand the moral of the story,' he said carefully.

'What I'm saying is, it was the fact it was *so* expensive that made us think going inside would be worth it. If you charged a door fee, people might be intrigued. You could get bouncers too.'

Arthur shook his head. 'I keep telling you, Lenni, the chapel is well attended. I spend a lot of time speaking with patients and relatives. People often come in to see me, it's just that—'

'It's just that by coincidence I always happen to stop by when the people aren't here?'

Father Arthur looked up at the stained glass window, and I could almost hear his internal monologue, asking God for the strength to tolerate me. 'Did you think any further on what we talked about during your last visit?'

'A bit.'

'You asked me some good questions.'

'You gave me some unhelpful answers.'

There was a pause.

'Father Arthur, I was wondering whether you would do something for me?'

'What would you like me to do?'

'Can you tell me one truth, one cool, refreshing truth? No church spin, no fancy wording, just something you know to your core to be true, even if it hurts you, even if you would be fired if your bosses heard you say it to me.'

'My *bosses*, as you put it, are Jesus and the Lord.'

'Well, they certainly won't fire you – they love truth.'

I thought he would need more time to think of something true. I assumed he would need to contact a pope or a deacon and check whether he was allowed to dole out and administer the truth without any official guidelines. But just before New Nurse arrived, he turned to me awkwardly. Like someone who's about to give a gift when they're not at all sure that the recipient will like it.

'Are you going to tell me something true?' I asked.

'I am,' he said. 'Lenni, you said you wish that this could be a place of answers and . . . well, I wish it were a place of answers too. If I had the answers, I would give them.'

'I already knew that.'

'Then how about this?' he said. 'I really hoped you'd come back.'

*

When I made it back to my bed, New Nurse had left me a note: *Lenni, talk to Jacky – social service's*.

I corrected her grammar with the pencil she'd left and then headed over to the nurses' station. Jacky, the heron-haired head nurse, wasn't there. That's when something caught my eye.

Beside the nurses' station desk, the recycling trolley was awaiting the return of Paul the Porter. It's a big wheeled bin. It used to have the words 'mean machine' penned in permanent marker on the handle, but that's been painted over now. Paul's trolley is not usually something I would find interesting, but the interesting thing about it that day was the elderly lady who was hanging halfway out of the bin, rustling through its papery contents with both hands, her small purple-slippered feet barely touching the floor.

Seeming to have found whatever it was she was looking for, the old lady straightened up, her grey hair fluffy from the effort. She slipped an envelope into the pocket of her purple dressing gown.

The door to the office made a clunk as someone pulled on the handle. Jacky and Paul were coming out.

The old lady caught my eye. I got the feeling she didn't want to be seen doing what she had just done.

As Jacky and Paul the Porter emerged from the office, looking tired and bored respectively, I made a yelping sound.

They stared at me.

'Hey, Lenni!' Paul grinned.

'What is it, Lenni?' Jacky asked. The part of Jacky's face where she really should have had a beak was set into a flat line of irritation.

I didn't want them to take their eyes off me as, behind them, the purple lady climbed down from the edge of the bin and began her extremely slow getaway.

'I . . . there's a . . . spider,' I said. 'In the May Ward.'

Jacky rolled her eyes as though it were my fault.

'I'll get it for you, darlin',' Paul said, and they both walked off past me into the May Ward.

Now safely at the end of the corridor, pulling the envelope from her pocket, the old lady stopped and turned. Then she caught my eye and she winked.

To my great surprise, Paul actually managed to find a spider in the corner of the window at the end of the May Ward. I wondered if it was a biblical sign. Seek and ye shall find. He captured it in a plastic cup and held his hand over it and let us have a peek. I noticed that the tattoos on his knuckles spelled out the word 'free'. Seeing the spider, Jacky told me to *man up*, and that if I wanted to see a *real* spider I should hang out in her back garden in the summer time when she has barbecues. Apparently, the spiders that live beneath her wooden decking are so big that if you try to trap them with a pint glass, their legs stick out of the bottom and end up getting severed. I politely declined the invitation and made my way back to bed.

Father Arthur's latest pamphlet was lying on the pile of similarly tragic offerings on my bedside table. A different Jesus on each one. Concerned Jesus, Jesus with sheep, Jesus with a group of children, Jesus on a rock. Each more Jesus-y than the last.

I drew the curtain around my bed and got into my thinking position. Father Arthur said that he wished he could give people answers. I thought how frustrating it must be for him to be in a position where people constantly ask you questions you can never answer. Being a priest without any answers is like someone who can't swim being asked for swimming lessons. And he was clearly incredibly lonely. I knew and had always known that I would not find the answers to anything behind those heavy chapel doors. What I had found instead was someone who needed my help.

It took a couple of days to draw up my many-pronged plan to get more patients to visit the chapel. I'd make some eye-catching yet mysterious posters, maybe even get a spot of media attention. The hospital radio station could probably be coerced into giving the chapel a shout-out. Instead of focusing on religion, I would emphasize the therapeutic nature of my chats with Father Arthur, and perhaps as a side note I would mention how cool the chapel is. The other patients would like that, because it seems there is some law that says hospitals must be kept just above a comfortable temperature at all times. Just hot enough so that you're always a bit clammy. Not so hot that you can toast marshmallows.

New Nurse took me to the chapel, and to make sure Father Arthur was in a suitable mood for a marketing meeting, I peeped through the crack in the door. But he wasn't alone.

Father Arthur was standing in front of a man in an identical outfit – the white collar, the smart dark shirt and trousers. As he and Father Arthur shook hands, the man wrapped his other hand protectively around their union, as though he were keeping it sheltered from cold weather or a strong wind that might tear them apart and undo whatever agreement was being made.

The man had dark eyebrows and dark hair. It was hard to tell his age. He was smiling. Like a shark.

'Is there someone in there?' New Nurse asked.

'Yeah,' I whispered.

It was then that the ageless man made his way to the door.
I had just enough time to straighten up as the door opened to
reveal Arthur and the man, staring at me.

'Lenni, what a surprise!' Arthur said. 'How long have you
been waiting there?'

'You did it!' I said. 'You got someone in.'

'Sorry?' Arthur said.

'You've got another customer.' I turned to the ageless man.
'Hello, fellow friend of Jesus, or Father Arthur.'

'Ah, well actually, Lenni, this is Derek Woods.'

Derek held out a hand. 'Hello,' he said smoothly. I shoved
my Save the Chapel project plans under my arm and shook
Derek's hand.

'Derek, this is Lenni,' Father Arthur said, 'a frequent visitor.'

'Lenni, it's a pleasure,' Derek said, smiling at me and New
Nurse, who was hovering awkwardly near the doorway.

'To be honest, I'm just glad that someone besides me
comes in here. You're the first person I've seen and it's been
weeks.' Arthur looked at the floor. 'So, on behalf of the Save
the Chapel focus group, I'd like to thank you for making the
chapel your religious destination of choice.'

'The focus group?' Derek asked, turning to Arthur.

'I'm sorry, Lenni, I don't quite follow,' Arthur said, glanc-
ing at New Nurse.

'It's fine. I'll tell you all about it in our next meeting.' I
turned to Derek. 'I hope you feel better.'

'Derek isn't a patient,' Father Arthur said, 'he's from the
Lichfield Hospital Chapel.'

'Hey, a bum on a seat is still a bum on a seat, and I have this plan to get some Christ—'

'Derek has just agreed to take up the position here.'

'What position?'

'Mine. Unfortunately. I'm retiring, Lenni.'

I felt heat rise up in my cheeks.

'But *I* would very much like to hear about your plans for the chapel,' Derek said, placing a hand on my shoulder.

And then I turned.

And then I ran.

Lenni and The Temp

In September last year, the hospital hired a temp.

The Patient Experience and Wellbeing department had taken a knock from two resignations and a pregnancy. The Temp, overqualified as most temps are, had just graduated from a Good University with a Good Degree in a Good Subject. The trouble was that the market was saturated with other Good Graduates from equally reputable establishments, so she jumped at the offer of the position of Temporary Administrative Assistant at Glasgow Princess Royal. It didn't matter that the work was in no way related to her art degree or career goals; she was happy to no longer be out in the cold with the other shivering graduates of the class of 2013.

The Temp was put to work immediately and spent several months toiling away at data entry and photocopying, while staring out of windows into the hospital car park yearning to be an undergraduate again. One day, when speaking to her boss, a wide man who wore faux designer perfume that he bought in the market, she mentioned an article she had recently read – and this was the part that piqued The Boss's interest enough for him to look up from his smartphone – about a charitable art foundation that was offering a considerably large donation to hospitals and care homes wishing to install art therapy programmes for their patients.

The Boss told The Temp that he would photocopy his own paperwork that afternoon, and within a few weeks the General Office Crap on The Temp's desk was virtually non-existent. She wrote the financial bid, organized quotes from contractors, spoke to art supplies companies, and filled out the endless health and safety documents needed to navigate the maze of putting seriously ill people in a room with craft scissors and pencils, upon which they might accidentally impale themselves.

The funding presentation to the art charity was at their head office in London. The Temp's palms were sweating so much as she waited to be shown into the board room that she left wet stains on the bottom of her document, and had to beg the charity temp to make her another copy.

The news came on a Thursday morning, just after eleven. She didn't read the first paragraph of waffle thanking her for applying but skipped to the second, which began: *Your grant will consist of* . . . She'd done it. There was going to be an art room in the Glasgow Princess Royal Hospital.

The Temp worked harder on the art room than she had on anything before. She bored her friends on pub quiz night with the latest news in medical arts and crafts. She spent her weekends painting plant pots for the flowers that the patients would draw. She designed three different posters promoting the new art room, and secured media coverage from two local papers and a regional news programme to get the word out.

The day before the grand opening, The Temp went into the art room to make sure everything was ready. The merging of two old IT store rooms meant that the classroom was a decent size, and it had the added benefit of natural light through big windows on two sides. There were cupboards with art supplies, books on art, a whiteboard for the teacher, tables and chairs of varying heights and comforts for the patients' needs, a sink to wash brushes, and a wall covered in display boards where string and fabric pegs hung at different heights so that patients could hang their work up to dry.

She circled the space. The art room was ready, it was waiting. The pencils were unbroken, the tables unmarked, the sink still bright white and the floor not covered in paint drips. One day soon, she thought to herself, this room would be alive with colour and buzzing with expression. It would give the patients somewhere to soothe their souls. Somewhere to be heard. A place they could stop being 'ill' people and just be people for a while. Before she locked the door, she breathed in the fresh paint smell of the walls and reminded herself that just a few months ago, this had been a badly managed stock room for IT equipment.

The morning of the grand opening, The Temp drove to work feeling as though she might be sick. She couldn't wait to tell people about the art room, but more importantly, she couldn't wait for the patients to see it. The one thing she hadn't been able to imagine was what it would be like when they got in and started to use it. What stories would those first paintings tell?

When she arrived at the office in her specially bought outfit, she couldn't understand why The Boss was so reserved, why he wasn't meeting her eye and why the atmosphere felt so ... low. She showed him the Twitter coverage on her phone and ran through the itinerary for the grand opening.

'Look, I hate to put you on the spot, especially today,' he said, running his fingers through what was left of his hair, 'but we're going to need an art teacher, and with the budget cuts, and temps needing holiday pay . . .'

The Temp's heart was racing; she would be lying if she said that she hadn't hoped he would ask. After all, it was obvious the art room would need a teacher and he had dragged his feet about hiring one. He knew she had a degree in art – who could be better? She squeezed her own hand tightly.

'Anyway, the woman I've hired is going to cost more than I thought, so we don't have the budget to renew your contract at the end of the month. But please do stay for the opening. And you'll have three weeks before your contract officially ends.'

The Temp smiled for about three or four seconds while her stunned brain tried to communicate with her mouth that this was not a time to smile.

Then came the time for the TV interview. She led the journalists into the art room and helped them set up shots with the poorly children who had been invited to the grand opening. ('Just broken arms and legs please, nothing too depressing, no cancer patients,' had been the instruction from The Boss.) The news presenter arranged The Temp with the children, and the camera panned across as she demonstrated how to paint a star, the children copying with thick yellow poster paint on black paper. Then the camera zoomed in on The Boss, who had arrived with a sense of purpose, reeking of fake Gucci perfume and letting everyone know that he was the department lead on the project. He was microphoned ready for his interview, which would air on the evening news at

6 p.m. and 10.30 p.m. The Temp rose slowly from her seat and exited the room.

She held back the tears all the way to the office. Emptying a box of photocopier paper onto the floor, she hurriedly filled it with her possessions: her mug, her photo frame, her box of tissues. She had much less stuff than she had thought, and even her personal papers and paint samples for the art room fitted neatly into the box. She placed her staff card on her boss's desk and shut the door.

Her head was blurry, stuffed full of emotion. She wanted to get out of the building before the TV crew and the children and the reporters came out into the corridor; she couldn't bear them seeing her. But without her staff card, she had to use the public door rather than the staff one and she couldn't remember how to get to it. As she made her way along the maze of hospital corridors, she broke into a run.

She didn't see the girl in the pink pyjamas until she had crashed into her.

The Temp managed to regain her balance but the girl in the pyjamas didn't. She tripped over The Temp and fell to the floor. A little heap of bones and pink.

The Temp tried to apologize, but all she managed was a strangled squawk. The nurse who had been walking with the girl crouched down beside her and called to a passing porter to bring over a wheelchair. The Temp didn't even get a chance to see the girl's face, but she noticed her thin arms as the nurse fussed her into the wheelchair and wheeled her away. She tried to shout an apology after them.

Those thin arms as the girl was lifted into the wheelchair were all The Temp could see when she tried to sleep, several glasses of Merlot chugging their way through her system but doing nothing to soften her thoughts. She couldn't go back there. But she had to.

The next day, The Temp telephoned the children's ward of the hospital to try to track down the girl in the pink pyjamas. All she could tell them was that she estimated the girl was about sixteen or seventeen and she had blonde hair and pink pyjamas. After nearly forty minutes of being on hold and being transferred and being interrogated about her intentions and several lies about how she was related to the girl, the hospital gave The Temp the name of the ward where the girl could be found.

And that was how The Temp came to be standing at the end of my bed, a look of remorse on her face and a posy of yellow silk roses in her hand.

Lenni and the Art Room

THE TEMP IS probably prettier than you imagined her. Taller, too. She was more nervous than she ought to be, though. She seemed surprised that she could sit on the edge of my bed without my bones shattering like glass. We have shared heritage, she believes, her father being Swedish too. Or Swiss. She couldn't remember. And that mattered, of course. But not as much as what she told me next.

New Nurse said that if I wanted to go to the art room, she would need to ask Jacky's permission. Jacky said it wasn't up to *her*, so New Nurse had to find a doctor who could confirm whether I was allowed in the newly built patient art room and that I wouldn't be at risk of disease or infection or rabid wolves gnawing at my drip tube.

But New Nurse didn't come back. While I waited, I read that morning's out-of-date newspaper. Paul the Porter sometimes leaves them for me on my bedside cabinet. I like the local newspapers best – where the rest of the world doesn't exist, and all that matters is the local primary school's new nature garden and an old woman who knitted a quilt for charity. Children are turning one year older, teenagers are graduating and grandparents are being laid to rest. Everything is small and manageable and everybody waits their turn to die.

When I'd finished reading the newspaper, I waited some more. At first I waited patiently, but then I started to think about it properly. A room, a cuboid space to which I had never travelled, existed. There'd be paints, pens, paper and (Vishnu willing) glitter. I might even be able to get my paws on a permanent marker for the graffiti I've been planning. Right above my head, on the shelf made out of sockets and switches, is the hospital's kind reminder of my impermanence. A whiteboard that says 'Lenni Pettersson' in red marker with a smudge near the final 'n'. The thing about whiteboards is that they're so easily wiped clean. They're designed to be used again and again and again for the names of the unlucky few who find themselves in the May Ward. One day, in just the briefest stroke of a dry whiteboard eraser, I'll be gone. A new patient with skinny arms and big eyes will take my place.

I waited some more.

I had a watch when I first came here, and even when I was wearing it, I spent most of my time asking people what time it was and then asking again because I didn't believe the reply. I thought I'd been in the May Ward for two months, only to find out it had only been a couple of weeks.

But that was several years ago.

After that morning, I waited for seven weeks for New Nurse to get back to me about the art room. I became anxious, frustrated, desperate, and then at peace with her absence. In that order. Twice. In the fifth week that I was waiting, I mentally designed the art room in my mind, using The Temp's descriptions. I never forgot the windows. The Temp had said there were large windows on either side of the room. In the weeks that I waited, the windows became larger and larger

34

until the whole back wall of the art room was one huge open window. The other side became a wall constructed entirely of paintbrushes – hundreds of them sticking out from the wall, just waiting to be chosen.

By the sixth week, I started to get excited again. I rehearsed in my head what I would say when New Nurse arrived to take me there. I deliberated over which pair of slippers I would wear (Everyday Casual or Sunday Best?). By week seven, I was calm and ready. With every day that passed, my confidence grew. I no longer needed to plan or imagine. She would come. New Nurse would come for me.

'Sorry I took so long,' New Nurse said when she came back. 'I hope you weren't waiting all this time?'

'I was,' I said. 'But it's okay, you're here now.'

New Nurse checked her watch. 'God . . . two and a half hours. Sorry, Lenni.'

I smiled and shook my head. The hospital is a cruel mistress. The International Date Line runs somewhere between the end of the May Ward and the nurses' station. The only way to fight Hospital Time is to never fight it. If New Nurse wanted to claim that she had only been gone for two and a half hours, then I would let her. People start to worry if you fight Hospital Time. They ask you what year you think it is and if you remember the name of the Prime Minister.

'Sorry about the wait, but it's good news,' she said, 'I can take you down there this afternoon.'

Without paying attention, I slipped on my slippers and then discovered my feet had chosen Everyday Casual instead of Sunday Best. Well, it's their decision after all.

'Shall we?' she asked as I closed up my dressing gown.

'We shall,' I said, and I took her outstretched arm.

Survival instincts are incredible things. I've taken to memorizing the routes to everywhere I go from the May Ward. I think my subconscious is worried that I am being held captive. So I can tell you that to get to the art room from the May Ward you go left at the nurses' station and down a long corridor, through a set of double doors and straight down another corridor, you turn right, and then you go down a long corridor. Then you come to a corridor crossroads and take a left and go up a very slightly inclined hallway. The art room is on the right. It's a nondescript door, but that's fine by me. The doors that don't make a show of themselves usually have the best stuff behind them.

New Nurse knocked and gave the door a push and there it was – the patient art room, and it was all waiting. The desks were white and waiting for spills and scratches and stains. They might hurt as they went on – like tattoos – but they would make each of the tables unique, and for the dying artists they would be poignant reminders of hands that held and painted and cut and inked. The chairs were waiting to cradle the poorly – to have the odd leg wrapped in plaster rested across them. The windows were there as promised – two of them. Most hospital windows are frosted to prevent captives from seeing out and to protect outsiders from seeing in. But the art room windows were clear and wide and the sun was streaming in through them as if, like me, it were excited to find a new room it had never been inside before.

Sitting behind the teacher's desk in front of the whiteboard was a woman, and she was waiting too. She had a black slate sign in front of her and a paintbrush in her hand. She stared down at it. Sensing she was no longer alone, she jumped and laughed at the same time.

'God, sorry!' she said. 'How long have you been there?'

'Oh, we didn't mean to intrude, we're here for the art class,' New Nurse said.

'I'm Lenni,' I said.

'Hi. Pippa.' The woman shook my hand.

'I can take it from here,' I whispered to New Nurse, and she nodded and left.

'Oh ... er ... oh.' Pippa stared at the door. 'Is she coming back?'

'Nope. They said the classes last an hour.'

'They do,' she said, pulling up a chair so I could sit beside her at the desk, 'but they don't actually start till next week.'

There was a silence.

'But no matter,' she said brightly, 'you can help me with this.'

How can I describe Pippa? Pippa is the kind of person who would give 30p to a stranger at a train station so they could use the loo. The kind of person who isn't afraid of the rain and enjoys a Sunday roast. The kind of person who seems like she might, but doesn't actually, own a dog. A sandy one. Pippa is someone who makes her own earrings for special occasions, and who has hundreds of incredible paintings that have yet to be seen or sold because she hasn't quite figured out how to use her own website yet.

I sat next to her. The slate on the table had a thick piece of rope going through it, ready to be hung.

'What's it going to be?'

'The sign for the art room.'

'What are you waiting for?' I asked.

'Inspiration.'

'How long does it take to get inspired?'

'Well' – she glanced at her watch – 'I only came in to place some paint orders and I've been here for an hour and a half.'

'Can I do it?'

She stared at me for a moment. I wasn't sure what she was looking for, but she must have found it because she slid the slate across the desk and handed me the paintbrush.

'What's it called?'

'Well, that's the thing. Technically, it's room B1.11.'

'Poetic.'

'Exactly,' she said, 'so I was trying to think of a name for it.'

'Are there any rules?' I asked.

She said there probably weren't, so I put the brush to the slate and started. When I was done, Pippa drew some white flowers around the name. As I watched her paint, I noticed a sandy hair on her cardigan sleeve and I wondered if it was from the dog she doesn't own.

'Not bad,' she said when we were both done. 'Not bad at all.'

By the time New Nurse came back, we had hung up the sign and applauded the newly named art therapy room of the Glasgow Princess Royal Hospital.

*

Even if she never came back, even if she spent many years searching for a job, even if her degree proved useless and she never got to make art, The Temp would always know she had a friend here, and that she had made a mark on the hospital. She deserved recognition, because it was she who created the Rose Room.

Runaway

IN HOSPITAL, THE day, as it normally functions, is distorted –
bent like a straw seen through a glass. Bigger in some places
than others, disconnected and yet whole. In the outside world,
the day starts when the sun comes up. In hospital, the busiest
hours can be the middle of the night. People sleep through
the sunlight; they wake in the darkness and go for walks, for
coffee, for a crafty cigarette, only to find it's several days later
than they thought and actually half past nine in the morning.

The hospital itself never sleeps. The lights of the corridor
are never switched off, which is something I realized several
weeks after I came here. It's the same with the lights in the
main entrance, and everywhere else. I imagine that occasionally a porter will come along to change a bulb, but the light
is relentless.

I'd been lying awake since two, but it felt like the middle
of the afternoon. I hadn't been able to get this one memory
out of my head. It was a memory of a TV advert I'd seen on
a hotel television in a foreign country where I didn't speak
the language. It was an advert for an adventure company, and
in it a group of children were white-water rafting on a river.
The children wore fluorescent orange helmets and they were
paddling themselves through the moving river and screaming

with delight. I told myself that one day I would go there and do that.

So, I decided it was time I made good on the promise and took myself rafting. I closed my eyes and walked with bare feet on the rubbery grass towards the edge of the water. I climbed into the inflated orange boat. It rocked a little, but the instructor held it steady for me. I pushed away from the riverbank and paddled. Once the boat had gained some momentum, I let my hand run along the surface of the cool water. It splashed up my sleeve, an icy but refreshing surprise. I could just about hear birds if I strained my ears over the sound of the rushing water.

As I paddled further down the river and past the lines of conifer trees on the cliff above, I realized I was alone. I'd forgotten to imagine having friends, and now I was in the boat by myself and it was too late to conjure anyone up.

In some of the daydreams, I would drift successfully to the end of the river. In others I would fall out of the boat, and in some of those I would be rescued by the handsome rafting instructor. Other times I would hit my head on a jagged rock and slip slowly into the dark water, blood swirling up above me.

At some point, the sun had started rising in the May Ward and I heard The Girl in the Corner's friends arrive. There were at least five of them and they had all adopted the gentle, hushed language that people reserve for the dead and the dying. No matter how hard I tried, I couldn't tune out their voices, and I couldn't get back to my white-water rafting. I supposed it was just as well; I had been at it for hours. If I wasn't careful, my skin would prune.

They knew everything. They shared stories and jokes. They brought her presents they knew she'd love. They took selfies with her. They missed her.

The girls I knew at my second Glasgow school weren't like that.

They were sweet to tolerate me for as long as they did. They let me come on nights out with them, allowed me to go to their parties. But they weren't mine. Just borrowed. I didn't get their jokes and they didn't get mine. I kept saying things that weren't right, even though I know my English is fine. And when I stopped going to school, it was easy.

I imagine they were relieved.

I know I was.

I listened to The Girl in the Corner's friends trying to talk without pity in their voices, trying to play down the significance and the fun of the group holiday The Girl in the Corner had missed. But I heard her voice shake when she spoke.

So, I tried to block out her friends and I stared at the curtains that surround my bed. They are green and awful. But no matter how hideous they may be, what always cheers me is the thought that for someone, somewhere, these are the ideal hospital curtains. That person had the responsibility of ordering curtains for the whole hospital and they chose *these* curtains from a catalogue, had the order approved. The order was placed and the material shipped, the curtains assembled, and all of the May Ward and most of the rest of the hospital was adorned with green chequered curtains featuring navy flowers with an odd number of petals.

'Lenni?'

There was a ruffling of fabric as someone made the non-sensical decision to knock at my curtain.

'Yeah?'

'Are you awake?'

'Always.'

'Are you decent? You have a visitor,' New Nurse whispered.

'I'm decent,' I said, wiping my mouth with the back of my hand, just in case things had got dribbly.

As New Nurse drew the curtain back, I was surprised to see that The Girl in the Corner's friends weren't there any more. She was alone and lying down with the covers pulled up over her head. Having friends must be such sweet sorrow.

New Nurse came in followed by my visitor.

'Hello,' he said, resting a hand on the end of my bed and then taking it off as though the bed had electrocuted him. He probably didn't want to seem over-familiar.

'Everything okay, Lenni?' New Nurse asked.

He looked at me and I at him. *Was* it okay? Apparently, it was my choice to decide. I mean, he was no group of age-appropriate friends who would while away my time with their chatter and gossip and nonsense, but even my mind raft was empty of friends.

'I'll be back in a bit, then,' New Nurse said, but before leaving she pulled both of my curtains back, so that I was released from my chequered cocoon of privacy and bared for all the ward to see.

Father Arthur, standing still like one of his holy statues, remained at the end of my bed.

'You can sit, if you want.'

'Thank you,' he said, taking my visitor's chair and pulling it away from the head of my bed so I could see him properly.

'Are you well?' he asked, and I laughed.

'I . . . you . . . haven't . . .' He cleared his throat and tried again. 'It's been quiet in the chapel over the last few days.'

I nodded.

'I've missed your . . .' He looked for the word, but I didn't help him find it.

'What's the name of that guy in the Bible who has the two sons, and he only loves one of them?'

'I'm sorry?' Arthur said.

'He's a guy and he has two sons. One is obedient all the time and the other son runs away. But when the runaway comes back, the father loves him more than the good one.'

'Ah yes, the parable of the Prodigal Son.'

'I always thought that didn't make sense. The good son does everything right and gets nothing. The bad son causes his parents worry and heartache, but when he returns he gets everything he wanted.' Father Arthur furrowed his brow but didn't say anything. 'It just goes to show,' I said, 'that people love a runaway.'

'Do they?'

'Of course! Look at us: I ran away from you, and here you are. You never visited when I was coming to the chapel all the time.'

'I suppose . . .' He looked at me intently, as though trying to work out exactly how much I had already forgiven him and what was left to go.

'I think, Lenni, the lesson of that particular parable is about asking questions. Those who ask questions and return to God are better than they who never ask questions and only pay lip

44

service to their religion.' He frowned, sighed, and then sighed again as though the first sigh had only served to remind him how much he enjoyed sighing. 'I'm sorry I sprung Derek on you,' he said after a while, 'I didn't realize that you would get . . . upset.'

'I wasn't upset.'

'Right. Of course not.'

'I was angry.'

'Oh. Well, I had intended to talk to you about Derek and my retirement, I just didn't—'

'Didn't he give someone a fish?'

'Derek?'

'No, the man with the prodigal son. Didn't he give the good son a fish and the bad son his empire?'

'I don't think so . . .'

'I think he did. I think it was one fish for the good son, his whole business empire for the runaway.'

'Um . . .'

'Come on, Arthur, you need to get better acquainted with your source material. The prodigal father is up there in heaven right now, holding his fish and hugging his runaway son and wondering why you don't know all the stories in that religion you're selling.'

'I'm not selling anything.'

'Well, you should. It's a terrible business model to give it all away for free.'

He laughed and then the smile drained from his face like water.

'I just want you to know that I didn't mean to deceive you. Or to anger you.'

45

'I can believe that. Hey, is that your true thing for the day?'

'It is.'

'It's a good one.'

'Thank you. You know, I will be in the chapel for several more months before my post ends, and I thought—'

'So running can be good?'

'You're going to give me a headache.'

'Running away. The message of the prodigal son is that if you run away when you want to run away, you'll be rewarded.'

'I'm not sure that—'

'Father Arthur?'

'Yes, Lenni?'

'I have somewhere I need to run.'

There's a difference between running and running away. They are oceans apart but nobody ever pays attention. They're only interested in telling me that if I keep *running away*, they'll take away my visiting privileges. But it's not running away unless I leave the hospital doors. And I never have.

I couldn't actually *run* from Arthur because my hip was still hurting from the crash with The Temp. Instead, I slipped on my Everyday Casual slippers and shuffled slowly in the direction of my destination. Arthur didn't give chase, which was kind because his walking speed is probably faster than mine and it would have been embarrassing for him to catch up with me before I even got out of the May Ward.

I wasn't running because I wanted an empire, or because I wasn't enjoying my talk with Father Arthur, but because I wanted to be somewhere else.

I peeped through the small window in the Rose Room door, and saw Pippa holding a piece of paper up to an elderly audience of three. She pointed her finger to the edge of the canvas and swooped her hand down in a sweeping motion. When she had finished talking, she put down the paper, and it was then that she waved and beckoned for me to go in.

I shuffled in, feeling the eyes of the room on me and my pink pyjamas. I should have gone for my Sunday Best slippers.

'Lenni, hi!'

'Hi, Pippa.'

'What brings you here?'

I struggled to think of how to phrase what exactly had brought me there. A long-dead man and his two unequally loved sons. A fish. A priest. An itching to do anything other than mind white-water rafting... None of those made enough sense to verbalize in front of a geriatric audience.

'Fancy doing some painting?' she asked.

I nodded.

'Pull up a seat and I'll bring you some paper. The theme this week is stars.'

I turned to find somewhere to sit and there she was. Sitting all alone on the table at the back. Her hair catching the sunlight and shining like a ten-pence piece, her cardigan a deep shade of purple and her eyes set on the paper in front of her, on which she was sketching with a nubbin of charcoal. The mauve miscreant, the periwinkle perpetrator. The old lady who stole something from the bin. 'It's you!' I said.

She looked up from her drawing and stared at me for the briefest of moments, letting me come into focus. Then, with recognition and delight, said, 'It's you!'

Lenni and Margot

I SHUFFLED OVER to her table.

'I'm Lenni.' I held out my hand.

She put down her charcoal and shook my hand. 'It's nice to meet you, Lenni,' she said, 'I'm Margot.'

The charcoal on her fingertips left several of her prints on the back of my hand.

'Thank you,' she said. 'You did me a great favour.'

'You're welcome,' I said. 'It wasn't really anything.'

'It was something,' she said. 'It was. I wish I had a real way to thank you, but all I have to my name right now are several pairs of pyjamas and a half-eaten fruitcake.'

She gestured for me to sit down.

'What are you doing here?' she asked, and I knew she meant the Rose Room, but I think it's best to be honest, so I told her the truth.

'They say I'm going to die.'

There was a moment of silence between us as Margot studied my face. She looked like she didn't believe me.

'It's a life-limiting thing,' I said.

'But you're so—'

'Young, I know.'

'No, you're so—'

'Unlucky?'

'No,' she said, still looking at me like she didn't believe it. 'You're so alive.'

Pippa came over to the table and placed some paint-brushes in front of us. 'So, what are we talking about over here?' she asked.

'Death,' I told her.

The crease that this word caused in Pippa's forehead made me certain that she needs to go on a few away-day courses about how to deal with the dead and the dying. Because she's not going to last long working at the hospital if she can't even bear to hear the word. She crouched down beside the table and picked up one of the brushes.

'It's a very big topic,' she said eventually.

'It's okay,' I said. 'I spent a whole day doing that seven stages of grief thing, and I got over it all in one go.'

Pippa pressed the dry bristles of the brush into the table-top and they fanned out in a perfect circle.

When I was in primary school in Örebro, I accidentally tore the corner off a page in a textbook. Me and a boy whose name I can't remember had been racing to see who could turn every page of the book the fastest. I'd been trying to turn the pages really quickly and one of them just tore straight off at the corner. My class teacher shouted at me and, I think because I didn't look contrite enough, sent me to the head teacher's office. It felt like I was being sent to the police. I was already sure that my parents would be told and that I would be in trouble for ever. My palms started sweating. Even walking along the corridor to the head's office while everyone else was in class felt wrong, like I was somewhere I ought not to be.

The head teacher was a sturdy woman with icy silver hair and a pursed pair of lips that were always dressed in oily lipstick. I pictured her shouting at me and I had to work very hard not to start crying. When I got to her office, she was in a meeting and the receptionist told me to wait on one of the green chairs outside her door. A boy several years older than me named Lucas Nyberg was already sitting on the left-hand chair.

'Are you in trouble?' he asked me (although of course he asked it in Swedish not English).

'Yes,' I told him, and I felt my chin start to wobble.

'I'm in trouble too,' he said. And he patted the chair beside him. He didn't seem scared or fazed about being in custody outside the head teacher's office. If anything, he seemed proud of himself.

As I sat beside him, I was relieved. It was comforting to know that someone else was in trouble too. Lucas and I were sharing a fate and it felt so much better than going it alone.

And that's exactly how I felt when Margot chose to break the silence by leaning towards me and whispering, 'I'm dying, too.'

For a moment, I met Margot's bright blue eyes and I felt that we were perhaps going to be cellmates.

'If you think about it,' Pippa said, finally placing the paintbrush down, 'you're not dying.'

'I'm not?'

'No.'

'Can I go home then?' I asked.

'What I mean is, you're not dying *right now*. In fact, right now you're living.'

Margot and I both watched her try to explain. 'Your heart is beating and your eyes are seeing and your ears are hearing. You're sitting in this room completely alive. And so you're not dying. You're living.' She took in Margot. 'You both are.'

It simultaneously made perfect sense and no sense at all.

So Margot and I, both alive, sat in the quiet of the Rose Room and we painted stars. Each on a small square canvas whose edges I forgot to paint, which would annoy me later when Pippa hung them on the wall. Margot's star was on a background of inky blue and mine was on black. Hers symmetrical, mine not. And in the quiet, as she carefully outlined her yellow star in gold, I got this feeling I've never felt with anyone. That I had all the time in the world. I didn't have to rush to tell her anything, we could just be.

When I was little, I loved drawing. I had an old baby formula tin full of crayons and a plastic table to work at. And no matter how terrible my picture, I would write my name and age in the corner. We'd been to an art gallery with school and our teacher had pointed out all the names in the bottom corner of the prints. I had this idea that because I was so talented, one day my pictures might be displayed in a gallery. Therefore, they'd need my name and the date. The fact that I was only five years and three months old when I drew a wonky Dalmatian copied off a VHS cover would only add to the art world's awe at my talent. They'd talk of the famous painters who took until their twenties or thirties to really get to grips with their talent, and then they'd say, 'But Lenni Pettersson was only five years and three months old when she created this work – how is it even possible she was already *that* good?' In honour of my own vanity, at the bottom of my painted star, in yellow and using the thinnest brush I could find, I wrote *Lenni, aged 17*. Seeing this, Margot did the same. *Margot*, she wrote, *83*. And then we put them side by side, the two stars against the dark.

Numbers don't mean a lot to me. I don't care about long division or percentages. I don't know my height or my weight and I can't remember my dad's phone number, though I know I used to know it. I prefer words. Delicious, glorious words.

But there were two numbers in front of me that mattered, and would matter for the rest of my numbered days.

'Between us,' I said quietly, 'we're a hundred years old.'

Lenni Meets Her Peers

SEVERAL DAYS LATER, a slice of fruitcake appeared on my bed-side table.

I'm not usually a fan of fruitcake. The way raisins burst in my mouth is exactly what I think it would be like to eat wood-lice. The way they are firm at first but then you pierce them and the sweet liquid spurts out, and then you're left with the skin-like casing.

But free cake is free cake.

I thought about Margot while I ate.

Between us, we have been alive for one hundred years. I suppose that's quite an achievement.

I'd noticed during our art class at the exact same moment that New Nurse had blushed her way into the Rose Room, accidentally smashing her hip into one of the desks by the door. New Nurse had whispered that she'd found Father Arthur sitting alone in my cubicle. She said I wasn't technically supposed to be in the Rose Room, and that technically if I didn't return immediately, I might get in trouble. Which was sweet. For New Nurse, trouble is being shouted at by Jacky. Trouble isn't the same thing when you're wearing nightwear in the middle of the day and you've named the tube that bur-rows your dinner into your vein. That's real trouble. And I'm already in it.

I followed her, though. Because it's best to leave people wanting more. The trouble I got in was small. I listened intently to it and I promised Jacky I'd stop wandering around. Or wondering around. Nobody was specific about the spelling.

The curtain around my bed drew back just as I was flicking the last of the fruitcake crumbs from my bed.

'Morning, Lenni,' Paul the Porter greeted me with a smile. 'Seen any more spiders recently?'

When I told him I hadn't, he gestured at my bedside table. 'They're going to replace all of these bedside tables over the next few months because they don't have enough weight in the base.'

I nodded because it was boring.

'May I?' he asked.

He pulled on the handle of the top drawer. He pulled harder and then shook it. The yellow silk roses from The Temp looked like they were doing a jitterbug dance. Finally, with both hands, he managed to open it, and as he did so out fluttered a piece of paper.

'Love letter?' he asked.

'Inevitably,' I told him. 'I'll just put it with the others.'

Paul picked it up and, failing to hide his opinion on his face, held it out to me.

Forgiveness: the Lord's light was printed in swirling text over the top of a pixelated photo of a dove against a cloudy sky with a sunbeam poking through the clouds. Beneath it, the times of the chaplaincy services were printed, and beneath that, scribbled in blue fountain pen, it said:

Lenni, before you ask, I didn't print this forgiveness
pamphlet out specially for you, it's just a coincidence.
I'm always here if you need a chat.
    Arthur

Even his email address was tragic: Arthurhospitalchap-
lain316@gpr.nhs.uk.

When I looked up, Paul smiled. If I were about ten years
older, and could overlook his wonky tattoos, I think Paul the
Porter and I would have made a great couple. Weird, but good.
The kind of couple you meet and think, *How did* they *get to-*
gether? He shoved the drawer closed, made a note on his clipboard and sighed. 'Take care, eh?' he said, as though it were in
any way under my control.

That afternoon, or several weeks later (who can really say?),
New Nurse came to get me for my first scheduled above-
board and totally legit trip to the Rose Room. I was going
to meet people my own age – people Pippa had previously
described as my 'peers'. I didn't actually know what that word
meant, but in my mind they were a group of people higher
up, more important, or cooler than me who would spend a lot
of time *peering* down, from on high.

The Rose Room was almost empty when I came in and the
sky outside the windows was the colour of nothing. Not grey,
not quite white, just an indiscriminate thing hanging above
us all.

'Afternoon, everyone,' Pippa said, sneaking me a smile as
I sat down by myself at my usual table. 'I'm Pippa and this is
the Rose Room. The rules are pretty simple: spill something,

please wipe it up, no diving, no horseplay. You can paint whatever you like, but I have some props that might inspire you, and sometimes we have themes. For example, this week's theme is leaves.' She held up a basket of brown leaves. 'If you feel ill or need medical attention, please tell me, and . . . um . . . that's about it?' Pippa has the habit of making the end of every sentence sound like a question. It makes me feel the need to reassure her.

There were only three other members of the class that day. I was the only one in pyjamas.

On the table by the window, two girls who were around my age, wearing normal outdoor clothes and with shiny make-up, were laughing at something on the shinier girl's phone. Opposite them was an older boy. He was chunky and wearing jogging bottoms and a matching T-shirt that looked both scruffy and expensive at the same time. He was resting his plastered leg on the chair beside him. Someone had drawn a massive penis on it in black marker pen.

Pippa asked the girls to put their phones away. They turned their phones over so they were screen-down, but didn't put them away. They didn't even notice when she put the leaves and paints on the table beside them.

The boy shook his head at the leaf Pippa offered him, pulled a biro from his pocket and started drawing.

Then Pippa came over to my table.

'Leaf?' she asked.

I nodded and she placed one in front of me. I was inspecting it, turning its crunchy self around to see which bit I wanted to draw, when I realized she hadn't moved.

She mouthed something at me.

'What?' I asked.

She leant forward and mouthed something else at me. It seemed like she was saying 'walk do hem'.

'*What?*' I asked again.

'*Talk to them,*' she whispered.

Then she went off and busied herself with something on her desk. I observed my peers at their table. The girls had picked up their phones again and were taking a photo of themselves holding up paintbrushes with open-mouthed smiles. The boy was colouring in blue biro so hard that the nib went straight through the canvas. From where I was sitting, he seemed to be drawing a knife.

I glanced back at Pippa. She had so much encouragement in her eyes that it almost hurt to look.

'How did you hurt your leg?' I asked. My words fell in the air somewhere between my table and theirs. And not one person acknowledged their journey.

I looked back at Pippa.

She nodded for me to try again.

I did. This time I knew they must have heard me, but nothing happened. In the end the shinier girl tapped on the boy's canvas.

'What?' he asked.

'I think she's talking to you,' the girl said, pointing, with the same embarrassment for me in her voice that the girls I knew at school used to have. I would say something that made perfect sense and was actually quite funny and they would look at me, embarrassed. And we would wait for the moment to pass.

He turned and all three of them observed me.

'Yeah?' he asked me.

'I asked how you broke your leg,' I said.

'Rugby,' he said. Then he turned back and carried on colouring in the knife.

'Where do you play?' the less shiny girl asked him.

'St James.'

'My boyfriend just started playing there,' she said.

'No way! What's his name?'

It turned out, much to everyone's delight, that the less shiny girl's boyfriend was one of the rugby boy's favourite new team members. Naturally, they had to take a photo of them all together and post it online and tag the boyfriend with the caption 'Look who we found!'

And then they moved, somehow, from that joyous discovery to the new series on Netflix that *everybody* was watching. The boy had already seen season two because it had leaked online, and the shinier girl screamed and put her index fingers in her ears because she didn't want spoilers. But the rugby boy was determined to tell them about the character whose death they would literally lose their minds over. None of them looked back over at me.

I picked up my pencil and wrote *FUCK* in capital letters in the middle of my piece of paper.

Pippa came over to my table and sat down on Margot's chair.

'If you're going to tell me to go over and sit with them and try again, I'm going to scream,' I said.

Pippa's face fell because that's clearly what she'd been planning on doing.

I put my head down on my desk.

'What is it?' Pippa asked gently.

I opened my eyes but didn't lift my head, and I peered at the table where the two upside-down shiny girls were laughing so hard at something the boy had said, and he was stamping green splodges of paint around the knife he had drawn.

'They have so much time.'

'So . . . ?'

'I don't.'

Pippa couldn't meet my eye.

'I'm not saying that to make you feel bad,' I said, 'I just want you to understand what I'm feeling. I have an urgency to have fun.'

'You have an urgency to have fun?'

'Yes. I have to have fun. It's urgent.'

'Okay,' she said eventually, 'what can I do to make it better?'

'You know when I came in here when I wasn't supposed to?'

'Yes . . .'

'When I met those old people.'

'The over-eighties group, yes . . .'

'I met Margot.'

'Yes . . .'

'I want you to move me into her art group. The over-eighties one.'

'But Lenni, that is the class for people in their eighties and over,' Pippa said.

'Yes. I understand that.'

'So it wouldn't really make sense to put you in that group.'

'Why?'

'Because you're not eighty!'

'But apart from that?'

'That's just the way we've decided to do it, so that the classes can be suited to people's interests and abilities.'

'Well, I think that's ageist.'

I waited. She was wavering, I could tell.

'I promise I'll be good.'

Pippa smiled. 'I'll see what I can do.'

Seventeen

WHEN PAUL THE Porter drew back the curtain, the old lady in the purple pyjamas looked up from her *Take a Break* magazine and asked sharply, 'Who are *you?*' She didn't seem pleased to be taking a break from her break-taking.

'That's not her,' I whispered to Paul.

'Sorry!' Paul said cheerfully while the woman scowled at us. 'We're looking for someone.'

The woman mumbled something. Paul drew the curtain back around her bed like he was shrouding an unwanted prize on *The Price is Right*.

When Paul drew back a different curtain to reveal a different elderly lady in purple pyjamas, she was sleeping, with a faint smile on her lips and a half-eaten slice of fruitcake on a paper plate on her bedside table.

'That's her.'

'You want a chair?' he asked, and began dragging a plastic visitor's chair across the ward before I could answer. The sound of the chair dragging across the lino didn't wake her, but Paul shouting 'Bye!' did.

Margot opened her eyes. 'Lenni?' She smiled as though she were remembering me from a dream.

She had several hardback books on her bedside table. Tucked between the top two was an opened envelope, and

I was sure I could see a letter peeping at me from inside. On the mini whiteboard above her head, her name was written by someone whose writing slanted strongly to the left. *Margot Macrae.*

Beyond Margot's curtain, I could hear the low murmur of people talking and some gentle classical music from a staticky radio. Through the gap in the curtain, we watched a tall woman with a tuft of grey hair sticking out from under an Alice band. She had a dark red dressing gown with the initials W. S. stitched in gold on the top pocket. She was making her way out of the ward leaning on a Zimmer frame. Her face was covered in age spots which made her look like a dappled, very slow racehorse.

'What were you like when you were my age?' I asked Margot.

'When I was seventeen?' she asked.

I nodded.

'Hmm.' She squinted her eyes, as if somewhere between her open and closed eyelids lived the images from so many years ago, as if she'd be able to see herself, if only she could get the gaps between her lashes just right.

'Margot?'

'Yes, dear?'

'You said you were dying.'

'I am,' she said, as though it were a promise she was proud to be keeping.

'Aren't you scared?'

She looked at me then, her blue eyes swaying left and right in tiny movements, like she was reading my face. The static of the radio died down and all that was left was the sound of a gentle lullaby.

And then Margot did something amazing. She reached out and she held my hand.

And then she told me a story.

Glasgow, January 1948
Margot Macrae is Seventeen Years Old

On my seventeenth birthday, my least favourite grandmother leant into my face and asked if I was 'courting'. Her face was so close to mine that I could see the dark purple mark on her bottom lip. I had always thought it was errant lipstick, but up close it was different. A bluish violet that looked like a stone, but bedded in, deep under the skin. I wondered if we could find a doctor who would be willing to scrape it out, just to see what it was.

Disappointed, she sat back in her chair and wiped the icing from the edge of the cake knife with her finger and put it in her mouth. I needed to hurry up, she told me. There were fewer men than women now and 'the pretty girls will have their pick'.

A week later she announced that she had arranged a date for me with a nice boy from church. I wouldn't know him, of course, given that my mother and I 'never visited the house of the Lord'. I was to meet him under the big clock at Glasgow Central Station at exactly twelve noon.

I recounted this interaction to my best (and only) friend Christabel as we hurried along my street towards the train station.

She scrunched up her face and her freckles moved, forming new constellations. 'But we never talk to boys,' she said.

'I know.'

'So, what are you going to say to him?'

This thought hadn't occurred to me and I stopped. Christabel stopped too, her pink skirt swishing. I don't know why she was dressed up too, when it was me who had the date. My grandmother had put me in a starchy floral dress and pointed black shoes that were pinching my toes. I felt like I was a child playing at dressing like an adult. She'd put a gold cross around my neck and told me to 'at least seem Christian'. I had no idea what that meant.

'You might be about to meet your husband,' Christabel said, and she bent down to pull her left sock higher over her bony knee. Satisfied, though her socks were still uneven, she put her arm through mine. 'Isn't that exciting!' As she said it my stomach twisted, but I let Christabel pull me onward towards the station.

I stood under the clock at 11.55 and watched Christabel, hidden behind the wall of the newsagent's. I don't know why she was hiding, because nobody was looking for her. She pulled up her right sock and stumbled into an old man with a spectacular hunch. He shook his cane at her and I laughed.

Over the next fifteen minutes, I watched Christabel's freckled face transform from excitement to impatience to pity. Across the station, I could see that she was biting down on her bottom lip. There were two little trenches on the centre of her lip because she did this so often. By a quarter past twelve, I knew he wasn't coming. My palms were hot and I felt that all the world was staring at me in my uncomfortable dress. I wanted to cry. I wanted to go home. But I found myself rooted to the spot, unable to move or to deviate from my instruction to stand under the clock and wait.

I looked for Christabel, but she was gone too. And then the tears came. I stood and watched the people hurrying about the train station with their coats and their cases. Some of them spotted the girl in the floral dress without a coat, crying under the clock, but most people scurried past oblivious.

Then I was aware of a hand on my shoulder and I jumped, momentarily expecting to see the face of a strange Christian boy. But it was Christabel. She stood beside me and looked out on the station.

'Do you ever wonder,' she said, as she kept her arm around my shoulder, 'if the boy you were meant to marry got killed in the war?'

I asked her what she meant.

'I mean, perhaps there was this boy who was perfect for you, and you were *supposed* to meet him in the future and fall in love. Only, he was a soldier and he died in the trenches in France, and now you'll never get to meet.'

'Do you think that about me?' I asked. 'That I'll never find someone to love?'

'Not you *specifically*,' she said, 'I think it about everyone. I think about all the people we'll never meet.'

'Well, I'm cheered up now,' I said.

Christabel laughed and held out two tickets to Edinburgh. 'Let's go to the zoo,' she said. 'I want to see Wojtek the soldier bear.'

And she pulled me by the hand to the platform and onto the 12.36 to Edinburgh.

The carriage was busy so we sat in a booth opposite a young man in a suit. I estimated he was probably about twenty-five and he seemed not to notice us until Christabel's pink dress, which had layers and resembled a soufflé, brushed against his legs. He looked up then, surprised.

Christabel tucked her dress under her knees and I thanked my stars that she didn't go to pull at her socks.

'That's a pretty dress,' he said, and Christabel shone red.

I said nothing, taking him in. He was very slim, and I had a feeling that when he stood up, he'd be tall. He was wearing a white shirt that looked as though it had been worn several times already that week, but his hair was neatly combed to one side and held in place with thick cream.

His eyes met mine.

'We're going to Edinburgh,' Christabel said, buoyed by his compliment.

'Me too,' he said, and he held up his ticket like he'd won a line at the bingo.

'I'm taking her to the zoo,' Christabel said, 'to cheer her up.'

'And why would you need cheering up?' he asked me, but Christabel answered, speaking quickly.

'Margot had a date today, but he didn't come.'

'You're Margot?' he asked, a slight smile on his lips.

I nodded, my face burning.

'You were just saying, actually, weren't you, Margot? That you might never find someone to love?'

His eyes didn't leave mine as he said quietly, 'I could love you, if you want.'

He offered his love like a cough drop. As though it were nothing at all.

~

The nurse was standing beside Margot's bed, squinting at us. He seemed like he might have been standing there for a while.

Margot lifted up her purple sleeve and held out her arm.

'Just the anti-sickness,' he said gently, as he snapped the protective top off the needle and placed it in her arm.

'Ooh.' She shut her eyes and breathed in through her teeth.

'All done,' he said. He stuck a dot of a plaster on her arm and helped her roll down her sleeve. 'Visiting hours are nearly up, do you need someone to come and collect you?' he asked me.

'Oh, no, I'm fine,' I smiled.

Once he'd gone, I turned to Margot.

'What happened next?' I asked.

'I'll have to tell you the rest later,' she said, and she pointed behind me.

New Nurse was standing at the foot of Margot's bed. 'Found you!' she said, with a look that was somewhere between amusement and annoyance.

As we made our way down the corridor and back towards the May Ward, I asked New Nurse, 'What were you like when you were seventeen?'

She stopped still, thinking for a moment, then she smiled and said, 'Drunk.'

That night, when I would usually take to the wild waters for rafting with the handsome instructor, who had recently purchased a pair of tropical shorts, I found myself pulled. Not by the water, but by Margot. I didn't go to the grassy knoll by the water's edge or lie in the raft with the sun warming my skin. Instead I took a little walk to a train station in Glasgow and I boarded the 12.36 to Edinburgh. I saw a pretty girl in a floral dress and a skinny man and the beginning of something.

And then, somewhere on the way to Edinburgh, I fell asleep, for the first time in years.

Lenni and Margot Get Happy

MY FIRST DAY as an octogenarian was surprising. My legs didn't feel any more tired and my hair wasn't grey. I had yet to develop a passion for the smell of lavender and my sleeves didn't contain any tissues. I had never had lunch in a Marks & Spencer café or shown pictures of my grandchildren to strangers on the bus. But there I was, among my octogenarian peers in the Rose Room, ready to do some painting.

Pippa had rearranged the tables again, this time into clusters of four. I sat beside Margot, and opposite us sat Walter, a retired gardener whose grey hair and rosy red cheeks made him resemble a garden gnome, and Else, who with her black pashmina draped over her shoulders and her short silver bob looked like she could be the editor of a French fashion magazine.

The table beside us was in my mind our competition, as it was made up of four real octogenarians in various shades of sensible pastel pyjamas, whereas on our table sat a gnome, a magazine editor, a fake octogenarian and a Margot. If there was a competition, which I hoped there would be, I was sure we'd win.

Outside the window, the hospital car park was drenched in grey, with half-hearted rain misting down on people as they ran to the payment machines, bowing their heads and opening umbrellas against the subtle deluge. I tried to remember the last time I'd felt the rain. And I wondered, briefly, if I could convince New Nurse to take me out into the car park next time it rained, or better yet, if I could stand in one of the shower rooms fully dressed and have her simulate the rain with one or two of the showerheads on their softest setting.

'I'd like it,' Pippa said, rolling up the sleeves of her floral top, 'if we could spend today thinking about happiness, and painting or drawing moments from our happy memories. I'll share mine first.' She tried to perch on the edge of her desk, but stood up fairly quickly because it was ever so slightly too high. 'One of my happiest memories is a walk my family took with our old dog. It was sometime around Easter but it was a surprisingly hot day. My grandfather was there too, and we just walked along a country road in the sunshine.'

'I knew you were a dog person!' I said before I really intended to.

She grinned and clicked off the lid of her board pen. 'So,' she continued, 'what I might draw for that memory could be the line of trees on the country road. People are hard, so if you're looking to finish the painting today, I'd steer clear of people, but then I might have the sunlight come through the leaves of the trees.' She sketched all of this out on the board as she talked, and even though it was just a whiteboard drawing, it still looked good.

'Or,' Pippa said, 'if you're more interested in object studies, the handle of our old dog's lead, perhaps with the back of his head, might be good.' She did another sketch beside the first, with a hand holding a handle and the back of a dog's head with fluffy ears. I felt cheated. Her sketches were so good that mine would never even come close.

'I've made us a CD for this week's theme,' she said, as she pressed play on her CD player. Judy Garland singing 'C'mon get happy' crossed the boundaries of space and time to enter our ears.

I felt a heat rise in my chest as everyone around me began drawing.

Walter had picked up one of the pencils and started sketching. He definitely has gardener's hands. There was a flap of skin coming loose on the knuckle of his first finger. And green stains under his nails. His brow was wrinkled as he pressed hard with his pencil onto the canvas. I wondered what he was drawing for his happiest memory. Perhaps it was the day that he made a wish and turned from a garden gnome into a human. Else was painting long strips of black paint onto her canvas. And Margot was holding her pencil and pulling it across the canvas so lightly that the marks it left behind were like the ghost of a drawing.

My canvas stayed white. I didn't know what to draw. Being aware of everyone around you successfully getting on with the task at hand is the worst feeling. It's just like school and it's itchy.

The first eye was impossibly real as Margot sketched out her happiest memory. It was clear and yet somehow shining. Instead of feeling angry at her for being so good at drawing, I was fascinated. She was capturing something, someone, who in eighty-three years of living she had been the happiest to see.

The tiny hands came next, one curled into a small fist and the other open and stretching out, reaching for us.

The blanket covered the little tummy and there were wisps of hair that stuck out from underneath a yellow hat. The button nose was so real that I couldn't quite believe she was drawing this from memory. All the while, Margot's face was soft, as though the baby she was drawing were lying on the table in front of her and she was watching it gurgle and kick and stare up at her with big, learning eyes.

When she was done, it was perfect. Just coloured pencils on canvas; she'd shaded the warmth in the cheeks and the soft blue blanket.

Then she put down the pencil and I saw her, though I don't think she knew, wipe a tear from her bottom set of eyelashes.

'Is it a boy?' I asked.

She nodded.

'What's his name?'

'Davey.'

As Pharrell Williams's 'Happy' forced its way into the room, I picked up a paintbrush. That was a key mistake, I learned later – starting to paint before sketching it out in pencil first. But I didn't care. I'd remembered something happy and I had to get it down.

While I was painting the memory I could see, I told Margot the story.

Örebro, Sweden, 11ᵗʰ January 1998
Lenni Pettersson is One Year Old

It's a memory I visit a lot.

It's my first birthday. My mother has plaited my baby hair wisps on top of my head and secured them with a Minnie Mouse clip. I don't watch it through my own eyes, but from the perspective of the video camera that frames my face in the shot as I point my finger at things and people, and make incomprehensible noises that are not yet words.

I'm sitting on my father's lap and looking up at him like he's the moon. He's talking to whoever's holding the camera and as he does, he sways me left and right on his knee and my cackle of delight makes him laugh. He turns to me and says something I've never been able to hear on the videotape that makes me point at the table and shout, 'Da!'

Though daylight is still streaming in through the windows, someone turns off the lights and the cake, with its single candle, glows its way from the kitchen into the living room, my mother's face illuminated. She places the cake on the table in front of me and kisses me on the top of my head. Then she steps back, standing behind me and my father as though she's not quite sure what to do with herself. I see her mouth 'Happy birthday, Lenni' in English to me, which she never spoke unless absolutely necessary. My father takes hold of my hands so I don't reach out and touch the flame.

The videotape always skips at this point, as together they begin to sing.

Ja, må hon leva!
Ja, må hon leva!
Ja, må hon leva uti hundrade år!
Javisst ska hon leva!
Javisst ska hon leva!
Javisst ska hon leva uti hundrade år!

Which means:

Yes, may she live!
Yes, may she live!

Yes, may she live for a hundred years!
Of course she will live!
Of course she will live!
Of course she will live for a hundred years!

Once I was old enough to understand it, the Swedish birthday song always made me sad. I didn't know anybody who had lived to one hundred, and I didn't think I would live to one hundred either. So, every year when my parents and friends sang to me, I felt this sadness that they were all celebrating something that wouldn't actually happen. They were hoping for the impossible. I would let them down.

In the video, having just blown out my first birthday candle and been fed some icing on a spoon by my father, I have no idea what the song means and I look so happy.

The One Hundred Years of Lenni and Margot

THE IDEA SLIPPED into my mind like a silverfish.

In the absence of a pen on my bedside table, I had to tell someone before it swam away again.

Her ward was in darkness and mostly silent, except for some spectacularly loud snoring coming from the bed of the woman with the monogrammed dressing gown.

I pulled back the curtain that hung around Margot's bed. 'The stories,' I said, taking in a gasp of air, 'your stories!'

Margot opened her eyes.

'We should paint them! One for every year!'

Despite it being somewhere between three and four o'clock in the morning, Margot pulled herself up in bed and squinted at me in the dark.

'We're a hundred, remember?' I said, in case she'd forgotten. 'Seventeen plus eighty-three. One hundred paintings for one hundred years.'

'Lenni?' she said.

'Yes?'

'I love it.'

*

After the night nurse, a sturdy man named Piotr with a twinkling earring in his left ear, advised me to return to my bed, I lay in the dark thinking about it.

I still hadn't been able to find my pen when I returned to the May Ward, so I stared up at the ceiling and hoped that at least one of the three of us – me, Margot or Piotr – would remember the plan when we woke up in the morning.

Somewhere, out in the world, are the people who touched us, or loved us, or ran from us. In that way we will live on. If you go to the places we have been, you might meet someone who passed us once in a corridor but forgot us before we were even gone. We are in the back of hundreds of people's photographs – moving, talking, blurring into the background of a picture two strangers have framed on their living-room mantelpiece. And in that way, we will live on, too. But it isn't enough. It isn't enough to have been a particle in the great extant of existence. I want, we want, more. We want for people to know us, to know our story, to know who we are and who we will be. And after we've gone, to know who we were.

So, we will paint a picture for every year we have been alive. One hundred paintings for one hundred years. And even if they all end up in the bin, the cleaner who has to put them there will think, *Hey, that's a lot of paintings.*

And we will have told our story, scratching out one hundred pictures intended to say:

Lenni and Margot were here.

A Morning in 1940

THE WARD WAS quiet. The morning visiting hours were over and visitors had been begrudgingly forced to leave. Someone had brought in a balloon for one of the May Ward patients and I had spent my morning enjoying the intense commotion it had caused. What resulted, in the end, was an irate uncle, who was angry at both 'Health and Safety' and 'Political Correctness' having simultaneously 'gone mad', storming out of the ward ahead of his family carrying a helium-filled *Get Well Soon!* sheep balloon. The young patient he had visited took the whole thing with a level of maturity the uncle would probably never attain. But that just made me sad because the May Ward has a way of doing that to children. Making them calm and measured and flat. Old before their time.

And I wondered, as I wandered down the hall towards the Rose Room, whether I am old before my time. The set of seven octogenarian faces that greeted me when I opened the door reminded me that, at the very least, I'm not quite eighty yet.

'Lenni!' Pippa rushed over to me. 'Look!'

In the corner of her whiteboard, she'd stuck a piece of paper on which she'd written in gold ink *Lenni and Margot's big idea*, and she had made two tally marks for Margot's painting of the baby and my terrible sketch of the video camera view of my first birthday.

'Two down, ninety-eight to go!' she said, as she picked up some sheets of paper and followed me to the table. Margot was already sketching out something that looked like a mirror, hanging against patterned wallpaper.

I sat beside her and, when Pippa had bustled away, we gave each other a smile.

'Shall I tell you a story?' she asked.

Cromdale Street, Glasgow, 1940
Margot Macrae is Nine Years Old

My least favourite grandmother had arrived at our house one afternoon in 1939, several weeks after my father joined the army. My mother actually let out a little scream when she opened the front door on a dim Sunday afternoon to find my grandmother standing there with a suitcase. My mother couldn't understand how it was that she had even heard about my father's deployment. My father swore, in a letter from his training camp near Oxford, that he hadn't mentioned his deployment to his mother and had no idea why she had suddenly appeared on our doorstep.

Now I don't know whether to pray for my safety or yours, he wrote. *There's a bottle of whisky hidden under the sink.*

I'd seen grandmothers at work and I knew them to be warm and sweet and kindly. Christabel's grandmother made her nice dresses. My mother's mother, who had died when I was five, had knitted a cardigan for me and another identical one for my doll so we could match.

The woman who stood scowling at us from the doorstep wasn't like that.

*

My least favourite grandmother had a special perfume she saved for Christ. It was tangy and it stuck to the back of my throat. Every Sunday morning, she would stand at the mirror in the hallway and assemble herself for Jesus. It was a very specific look.

One Sunday morning in 1940, when the days were getting darker, I listened at my bedroom door. I could hear the ragged sound of her pulling a hairbrush through her thick mane. It sounded scratchy, and I often wondered how it was that she hadn't ended up bald from the fury with which she brushed.

I could hear my mother clanking in the kitchen, recognizing the sound of the pan that she used to try to resurrect powdered egg into something resembling food.

I crept down the stairs, hoping my grandmother wouldn't notice me.

She was pinning her Sunday hat to her head, sliding grips all around the edge. She fixed me with a stare.

I carried on down the stairs and found my mother in the kitchen. Her face was pale and drawn and she was staring down at the powdered egg in the pan, not moving.

'Did he die?' I asked. My father was in France now and when my mother's face looked like that, my stomach would twist and I would prepare for the telegram.

'No,' she said quietly, her eyes fixed on the pan.

'Are you talking about your father?' my grandmother called from the hall, where she was now staring, unblinking, into the mirror as she curled her eyelashes with a terrifying metal contraption.

'He might be dead, you know,' she said. 'In pieces on a field somewhere.'

At this my mother looked up, and I saw that all around her eyes was red.

'And you can't even be bothered to pray for him,' my grandmother carried on, clamping the metal down on her lashes.

My mother opened her mouth as though she were going to say something, but closed it again.

'Imagine that,' my grandmother said, 'a wife and daughter who can't even take the time to ask God and all his angels for their dear father's protection.'

My mother put down the wooden spoon and used her hands to wipe the tears under her eyes.

'Only God can help your father now, Margot,' my grandmother said, placing the eyelash curlers down and leaning closer in to the mirror to inspect her work. Satisfied, she pulled the thin glass bottle of her sickly perfume from her vanity bag and began spritzing it on herself. Three sprays on the left wrist, three sprays on the right. Three on the neck, three at the waist. As she did, she began singing. She had a thin, watery voice, but it carried.

'*Soldiers of Christ, arise and put your armour on.*'

My mother went to the cupboard for salt and pepper as more tears came.

'*Strong in the strength which God supplies.*' My grandmother sprayed perfume all around her hair and then finished with three sprays on the brim of her hat, singing, '*Through His eternal son.*'

My mother sprinkled salt and pepper onto the powdered egg and closed her eyes.

'*Strong in the Lord of Hosts and in His mighty power.*' The last thing left for my grandmother to do was to pin the red brooch to the left of her blouse.

The tears were coming faster than my mother could cope with.

I walked up to my grandmother.

'Do you have a tissue?' I asked.

She fumbled in the pocket of the long wool coat she was wearing, which was my mother's favourite and had been summoned from my mother's wardrobe to keep my least favourite grandmother warm while she prayed. She pulled out a pink hankie and a scrunched-up scrap of paper. She handed me the hankie with distaste and threw the paper in the bin.

'What do you want with a hankie anyway?' she asked.

'Ma's crying.'

She leant in closer, peering into the kitchen to inspect her work.

Satisfied, she left for church.

After she left, I pulled the paper from the bin and unscrunched it. In my father's blotchy writing were the lyrics to my mother's favourite song:

How much do I love you?
I'll tell you no lie
How deep is the ocean?
How high is the sky?

I flattened it as best I could and took it up to her bedroom and placed it under her pillow.

It was the first one we found.

As it turned out, he'd left love notes for her everywhere. Inside the left shoe of her prettiest pair of high heels, at the back of the pantry weighed down by jars, behind the books on the living-room shelf. Slotted between their favourite records. Some of them had more song lyrics, some had jokes, some had pleas to remember him.

My mother collected them all and put them in a Mason jar on her dressing table. Every time we found a new one, she would smile in a way I hadn't seen her smile without him. When I discovered one in the bottom drawer of my bedside table, I kept it hidden so I could make her smile when we ran out of new notes to find. Or when the telegram came.

Lenni and New Nurse

'WHAT DO YOU write in that notebook, Lenni?'

'This?' I asked, pulling it from my bedside table and wondering briefly when she had seen me writing in it. New Nurse was sitting on the end of my bed. She'd kicked off her shoes and her odd socks (one pink with red cherries on, one striped with a pug's face on the toes) were swinging over the side of my bed. I knew she wanted me to let her see the notebook, but I didn't.

'I'm writing the story.'

'Of . . . ?'

'My life. And Margot's life.'

'Your one hundred years?'

'Exactly. Although I started writing it before I met Margot.'

'So, it's like a diary?' she asked.

I turned it over in my hands. It's shiny on the outside, all different shades of purple. I have to write on both sides of the paper because I don't want to run out of space before I get to the last page, so the pages crinkle when I turn them. Sometimes I just turn them back and forth because the crinkling is so satisfying. 'I suppose,' I said.

'I used to have a diary,' New Nurse said, and she pulled a lollipop from the top pocket of her uniform and unwrapped it. She passed it to me. I couldn't remember the last time I had a lollipop. It was cola flavoured.

'You did?'

She unwrapped another lollipop, a pink one, and popped it in her mouth. 'Mmm,' she said. 'It was boring stuff, though. *This girl said this thing behind my back and so I said this thing behind her back, so she tried to fight me, so I kicked her.*'

'You did?'

New Nurse looked a little proud, but said, as though she were worried I might go on a New Nurse-sanctioned kicking spree, 'Kicking is wrong.'

'Did you get in trouble?'

She twisted the lollipop in her mouth. 'Probably.'

'I write it when I can't sleep,' I told her. 'Since I'm not very good at painting, I figured I would write down our stories in case people can't tell what they are.'

'Am I in it?' she asked.

'If you were, would you want to read it?'

'Of course!'

'Then no, you're not in it.'

'I am in it, really, aren't I?'

'Who can say?' I said.

She got off my bed and slipped her shoes back on. 'If I'm in it, can you make me taller?'

I just gave her a look.

'Goodnight, Lenni,' she said.

And she left me alone with my diary. To write about her.

An Evening in 1941

'I DID THIS one in the same year.' Walter was showing Margot and me a picture of a hedge cut into the shape of a swan on his smartphone, which had incredibly big button graphics.

'What's the weirdest animal you've ever made?' I asked.

'A unicorn. For a woman who was selling her home but wanted to leave her mark.'

'That's the kind of woman I'd like to be,' I said.

'But really, my favourite thing is roses. I managed to get some almost perfect Ophelias and some hedgehog roses, which we don't often see in our neck of the woods. They still grow at the end of my garden, but I can't tend to them like I'd want, what with my knee. The white ones, my Madame Zoetmans, always come out the best. They're fluffy. Like sheep on a stick.'

'Oh, I love Zoetmans!' Else said, coming to sit with us in a burst of woody perfume. Walter stared at Else with delight. Like she was a unicorn hedge. So we left them to it.

Margot turned back to her drawing.

'Where to?' I asked, while she shaded the dark outer corners of what appeared to be a tin bucket.

'You'll like this one,' she said, as she used her thumb to smudge the dark shadows cast by the bucket onto the floor.

'We're going back to the house I grew up in,' she said, 'to an evening in 1941.'

Cromdale Street, Glasgow, 1941
Margot Macrae is Ten Years Old

I was in the bath when the air raid siren went off. My mother swore very quietly under her breath and stubbed her cigarette out on the soap dish.

My bathwater was still hot, and we'd filled it up to the line drawn in black paint that went all the way around the tub.

'How will they know?' I'd asked, when my mother had painted the wobbly line the year before.

'Well,' she said, 'they won't know.'

'So we could fill it all the way to the top?' I asked.

'Not past the overflow,' she'd said, trying to navigate the paintbrush past the plug chain without painting it too.

'We could fill it up all the way?'

'Yes,' she'd said, 'I suppose.'

'Why don't we just do that then?'

'Because,' she said, '*they* might not know, but *we'd* know. And how could you face your class at school knowing you'd had a big hot bath and they'd all had to clean themselves in puddles?'

I didn't say anything, but I felt that I probably wouldn't have minded that as much as my mother expected.

The air raid siren screaming, my mother scooped me up from the warm water and roughly rubbed at my arms and legs with the towel. I whined that she was hurting me and she told me she was trying to be fast.

'Come on, Margot,' she said in the sing-song voice that she used whenever she was trying to cover her fear, and she hurried me down the stairs, out of the kitchen door and into the back garden.

Outside it was icy; even the grass underfoot had frozen. My breath danced away on the air and I stopped still.

'Come on,' she said, the pressure beginning to really tell in her voice.

I was dressed only in a towel and standing in our garden in the middle of winter, and I had no desire to go down into the cold, damp Anderson shelter. I started crying.

When the war was still new, my mother had made a game of the air raids, by marking down in a notebook every time we used the shelter. 'Our fifteenth visit,' she would say, as though we were having fun and not hiding from fire falling from the sky.

We'd built the Anderson shelter with the help of some non-combatant soldiers provided by the local council. I'd watched as they'd packed the earth on top of the roof, so that what was once a square, simple garden was now home to a human rabbit warren. They'd talked to my mother about keeping it dry, and what necessities to store inside. They'd warned her not to smoke down there because the air would become thick.

Before they left, the larger of the two soldiers had asked me if I had any questions for them.

'Can we get out to go to the toilet?' I asked.

He laughed. 'You can't get out for any reason until the siren stops.'

'Then how do we go to the toilet?' I asked.

The answer was revealed to be – any way you wanted. My mother's solution was a large tin bucket. It lived in the corner of the shelter beside some magazines and newspapers, which were mostly for reading but also functioned as toilet paper.

'I shall be very proud of you,' my mother said when she installed the bucket, 'if you never have to use this bucket. You can have my jam ration any day that we come down here and you don't use it.' Jam was a big incentive for me at the time so I'd never used the bucket.

'Hurry up, Margot,' my mother said. Standing only in my towel in the bitterly cold air, I fixed her with a scowl and slowly followed her. She pushed open the corrugated iron door to reveal my least favourite grandmother squatting in the middle of the shelter, her knickers around her ankles and her skirt hitched up around her hips, urinating into the bucket on the floor.

For a moment, it seemed that even the air raid siren had fallen silent, and all I could hear was the hiss of my least favourite grandmother's urine hitting the inside of the bucket. In the unfortunate lighting from above, we could see the specks of wee that were splashing onto the floor. My grandmother's face was set in a picture of horror.

My grandmother finished urinating and then had to grope about for some newspaper. After dabbing at herself with an article from the *Telegraph*, she un-straddled the bucket and pulled up her knickers. Then she picked up the bucket, which now had a good few inches of wee sloshing around in it and a sodden strip from the *Telegraph* floating on top, and carried it very carefully to the corner of the shelter. Not making eye contact with us, she sat primly on the bench on the right-hand side of the shelter and smoothed down her pleated skirt, as though she were sitting in church on Sunday. From beside her, she picked up a novel and opened it. She held it in front of her face, but her eyes were staring, unblinking, into the distance.

My mother and I both wordlessly took a seat on the bench opposite. Sitting down, I could see the flush of my grandmother's cheeks. The bitter stink of urine wrapped itself around my nose and, I imagine, my mother's and grandmother's noses too. It made itself the fourth occupant in our tiny shelter.

My mother gently brushed my wet hair and then coaxed me into the spare dress she'd stored away under the bench for emergencies like this. Despite my skin being damp and the shelter being so cold, I made no protest.

'I thought,' my grandmother said into the silence, as she turned another page in her book, 'you were out.'

My mother caught my eye and I knew that if I managed not to laugh, I'd get her jam rations for a week.

I laughed anyway and so did she.

Lenni and Forgiveness, Part I

'Did you miss me?'

Father Arthur let out a scream not befitting an elderly clergyman.

'Lenni?'

'I'm back!'

Having leapt to his feet, he stood with his hand on his heart and clambered out of the pew without much grace. Panting as though he were just crossing a marathon finish line, he swallowed, and then said in a hoarse voice, 'Yes. I can see that. I'm old, you know. You shouldn't surprise old people like that.'

'Did you miss me?'

He wiped the back of his hand on his forehead. 'It has been a little quiet in here lately.'

'Do you need medical attention?' I asked him. 'I've been here a while, I've picked up a thing or two.'

'I'm fine, thank you.'

'I'm fairly certain I can hook you up to a drip.'

He chose not to comment, and instead asked, 'To what do I owe the pleasure?'

'Well,' I said, 'may I sit?'

'Of course.' He offered me a pew and then nervously hovered until I invited him to sit beside me.

'Are you well?' he asked.

'Of course not.' I smiled. 'I've been thinking a lot about forgiveness.'

'Really?'

'There are lots of stories in the Bible about forgiveness, right? Wasn't there one about a milking cow and a vine? Or was it a mouse who couldn't sew? Anyway, I'm not very good at forgiving people because I find it hard to forget. Also, if you forgive, you can't have the fun of getting revenge, and revenge, I have found, is so much more satisfying than forgiveness.'

'I see.' Father Arthur folded his arms across his round tummy. I wondered if God deliberately has all of his priests slowly start to resemble Father Christmas to endear them to the local community.

'So, what do you think?' I asked.

'About what?'

'About all of it; forgiveness, punishment, redemption.'

'I think you raise an interesting point: forgiveness is a huge part of the example Christ set for us. Although I am not sure I agree with the part about revenge being more fun.'

'But God spends half the Bible getting revenge on people – what about the plagues and the ghosts and that thing with the parrot?'

'The parrot? Lenni, I don't think you've . . .' He thought, coughed, and then he asked, 'Where exactly did you read the Bible, Lenni?'

'At school.'

'At school,' he repeated. 'Okay.'

'Well, they read it *to* us. You know, Sunday school. They would take us out of church and sit us all on the carpet and read to us.'

'And were these books always the Bible or were they sometimes something else?'

'Something else like what?'

'I don't know.' He stroked his chin. 'Something perhaps like a fairy tale or a children's book?'

'Nope, they were always from the Bible. It had gold edges.'

'Uh-huh.' Father Arthur looked sceptical.

'Forgiveness, then?' I asked, to give him a bit of a hint and get him back on track.

He went on, 'I'm not sure I agree that forgiveness is less satisfying than revenge, as you put it. And I might add now, I sincerely hope this conversation doesn't involve any revenge you hope to enact on me. Anyway, perhaps in the heat of the moment it might seem that revenge is the only thing you can do to satisfy your anger, but you might find that after time has passed, forgiveness is what has done you the most good, is what you are most proud of.'

'But,' I said slowly, 'I might not have those months or years to look back on my actions. I might never see the day when I am proud of my forgiveness. I'm only living in the short term, so shouldn't I just get my fun wherever I can?'

'When you say *fun*, do you mean revenge?'

'Yeah, in a way.'

'Can I ask, Lenni,' he said, 'who are you thinking about forgiving? I know it isn't me.'

'You do?'

'Yes.'

'How did you know I've forgiven you?'

'You came back,' he said with a smile, gesturing to the empty chapel.

Nothing dramatic had changed: there was the same stained carpet, the electric piano in the corner draped with its beige cover, the altar with its flickering candles and the noticeboard with more pins than notices. Maybe I'm like the noticeboard. More pins than messages. More contact slots in my phone than friends. More growth in my bones than I'll get to see. More revenge than forgiveness.

'So, who are you wanting to forgive?'

'I'd rather not talk about her,' I told him. 'I haven't seen her in years.'

'Of course,' he said, but I could tell he was curious. 'So apart from ruminations on forgiveness, what else is fun?' he asked.

'I've made a new friend.'

'That's wonderful.' And he said it without envy. And I saw that he was worthy of my forgiveness. He was deserving of New Testament Lenni.

'You'll like her. She's . . .' I paused to examine his face properly. 'About your age.'

He laughed. 'I'll withhold a reaction to that until I meet . . .'

'Margot.'

'Margot.'

So I told him about The Temp, about the art class and the Rose Room, about Margot and our plan to leave something behind before we die.

'The problem is,' I said, 'what if we die before we finish?'

Father Arthur tapped his nose. 'What if you don't?'

I saw his point: maybe we will hit the one hundred. Of course, if we both pop our clogs before it's done then there's not a lot we can do about that.

'If it helps,' he said, 'I will have a word,' and he pointed up to the ceiling.

'Human Resources?'

'I meant God.'

I inhaled the smell of the chapel – the sweet sadness of the wilting floral arrangement on the altar, the musty smell of the carpet, the dust on the pews.

'Father Arthur?'

'Yes, Lenni?'

'Did you miss me?'

'Yes, Lenni. Lots.'

Margot and the Night

Cromdale Street, Glasgow, 1946
Margot Macrae is Fifteen Years Old

IT WAS THE middle of the night when the bomb came through our window. It shattered the glass and landed at the foot of my parents' bed. My father woke in an instant, the muscle memory of the trenches kicking in, and he leapt up. Scrabbling around in the bed clothes, he was grabbing, searching for the bomb, but it was too dark to see.

'Helen,' he was screaming, 'the bomb! There's a bomb!' but my mother didn't stir.

He knew the pin had been pulled from it; he could hear the ticking and he knew the terrible sound that was coming, knew the sight of legs and arms strewn across the ground without anyone to claim them, knew the sight of half-burned faces, melted eyes. He had only seconds before the explosion.

He pulled himself from the bed and threw himself on the bomb, trying to use his body to cover the blast. To protect his sleeping wife and his daughter in the next room from the burst of flame.

And then there came light.

By the time he was breathing again he was on the bedroom floor, his back to the dresser, his body covered in sweat, and in his arms my mother's slipper.

Having heard screaming and banging, I stood in the doorway of their bedroom, and in the silence I watched my mother watch my father and I wondered if they knew, between them, how to fix him.

Lenni and Forgiveness, Part II

MARGOT WAS POISED, ready for my story. In front of her was a loose pencil sketch that she'd been doing while I drew my own design, and thought of the words to tell the story. My story had happened mostly in Swedish, so I had to make sure I had the right words to tell it.

Margot was wearing a plum-coloured jumper. It looked warm and itchy at the same time. I wanted to wear it, but also, to never have to touch it.

My picture wasn't very convincing, but nevertheless I drew the final plate on the wonky table. The table wasn't wonky in real life; it was heavy – a dark glossy wood, and neither a rectangle nor an oval but something in between.

When I started talking, Margot paid me her full attention. I liked that. She clasped her hands together, her fingers interlocking, and she fixed me with her bright blue eyes.

Örebro, Sweden, 2002, 2.42 a.m.
Lenni Pettersson is Five Years Old

I woke up in the middle of the night to the sound of an almighty crash. All the pots and pans from the messy cupboard in the kitchen had probably fallen on the floor, but in my five-year-old mind, something terrifying had happened. A bomb had gone off. A car had crashed into the house. A stranger had shattered a window and was climbing inside, ready to offer me sweets and tell me to get in his van (we had just learned about strangers at school).

Then there was clanking, and scraping and thuds.

In all the films and all the books, nothing good happened to curious children. But I didn't even think about staying in my bed. From the top of the stairs, I could see that a light was on, somewhere quite far away. The clanking had stopped, but now I could hear something else. A hiss. And chopping.

I stayed at the top of the stairs, listening, as slowly the salty smell of bacon danced its way up the stairs to meet me. And then something more acidic came too, oranges and onions. I sat at the top of the stairs and listened as the toaster popped and there was scraping. Lots of scraping.

I tried to picture him down there. The man in dark clothing we had learned about in assembly. He would try to get us on our own, they said. He would offer us sweets, or kittens or toys, but tell us there were more in the back of his van. He would try to get us to follow him, and then he would put us in his van and take us away. I wasn't sure what he would do next, but whatever it was, it seemed like he would do something you wouldn't want him to do. They said he would try to trick us. But they didn't say anything about him sneaking into our houses at night to cook us a meal.

I scooted down one step on my bottom. And then another. I heard the knocking of bottles as he opened the fridge and the rustle of a bag. Maybe something with salad in it. I kept going, scooting down one step at a time in the way my father had told me not to do because it was going to pull up the carpet. When I reached the bottom of the stairs the toaster popped again, but this time he pressed the lever and I heard the toast slide back into position.

I padded through the dining room, ready to confront him, and I wasn't scared.

But it was her. Dressed in a dirty white T-shirt and knickers. My mother. And then I was scared.

There was more clanking as my mother placed a new frying pan on the hob, and then she started cracking eggs straight into it. Her eyes were different. As though her real eyes had gone away on holiday, and what was left behind were some placeholder eyes that weren't hers but would give the impression of seeing for the time being. A small snake of smoke was rising from the inside of the toaster. The smell of burning was getting stronger.

I heard someone on the stairs and my father, in his faded pyjama bottoms, came and stood beside me. He put his hand on my shoulder and we watched her. He had this expression on his face like he was watching someone far out in the ocean who couldn't swim. He knew she was drowning.

And then the fire alarm started screaming.

My mother jumped and dropped her wooden spoon. Turning around, searching for a towel to flap at the fire alarm, she saw us and she froze.

The next night, when I heard crashing and chopping and sizzling, I stuffed my blanket under the door so I couldn't hear or smell anything that was going on in the kitchen, but I lay awake anyway.

And what started as something so strange very quickly became something that the Pettersson family did every day. I would lie in bed at night trying to get to sleep before it began, because once she'd started she could be cooking for hours.

When the morning came, my dad would always come to get me out of bed, and he'd pick me up even though I was far too old to be carried, and I'd smell the aftershave on his neck and let him carry me down the stairs.

The table was always the same, starting with the white tablecloth, then moving up to the plates, which always matched, and what was on them: ham and cheese, folded like fans; fruit in all shapes, arranged in colour groups; bacon, browned and crispy and laid in straight rows in the casserole dish; white sliced bread cut into hearts. The omelette was always whole, its thick topping only just revealing a peek of the bright colours of the peppers and onions within. Then there was a large serving bowl full of porridge set next to three stacked, striped bowls. In jugs at the top of the table were the coffee and juice, and on either side of the table our names written on place cards in black calligraphy.

Then my father and I, he in his smart suit and me in my pyjamas, would take our seats.

My father would make his choice – a slice of omelette, a handful of grapes, on rarer occasions the cold, crispy bacon followed by a bowl of porridge and perhaps a slice of the thin cheese on the heart-shaped bread. Whatever he chose I would copy, even if he'd chosen it every day that week, even if I didn't like it very much. I needed a guide and he was mine. He knew it, and so he'd always choose juice instead of coffee so I could copy.

She never joined us, not once. She would stay in the kitchen. In the summer, she could stare out of the window over the sink to our small garden. In the winter, she'd stare out into the darkness, at her own face reflected back in the glass. I remember trying to get her to join us a few times and not recognizing the look in her eye as she gazed out of the window. A teacher once told me that I had very dark bags under my eyes and I was convinced it meant that I had the same disease as my mother, whose dark circles were green at the edges in certain lights. They haunted her pretty eyes. I was sure that one day I'd be downstairs with her, well before the sunrise and catering for an unknown event for people who were growing steadily more afraid of me.

Sometimes, when he thought I wasn't looking, my father would watch her, with that same expression he had on that very first morning. As though he wanted to pull her drowning soul to safety, but she was too far out. It made him grey.

Eventually, she must have seen a doctor. Perhaps by choice, or perhaps someone – maybe her parents, maybe my dad – made her go. Probably not my dad. He was never very good at that kind of thing. One morning when I was almost six, we came downstairs and the table was naked – no tablecloth, no buffet of breakfast. Bare except for my mother who was slumped at the table, her head resting on her arms. Her dark hair blended with the wood of the tabletop. I thought she was dead and started to cry, but my father told me that she was only sleeping. I knew from the sound of his voice that this was a good thing. 'Come on, short one,' he said, and he found me some cereal and a bowl and, with me sitting on the kitchen counter and him standing by the window, we had our first normal breakfast. 'You have to forgive your mamma,' he said.

I didn't know how to reply, so I said, 'Okay.'

'She was poorly,' he said.

'Is she better now?' I asked.

'She might be.' He dunked his spoon into his bran flakes. 'She loves you, pickle.'

The First Kiss of Margot Macrae

PAUL THE PORTER and I thought it would be funny to pay another visit to the furious *Take a Break* lady on our way to see Margot. But when we got there, Paul drew back the curtain and the bed was empty.

And it wasn't funny.

Paul pulled the curtain closed, and we couldn't look each other in the eye for the rest of our walk to see Margot.

What if she's gone too? I thought on a loop, as we chicaned around the corridors to the Newton Ward.

I could see, without seeing, her empty bed. Her name smeared off the whiteboard, her old books piled and bagged up to be given to charity. Her purple pyjamas folded neatly and her slippers having no more journeys to make.

Paul's staff badge added a certain amount of ease to getting about the hospital. We didn't have to be interviewed on the intercom to get in anywhere. We could just stroll right into any ward we wanted. I made a mental note to try and procure one of my own. He gave a friendly, unreturned wave to one of the porters sitting at the nurses' desk and then we turned right into her little alcove of beds.

'No,' I said under my breath to nobody in particular, bracing myself for the impact of her absence.

But she was there, sketching in biro on the back of a piece of paper torn from a crossword book. She was drawing a door. So I sat beside her and waited.

Cromdale Street, Glasgow, 1949
Margot Macrae is Eighteen Years Old

The slim man on the train who had offered me his love like a cough drop was much younger than he looked. He was only twenty where at first sight I thought he was twenty-five or twenty-six. Perhaps it was the suit. He'd been travelling to his apprenticeship interview at a glassworks in the city.

He was different to the man I thought I'd met, who I'd had a sneaking suspicion might have been a bit of a cad. He was quiet. Thoughtful. He took things to heart. When I told him on the train about my least favourite grandmother lamenting how a boy had never brought me flowers, he'd remembered and turned up to meet me for our first date with a corsage of pink flowers on a ribbon that he tied to my wrist.

We walked around Glasgow Green, side by side but never touching. When we got to the McLennan Arch, he told me that his mother always made him and his brother Thomas make a wish when they walked under it. And so we walked under the arch and we made a wish and I wondered if his was the same as mine. It might have been, because the next week he telephoned and asked me out to dinner on Saturday. He would pick me up at my house at eight o'clock.

*

With the words 'books, music, Christmas' pinned to the mirror on my wardrobe door as conversation starters I felt I might need, I did my best to put on my mother's burgundy lipstick.

My mother was hovering in the doorway of my room, watching. 'Will you want a jacket?' she asked. 'It's cold.'

I blotted my lips on a piece of tissue as I'd seen my least favourite grandmother do, and shook my head.

'Should I have met his parents?' my mother asked. 'Should I have invited them to tea? Will you be safe with him, unaccompanied?'

'Ma, stop it!'

Her nerves ignited my own, and I found that I was shaking as I opened the front door.

Johnny was standing there, but something was different. His smile seemed strange. His shoes were untied and he had a big ink stain on his shirt.

I knew my mother was appraising him. But I was too, and something was making me feel like I was in a dream. Behind him, Johnny came running down the path to our front door.

'Margot!' He was breathless. 'I'm sorry.'

The boy on the doorstep grinned, and he was Johnny but he wasn't. His not-quiteness was alarming. They had the same eyes, the same nose, the same hair, but the boy on the doorstep's smile was crooked.

'This is my brother, Thomas,' Johnny said and, catching him up at the doorstep, he punched Thomas hard in the arm. My mother gasped but Thomas cackled. Now Johnny and Thomas were side by side, I could see that Johnny was taller by at least a foot, maybe more.

'I'm so sorry,' Johnny said, 'I told Thomas I was picking you up and he thought he'd be funny and get here first.'

Johnny caught sight of my mother and smiled, but he said nothing and neither did she.

'Nice to meet you,' Thomas said, his grin still illuminating his face, as he held out his hand for me to shake. 'You're very pretty,' he said.

'Get away!' Johnny hissed. Thomas ducked past Johnny's attempt to bat at his head and ran down our road with his hands in his pockets, laughing.

'I'm sorry,' Johnny said again.

And then, with my mother standing behind us in the hall, Johnny leant forward and kissed me. It was brief, but I felt the strange sensation of his warm lips against mine and the taste of what might have been Dutch courage.

'Shall we go?' he asked, and I nodded because I couldn't speak. He took my hand and I closed the door without looking at my mother, because I was far, far too embarrassed.

Margot's Getting Married

'WERE YOUR PARENTS married?' Margot asked.

'Yes, I attended the ceremony in utero.'

'And . . . where are they now?'

'Would you like a gummy worm?'

'Sorry?'

'New Nurse bought them for me at the gift shop.' I held out the packet, but she shook her head.

'Those would pull my dentures right out.' She laughed and, adding some light patches to the gold wedding ring she had painted, she asked if I would like her to tell me a story.

Cromdale Street, Glasgow, February 1951
Margot Macrae is Twenty Years Old

'Margot's getting married.'

My mother whispered the words to herself as we sat at the kitchen table – Johnny and I on one side and she on the other. In between tears, she told us she was happy. She told us there was so, *so* much to look forward to.

She offered us a plate of biscuits, arranged in a semi-circle. As we crunched with dry mouths, she asked Johnny to invite his mother to tea so they could meet. She asked Johnny whether his younger brother Thomas might be serving as best man and what church he thought his family would be most happy with. She asked us if we wanted a summer or an autumn wedding and whether she should make sandwiches for the wedding breakfast.

When Johnny had answered as best he could, she offered me her mother's wedding dress. It would need cleaning, but it would fit me quite well, she said. I would have said yes to getting married in a paper bag if it had got her to smile.

'I could make you some lace gloves.' She took my hand in hers. I'd forgotten what it felt like to have my mother's hand in mine. How soft her skin was and how cool her touch.

She turned her hand in mine and ran her finger across the gold band of my engagement ring. It had a small square emerald set in the centre. It felt odd on my finger.

'Such a pretty ring,' she said. I looked down at my hand and tried to imagine a second ring there. A permanent one.

'It's my mother's,' Johnny said. Then, as though he'd made a mistake, he said, 'Well. I mean, it *was* my mother's. It's Margot's now.'

'Well,' my mother said, 'how kind of your mother to give it to Margot.'

Johnny smiled at me. Sometimes, my breath would catch at the thought that one day soon this young man would see me naked.

'Well,' my mother said, 'shall we have some tea?'

She picked up the pot and successfully communicated some tea into her best china teacups. They were the ones she put out when she wanted to impress someone. I was wary of the cups, associating them as I did with doctors' visits, with unpleasant and non-biologically related 'aunts' and my least favourite grandmother, who, unable to continue searching for her son within my father, had moved back to her house by the sea.

My mother sipped her tea and I felt a wave of guilt wash over me. I was doing this to her. I was leaving her alone with only my father for company. But that was what people *did*. They met someone and they got married. That was what we were taught to do. Mine and Johnny's courtship was long for the time. As we sat at my mother's kitchen table, Christabel was almost a year into her marriage and living in Australia with a soldier she'd tripped over at a tea dance. So, it turned out that her future husband hadn't died in France. Or, at the very least, she'd taken someone else's.

'Perhaps, once we're married, we could live here?' I said to my mother.

Even that didn't work.

'No, pet.' She patted my hand and the emerald winked in the light. 'A married couple need a home of their own.'

I nodded, knowing there'd be no hope of a smile now.

She half stood to take the tea tray to the sink when the creak on the fifth stair announced a fourth presence among us.

My mother stopped, glanced to the hallway and sat back down. Johnny gave my leg a squeeze.

My father, topless, tired, came into the kitchen, his stomach hanging over the waistband of his stained striped pyjama bottoms.

'Margot's getting married,' my mother said, looking to my father for eye contact, but finding that he didn't have any to spare.

He took a dirty glass from inside the sink and filled it with water.

'I know,' he said.

'You do?' my mother asked.

'The boy asked for her hand.' He waved his own hand in the general direction of Johnny, but he didn't turn to look at us.

My mother smiled weakly at us. 'Oh, of course,' she said. 'How sweet of you to ask for her hand in marriage. Traditional. I wasn't thinking.'

The thousand-yard stare was one of the things I'd read about in the book on what they called 'combat stress reaction'. My father would sit and stare for hours. He was doing it then. Staring down to the garden, to the patch of brown earth where the Anderson shelter used to be. Where my mother and I and my least favourite grandmother had sat and waited for death or morning.

Watching him at the kitchen window, I marvelled at the idea that this man whose pyjamas we were *not allowed to wash*, this man who hadn't left the house in weeks and who had been sleeping on the sofa since the bomb came through the window, was responsible for giving away my hand in marriage. And now that hand wore a ring.

Father Arthur and the Sandwich

FATHER ARTHUR WAS sitting at his desk eating an egg and cress sandwich in complete silence.

'You eat the crusts first?' I asked.

'Christ!'

As Father Arthur pushed his chair backwards in surprise, some of the nonsequential sandwich crust caught in his throat.

'Lenni!' He wheezed, his face swelling red.

He coughed and lowered his head between his legs.

'I'll get New Nurse!' I shouted.

I was almost at the door to his office when he weakly said, 'No, I'm all right.' He wheezed again, unscrewed the lid of his red thermos flask, and poured out some tea.

'I'm sorry,' I said, and he waved me back into the office as though it were all fine.

As he sipped more tea and wiped tears from under his eyes, I inspected his office. He had two dark wood shelves with Bibles and songbooks and files. A picture of Jesus looking exhausted on the cross, in a frame with the remnants of a price sticker stuck to the corner of the glass. A photograph of a black and white dog, and a photograph of Arthur with *other people*, in which he is wearing an inordinately colourful jumper.

Arthur's office window was tiny and there was a grey layer of dust on the slats of the half-open blinds. When I pulled one back, I could see the car park. But that didn't seem right. How could the car park be outside the window of the chapel office and also outside the Rose Room and also outside the window in Margot's room? When I first came here, the car park was only on one side of the building.

'The other day I read,' Arthur said, as he noticed me staring out at the car park, 'that there are more cars in the world than people.'

'You need to dust your blinds.'

I drew an L in the dust.

Arthur took a tentative bite of his sandwich and I compelled myself not to try to make him jump a second time.

I drew an E beside the L.

'Do you think if Jesus had had a car, he'd have driven it around?'

Arthur frowned and smiled almost simultaneously.

'I mean,' I said, 'it would have saved him the work of appearing everywhere.'

'I don't—'

'It's odd that he didn't tell the folk in Jerusalem about cars – you know, give them a heads up of what's to come. Give them a clue that would lead to the invention of the motor car. Help them get there quicker.'

'How do you know he didn't?'

I gave Arthur a smile to let him know that was a good response.

I waited for Arthur to speak again, but now that he had the chance to not be interrupted, he didn't say anything. I drew two Ns in the dust on the blind.

'To tell you the truth, Lenni,' he said, 'I can't imagine Jesus behind the wheel of a car. It just seems odd.'

'But when he comes back, if he comes back, won't he want to drive anywhere?'

'I—'

'I suppose he can just ask for lifts. Nobody would turn Jesus down.'

I drew the I on the blind and then turned.

'But then, what if they don't know he's Jesus because he's dressed up like an old beggar woman, and then nobody helps him because nobody picks up hitch-hikers any more and he's just stuck on the M1 for hours? And then the more bedraggled he looks with that beard and everything, the more he resembles a homeless man. And then he just starts walking and the police pick him up because they think he's a drug addict. Then when they try to put him in rehab, he's telling them, you know, "I'm the Son of God." But nobody believes him, because why would they? And he gets put in a detention centre with a load of other people all claiming to be Jesus and nobody can tell who the real one is.'

A small crumb of bread had got stuck in the corner of Father Arthur's mouth. He wiped it off. 'Why would Jesus be dressed up like an old beggar woman?'

'To see if people are really kind or if they're just being nice to him because he's Jesus.'

'And he'd need to be dressed up as an old woman to find that out?'

'Yes, and then he gives them a rose if they're good.'

'Isn't that the plot from *Beauty and the Beast*?'

'Hey, you're the priest, you tell me.'

The First Winter

Church Street, Glasgow, December 1952
Margot Docherty is Twenty-One Years Old

JONATHAN EDWARD DOCHERTY and I were married at 12.30 p.m. on the first day of September 1951 on shaking knees and with a borrowed ring. My mother had cried for all the wrong reasons. And then we'd moved into a tiny tenement off Church Street.

I was working in a department store and Johnny's apprenticeship had led to a job at Dutton's – a glassmakers that specialized in windows and mirrors, which made perfect sense because Johnny was both a window and a mirror to me. Sometimes, I felt I could see right through him, and other times, when I looked for Johnny, or at Johnny, all I could really see was a reflection of myself.

He was still tall, still slender, still thoughtful, but he was different to me now that I knew how his mouth hung open when he was drifting off to sleep. Now I knew the one song he would whistle over and over again. He was less interesting to me now that I knew he could sit with me for hours and not say a word. He was less charming now that I'd seen him swearing when he couldn't screw the living-room lightbulb back into its casing. He was sillier to me now that I'd seen him in church on Sundays in his odd-fitting suit, his hair combed into a side parting, kicking his brother Thomas in the shins for stealing his hymnal.

Johnny's mother insisted the whole family went to church every Sunday: Johnny's mother, his aunt, Thomas, Johnny and me. We would always have the same pew, the one on the right next to the statue of Baby Jesus in the arms of Mary. We would have to be seated by 8.20 in order to secure it for the nine o'clock service.

For our first wedding anniversary, he saved up for an overnight train trip in the Highlands. We'd packed a picnic to have beside the loch, and while we'd set off on our trip a twosome, we'd returned home a trio. Everything was happening as it was supposed to. I was married and there was going to be a child.

I didn't tell Johnny until December. In fact, I didn't tell him at all. I let the dress tell him. A white dress with sailboats stitched on the hem. It was silk and soft and delicate. Perfect for a girl or a boy. On Christmas Eve, as I folded it inside the tissue paper and then carefully placed the package inside the box, I began to feel sad that the baby and I were about to lose the confidence of each other's existence. In all the world, only I knew my baby existed. And to my baby, I was the whole world. Every sound and sense of his was mine.

On the morning of the twenty-fifth, Johnny pulled back the tissue paper and stared at the inside of the box. I thought I could see him smiling, I thought I could see excitement, but that might have only been a reflection of my own feelings.

So, the baby and I waited for his response. In the end, he put down the white dress, came over to me and scooped me up in his arms. He told me it was wonderful and then insisted we put our coats on and go round to tell his mother.

Lenni Moves to Glasgow

Örebro to Glasgow, February 2004
Lenni Pettersson is Seven Years Old

THERE'S A VIDEO of this, too.

I'm standing beside my mother in a pair of dinosaur pyjamas with a coat on over the top. In one hand is my beanbag pig, Benni, and in the other is my passport, which I was allowed to be in charge of on the trip on account of how I was now a big girl.

'Wave bye to the house, Lenni!' my father says from behind the camera.

I do it half-heartedly.

'Say, "Bye, house!"' he tells me.

At this point I stare at the video camera.

My mother crouches beside me, puts her arm around my squishy coat and joins in.

'*Hej då huset!*' We wave at the locked front door.

Then, the camera follows us as we all climb into the back of the taxi. The driver seems harassed by the wait. My father passes the camera to my mother as he struggles to get my seatbelt to clip in.

Then, blackout.

The camera springs to life again in the airport departure lounge. Quite the film-maker, my father pans across the shuttered shops – perfume, surf wear, expensive sweets and snacks. They are all closed because it's 4 a.m. and no human wants to buy perfume or overpriced swimming shorts at this hour. My mother is asleep on a chair; she is almost translucent. I am sitting beside her, crying.

'Don't cry, sweetheart!' my father says, and I look up at the camera.

Then, blackout.

There's incredibly shaky footage of the plane taking off from the window, but because of the darkness all you can see is red and white dots shaking and then disappearing down the bottom of the screen. 'And we're off,' my father says quietly into the camera, as though it is a secret they're sharing. Then he turns the camera on me. I'm holding on to Benni tightly. I have my nose pressed against his beanbag snout.

'It'll be okay, pickle,' my father says softly.

Panning from the front door and around the living room, where there are boxes and suitcases and a distinct lack of furniture, my father narrates, 'Well, here we are!' And he does a tour of the house – the kitchen with only one working light-bulb and the bathroom, where the previous owners have left peach-coloured toilet paper and a shower radio in the shape of a seahorse, then into the bedroom with the double bed, where my mother is unpacking clothes. Then he goes into my bedroom where, clutching Benni, I am finally asleep.

*

The camera turns on about a week later, as I run in through the front door of the house in my new school uniform. Having not worn a uniform at my school in Örebro, I am strangely proud of my blue jumper and my pleated skirt in the colour of sadness.

'Lenni's smiling!' my father narrates to the video camera. 'How was your first day?'

I hold up a lollipop to the camera – it's one of those pink and yellow chewy ones and I'm smiling as though nothing in the world could ever top this moment.

'Did you make any new friends?' he asks. I open my mouth to answer and then, blackout.

May Flowers

ELSE AND WALTER were sketching the wooden mannequins Pippa had placed on our table. Beside Else was a single long-stemmed white rose, tied with a black ribbon. It was fluffy. Like candy floss gathered up on a stick. She and Walter were avoiding looking at each other and I was quite sure that under her tasteful make-up Else was blushing.

Pippa smiled when she saw the rose, but didn't say anything. Instead, she placed a mannequin in front of me and explained that artists use the mannequins to get the proportions of a human body right. She let me draw a face on mine with a felt tip – I gave him a pair of wide eyes and a grin. I arranged him so that his arms were up in the air, waving to the mannequins on the table opposite. Then I drew shoes on him, with the laces done up in a bow. I gave him a smart shirt and tie. I imagined he was courting a mannequin on the opposite table.

In the quiet, Margot was painting. She filled her canvas with yellow flowers. I don't know their names, in English or in Swedish, but they were beautiful. It was as though she had access to a private field of yellow flowers that only she could see. They crowded together so tightly that there were only a few gaps of white space left on her canvas. They were so bright they seemed to generate their own light.

St James Hospital, Glasgow, 11ᵗʰ May 1953
Margot Docherty is Twenty-Two Years Old

He was so chubby when he was born that he didn't fit into any of the clothes we had brought to the hospital. My mother had knitted him a whole wardrobe of outfits. Her favourite was a pair of dungarees (in private, Johnny had said, 'What will the child want with woollen dungarees in summer?') but the only thing we could get on him was a yellow hat, and even then it would only stay on for a short while before it rose up and eventually popped off his head.

Johnny had borrowed a camera from his boss, Mr Dutton, for the day. At the glassworks, they took a photograph of every installation they did and they had a wall for customers to examine their previous work. Johnny said it helped build confidence. The camera was boxy and much heavier than it appeared. It had dials and numbers that Johnny had promised Mr Dutton he wouldn't meddle with.

'Smile,' he said. And I did. Holding the human we had made. Wrapped in blankets and wearing only a nappy and a yellow hat.

We named him David George, the first name for Johnny's father and the second for the King, who had died the year before. Good role models, we thought then. I have had many years to think about it, and I wonder if the name had too much turmoil in it – both men dead, both so strongly connected to the war. David had died in 1941 and King George had been the one he was fighting for.

Davey had been in the world for about three hours when my mother came to the hospital with a bunch of yellow carnations. '*April showers bring forth May flowers*,' she said as she kissed me on the cheek, the flowers pressed between us giving off a glimmer of sweetness and sunlight.

My father wasn't with her. He had entered a voluntary treatment centre for men with shellshock. He wrote sporadically, and I felt guilty that I was relieved when his latest letter didn't mention any imminent plans to come home.

'Smile,' Johnny said again, and my mother placed her arm around me. I looked down at the sleeping Davey, still dreaming. The love I felt for him, this little pink thing, it was celestial. And for my mother too, who had done this all before and had done most of it alone.

'Your turn,' my mother said, and Johnny took her place beside my bed. I handed him the baby and he held him tentatively, as I had seen him hold sheets of white glass with their razor edges before they were sealed into windows. And we smiled.

'I'll take another, just for luck,' she said.

This one was just of me and Davey. I pulled the yellow knitted hat onto the head of my son. My boy. It still felt so strange to think that he was mine, that we had made him. As I smiled for the boxy black camera in my mother's inexperienced hand, in the corner of my eye I could see that Davey's yellow hat was rising higher and higher up. Just after the flash, it popped up.

In the picture I am laughing, and Davey's eyes, perhaps startled by all of the flashes, have opened for the first time.

And that photograph is still in my purse.

The First and Only Kiss of
Lenni Pettersson

KLIMT's *THE KISS* was lying in poster form on our table in the
Rose Room. I'd seen it before somewhere, at school probably,
but this was the first time I'd really *seen* it. Even though the
poster print wasn't shiny, the gold was so warm it seemed like
light was shining out of it. Pippa told us about Klimt's scan-
dals with his earlier works, and how this was by contrast very
well received. It depicts a romantic embrace, she said.

But I disagree entirely and I can't believe nobody else
could see it. The woman in the painting is dead.

She has flowers in her hair and her eyes are closed, and
while the man is kissing her and pulling her to him, her face
is blank. The leaves at her feet are vining around her ankles,
pulling her into the flowers of the earth, where she now belongs. The earth is reclaiming her to bury and he is desperate
for her not to go. His kiss is a wish. A wish that she still be
alive for him to love.

So, thinking about kisses, I began drawing, using felt tip
pens because they had looked so irresistible in their pot, and I
told Margot the story while I drew.

Abbey Field Secondary School, Glasgow, 2011
Lenni Pettersson is Fourteen Years Old

I had an English Literature teacher who, school legend has it, kissed a pupil at prom. I took these rumours with a pinch of salt, because another rumour at a neighbouring school told that there was a science teacher who'd had sex with a pupil in the biology supply cupboard. While the teaching skeleton watched. I could never get the picture out of my mind – the two passionate lovers frantically cavorting beneath the hollow, shocked grin of the skeleton.

If I had had any suspicions about our English teacher, they were instantly increased when, in the middle of a class on *Romeo and Juliet*, he sat on the edge of the desk I shared with a girl I didn't know, and in a faux casual manner asked the class, 'How do you know when it's okay to kiss someone?' This was met by baffled silence.

'How do you know when it's okay to kiss someone?' he kept asking throughout the year, as though he had some resentment about a long-passed assessment of the appropriateness of a kiss. Every time he asked it, my face would burn. Partly because I found it funny that the rumours might be true, but mostly because I didn't know. I had never kissed anyone in my life.

I think everyone has ideas about what their first kiss will be like. For some reason, I always imagined mine would take place under a tree with a boy whose face and hair and appearance didn't matter. The tree was always green and lush and the grass beneath us was dewy and wet and I was always barefoot.

Even though I had this vivid image of how it would be, I never actually tried to make the vision come true; I didn't hang around in lush parks searching for boys to kiss.

So I was surprised when my first (and only) kiss didn't happen like it did in my imagination. There were no trees or lush green grass.

Walking home from a house party that had ended when the neighbours called the police, the group of girls who let me hang around with them, for reasons I still don't fully understand, thought it would be fun to break into the school grounds. The very place we could never wait to escape, we now – in our free time, and drunk on spiced rum stolen from a father's alcohol cabinet – decided we wanted to visit. A party took place under the fire escape (if you can call twelve drunk teenagers playing drum and bass through a phone's external speakers a 'party' – which we did).

I had no interest in him. He didn't repel me, but I was about as attracted to him as I am to, say, a chair or a table. But when my friends and I were dancing, he danced behind me, put his hands on my hips and asked me if I wanted to go with him somewhere, so I followed him. Outside the science classroom, away from the friends whose tinny music we could still hear, he put his wet mouth on mine and I tried my best to keep up.

I walked home from the 'party' barefoot. One of the girls had lent me some high-heeled shoes and I couldn't walk in them. I heard some of them laughing about it. When the kissing was over, I took the heels off and handed them to her. 'You could just give them to me at school on Monday,' she said, but I told her she might as well have them back now because

I'd be walking home barefoot anyway. I made my way home alone along the gravelly pavement with nothing between my feet and the concrete. The cold of the ground was nice, actually. Soothing.

I let myself in through the back door.

She was asleep at the kitchen table.

'Mamma?'

I tucked her hair behind her ear and lifted the end of her curls out of the plate of toast crumbs. Her tea was cold. The milk had formed a little island in the middle of the mug.

I tried to clink about so she would wake up. I poured her cold tea down the sink and dusted her toast crumbs into the bin.

She didn't stir. She took a long breath in.

I put the butter back in the fridge and screwed the lid on the jam. Then I turned and watched her for a moment. Her shoulders rose gently. She looked peaceful, but the ghosts under her eyes were back. They had started haunting her again after she had asked for a divorce and we moved out of my dad's house. They were like bruises.

'I kissed a boy tonight,' I told her.

She didn't wake.

'It was my first kiss.'

She carried on sleeping.

'It wasn't what I thought it would be.'

I went to check that I'd locked the kitchen door. I put her plate and her mug in the sink.

'I thought I'd feel something, you know? But it was just weird. He had very wet lips.'

She breathed deeply again, her dreams making her eyelashes flutter.

'I thought it would mean something.' I turned off the kitchen light and picked up my bag. 'But it didn't really mean anything.'

She moved a little, adjusting her head on her arms.

'I just thought you should know,' I said. 'I had my first kiss tonight.'

I felt better for having told her.

I closed the kitchen door and went upstairs to bed.

Now my first kiss lives on for ever in an otherwise inexplicable felt-tip-pen rendering of a science classroom lit by moonlight (I embellished the skeleton in the window – he wasn't really watching . . . as far as I know). And the following Monday, as my English Literature teacher swung his leg over my desk and asked, 'How do you know when it's okay to kiss someone?' my answer still was, and still is, 'I don't know.'

Margot and the Man on the Beach

PAUL THE PORTER began with the snake and then, via some very inaccurately drawn Disney characters and a large Celtic cross, arrived at the ace of spades. 'Now this one, I don't remember,' he said. 'I was on a stag do, and when we left for the restaurant I didn't have a single tattoo on my shoulder, but when we got back to the hotel I had the ace of spades.'

'Do you like it?'

'No. I'm glad it's on my shoulder, cos I don't have to see it unless I'm looking at my back in a mirror.'

'Which I can imagine is not that often,' I said.

'It's not. Now this next one,' he said, pulling the sleeve of his polo top back down, 'is my favourite.' He turned over his left arm and in the crook was a baby, with brown eyes and only one dimple.

'This is my girl,' he said. Underneath the baby in curling cursive script was the name 'Lola May'.

'That one looks so real!' I said.

He grinned and pulled out his wallet, holding up an almost identical photo. 'I told Sam—'

'Sam?'

'He did all the Disney ones.'

'Yikes.'

Paul laughed. 'Anyway, I told him, *You cannot fuck this one up. I want only your best work!*'

'Well, he nailed it.'

'He did. Thinks it's up there with the top ones he's ever done.' Paul could not have been prouder.

'How old is Lola?'

'She's three. She was born here, you know,' he said. 'Proudest day of my life. She wants me to get a Winnie-the-Pooh tattoo, so I'm doing it for her fourth birthday. Probably on my calf cos I'm running out of room on my arms.'

There was a loud fuzz of static on his walkie talkie, and then someone said something that was muffled but seemed pretty urgent.

'Oops!' he said and jumped up. 'Come on, trouble, let's get you to the Rose Room.'

Once we were settled together in the Rose Room, Margot rolled up the sleeves of her purple cardigan and fixed her eyes on the car park outside the window. 'It's so strange, Lenni, to think that your parents probably hadn't even been born when I was standing on that beach, let alone you.'

She started sketching. Black charcoal on white.

Troon Beach, Scotland, November 1956
Margot Docherty is Twenty-Five Years Old

He'd suggested we go for a walk on the beach in such a way that I didn't think to argue with him, even though something somewhere between rain and snow was dancing diagonally outside our window.

The beach was deserted. And beyond the sand, the long grass was fighting against the strong wind. We stood silently for a while, watching the violent waves sweeping sand into the sea.

'I'm leaving,' he said.

I thought it was a joke, but then I saw that he was crying.

'I'm going,' he said. 'I've got to get out.'

The wind roared through me. I searched his face for sunlight. But I couldn't find it.

We were still living in the tenement and it was cramped and noisy; the neighbours had dogs and arguments. But worse than that, they had a baby. Her screams raged their way through the wall to our bedroom and we would lie in silence, fighting the urge to go and comfort a little life that wasn't ours.

We walked along the shoreline, not hand in hand but close enough to touch. My boots sunk into the sand. The air was much colder but no less claustrophobic than our tenement; the wind was strong as it circled us, throwing my hair across my face, filling my mouth and my ears with the roar of the elements. My fingers had curled into my palms in an act of self-preservation. I couldn't feel them any more anyway. We had to shout to be heard and that didn't suit Johnny and me. We weren't shouting people. It must have made it all the harder for him to shout it when he finally did.

'I just can't, Mar, you—' He stopped himself. 'I can't stay here.' He wiped tears from his face, and my fingers flexed out of instinct to reach for him.

'Why not?' I shouted over the waves.

All the wind in the world seemed to swirl around us and fall down into nothing. And, for a moment, everything was still.

'He had your eyes,' Johnny said quietly.

~

Margot smiled sadly.

I closed my eyes and took myself there – to stand with Margot on her beach, the freezing November air cutting into my skin, whipping through my dressing gown and into my pyjamas as I watched a young Margot, dressed in a brown coat, sitting in the sand and crying as the wind carried away all sound. I dug my pink slippers into the wet sand and dragged them out to my side, making an arc. A circle around myself. Margot looked so different with the dark hair that was swirling in the wind. As she buried her head into her skirt, her legs hitched up, I went to reach out and touch her . . .

'You'll be okay,' I said.

'Thank you.' She smiled, and we were back in the Rose Room. The rest of the class were doing a good job of ignoring us. I wondered whether Walter and Else had been listening as they etched and scratched and smudged.

Margot picked up the charcoal and darkened the grass at the top of the cliffs. Then she took a tissue out of her sleeve, but instead of blowing her nose or wiping her eyes, she used it to carefully blur the edges of the charcoal Johnny, who was tall and thin and with his back to the picture, faceless.

'So he just left you all alone with the baby? I'd have been furious.'

'No, it wasn't like that.'
'But he did leave?'
'Yes.'
'So where was the baby?'

Father Arthur and the Motorbike

FATHER ARTHUR WAS sitting at the electric piano in the corner of the chapel. He pressed a key and a dulled note came out. He pressed another. Then he pressed them together. It didn't sound good. He sighed and stood up.

'Don't stop, it was pretty.'

'Good God!' Arthur staggered and sat back down on the piano stool, his hand on his chest. 'I will never understand how you manage to sneak through that door so quietly.'

I came over to the piano.

'Do you play?' I asked.

'No. I was just dusting it and I decided to have a go. I'm not sure why it's here, actually, because we don't have a chapel organist.'

I sat beside him at the piano stool and pressed a note. It sounded like it was coming through a blanket. I pressed a few more.

'When you retire, you could take up lessons,' I told him.

He pulled the cover down over the piano keys. 'Perhaps,' he said.

'That's what retirement's for, isn't it? Doing the things you always wanted to do but never dared.'

'So I should take up motorbiking?'

'Would you be able to get on a motorbike in one of your dresses?'

'They're not dresses, Lenni.'

'Are they not?'

'No! I've told you this before. They're vestments.'

There was a pause as I wrestled with the image of Father Arthur attempting to get his long white vestments over a motorbike without showing too much leg. Then, his robes billowing absurdly as he motorbiked around the city wearing old-fashioned goggles with a gang of Harley-riding clergymen following behind.

Father Arthur looked a little sad. 'I actually won't be needing my vestments after I retire,' he said.

'You could take up gardening? Your robes would be great for that – they'd give protection from the sun but you'd still get a nice breeze.'

'I can't garden in my vestments!'

'You can't?'

'They're sacred garments.'

'Are they?'

'Yes! I can't use them for anything other than religious duties.'

'That's a shame because I bet they'd make very comfortable nighties.'

'I tend to prefer pyjamas,' he said.

Father Arthur got up from the piano and went across the chapel – the purples and pinks of the stained glass window fell across the carpet, and as he stepped into the patch of purple and pink, for a moment he was purple and pink too.

'So, Lenni,' he said, as he picked up a wayward Bible someone had left on a pew, 'tell me about your one hundred years.'

I lifted up the piano cover again and pressed the highest note and the lowest note together. 'Our tally on the wall of the Rose Room is up to fifteen now,' I said.

'That's splendid,' he said. 'And Margot?'

I pressed three keys in a row, from left to right so that the notes stepped up. It sounded quite nice.

'She's well,' I said. 'She's very good at painting. If I'd known she was this good, I might not have signed up to have my pictures placed next to hers for everyone to see.'

'Lenni,' he said softly, from somewhere behind me.

'So I'm writing them down, the stories. To make up for my lack of artistic talent.'

I pressed another three of the little black notes.

'What's she like?' Arthur asked.

'She's like nobody I've met before,' I told him.

I pressed the notes quickly so they sounded like tinkling bells.

'I think her baby died.'

The Second Winter

'WE CAN'T GET hold of your husband,' the nurse said as she stopped at the doorway, out of breath. I didn't just hear her words, I could see them, shimmering across my eyes in dots of white and black. I could feel her movements too. As she came towards me, the fizzes in my cheek moved with her.

I held my hand over one eye and I nodded.

'Are you okay?' she asked, coming closer. She faltered. 'I mean, your eye, is it okay?'

I nodded, hand still over my eye, and willed her to leave but she came closer. 'Is there something wrong with your eye?' she asked again.

I turned away from her, hoping it would make her leave, but it didn't and I couldn't remember the words to make her go.

She knelt down in front of me, and I felt the reverberations of her movement all across my face.

'Look at me,' she said, and I did. Her mouth and her chin were gone, replaced by a grey nothingness. 'Blink,' she said, and I did. Though she was in front of me, she felt very far away.

'Follow the end of my pen,' she said, and I tried to but the pen kept disappearing.

'Doctor?' she said in an even voice, but I knew there was concern in it.

The shape of a man came and stood beside her. 'She can't see,' the nurse said.

'I'm fine,' I tried to say, but it came out very long and slow, I couldn't get to the M, so I settled for a B. 'I'b fiy.' I knew it was wrong, but it wasn't clear how to fix it. I wanted to say something else, but I didn't know what it was.

The doctor made an interested sound and repeated the steps made by the nurse. Just like her, parts of his face were missing; there were grey gaps where his forehead and chin should have been. And what little I could see flickered with the flash of a photograph nobody had taken.

He had me open and close my jaw, turn my head. He asked me to tell him my name. I knew it, it was in my mind, but I couldn't find shapes to match it. I wanted to tell them to leave me, that I was fine, that my time was precious, but I couldn't.

From somewhere, the hissing snake of the word 'stroke' slithered its way to my ear.

'Stroke' is a lot like the word 'snake', only I'd never noticed before. This I clung to, and I thought it over and over several times. As though I were remembering my telephone number. I felt that I would need it later. Stroke and snake. So similar. Why had I never spotted that?

'Do you feel sick?' he asked.

I shook my head. I was lying. The sweet taste of stomach acid was already filling my mouth. I would have asked for a glass of water if I could remember how.

Stroke slithered back into my ears with an echo. Stroke snake stroke snake.

'No,' the doctor said firmly. 'It is most likely a migraine.' The words meant nothing to me – as though I'd heard them in a foreign tongue. I tried to separate them into pieces to find the meaning. *My-grain.*

'The child's prognosis?' the doctor asked.

'The consultant said it will be a matter of hours,' the nurse replied.

'Madam,' the doctor said, and I felt the weight of something on my left shoulder, presumably a hand. 'I believe you are having an ocular migraine. Have you ever experienced these symptoms before?'

I shook my head.

'They can be brought on by stress. I can give you something for the pain, but it will make you drowsy, you may fall asleep. Given the, um, the present circumstances, do you want me to do that?'

'No,' I managed. How similar 'no' was on the tongue to 'know'. They were almost the same. Perhaps they were the same.

'I understand,' he said. 'You may find you need to vomit. If you do, there is a container here. Other symptoms may include an aversion to light, intense head pain and confusion. You need to alert us if your symptoms change or worsen.'

I nodded.

'I will ask the staff to continue to search for your husband.'

He lifted his hand off my shoulder and spoke quickly to the nurse, but the effort of decoding the sounds into meaning was too great.

'I'll be here if you need me,' the nurse said, and I heard her draw the curtain around the bed. The tips of my fingers were tingling as I leant forward and felt for the edges of the mattress.

In front of me lay a baby. My baby. And it was time to say goodbye.

'Davey,' I said, my tongue able to remember him when nothing else sounded right. With what was left of my vision, I could see that his little eyes had opened. He was still pale, his body all wrapped up in his sleepsuit and his blanket. He looked up at me. What a sight I must have been. His mother with her hand covering her left eye. I wondered if he remembered the games of peekaboo we had played, and if that was what he thought we were doing.

I don't know how to say goodbye to a child. I didn't then and I don't now. So instead I talked to him. I told him of the life he would lead, of the school uniform he would wear, of his days in the summer sunshine when I would take him to the park. I told him how he would get a part-time job in a greengrocer's and eventually buy the place and run it himself. How he would meet a young lady who came in to buy a pineapple and they would fall in love. How they would marry and I would wear a yellow hat at the wedding. I told him of his own noisy three children and how he would grow old with them helping out in the shop, using apples to teach them to count. And his eyes stayed fixed on mine while I told him, softly, of how he'd be so incredibly happy and how he would come to visit me when I was old and grey.

I laid myself down on the bed beside him and I kissed his cheek. It was so soft and spongy. It had become one of his favourite games, where I kissed his cheek and tickled him beneath his chin, so I lay there and I kissed his cheek over and over. And I told him about my eternal love. How I would love him for ever. For the rest of my days and more.

Whatever grey absence had been dancing in my eyes grew wider until it had taken everything. Where Davey's sweet, sleeping face should have been was nothing. I closed my eyes and made an appeal to whatever gods in the universe were listening.

I stroked Davey's head so that he could be sure I was still there, and so that I could be sure he was still there. I rested a hand on his tiny chest and felt the gentle rise and fall of his breathing. How could there be something wrong with his heart when I could feel it beating stronger than my own? I reluctantly closed my eyes. I let the tears spill onto my arm and my sleeve, and I stroked his hair and I kissed his cheek and I told him more stories about the world, about jungles and animals and stars.

When I woke up, the migraine was gone.

Davey was gone too.

Lenni

'LENNI, CAN YOU hear me?'

'Lenni, talk to us, sweetheart.'

'Lenni?'

The bed was laid flat beneath me; there were more voices.

'It's okay, Lenni, we're here. Just stay calm.'

PART TWO

Lenni

WHENEVER I GO under general anaesthetic, I have the most vivid dreams. They are so vivid that in the past I have been accused of inventing them. I remember telling another girl in a different hospital in a different country about my dream, and she didn't believe it. This dream, though, is incredible and it feels like it lasts for days and days. There is an octopus and we are the fiercest of friends. He is purple, and everything is bright and extraordinary. And I can hear the most wonderful music.

Margot and the Diary

Hello, Lenni, it's Margot.

I've missed you.

Your red-haired nurse came into my ward yesterday. She said you'd asked, before they took you in for the operation, that I be given your diary. She said you write in it all the time and she suspects she might be in it. She said you wanted me to write you something.

I'm honoured you trust me with it, but you should know I've only accepted this book as a loan. If this is being bequeathed to me then I want no part of it, young lady.

You'll take this surgery in your stride, I know it. Nothing scares you. I'm quite the opposite.

But here is a story for you to read when you wake up:

This week in the Rose Room, I painted the first place I lived that I really, truly loved. It was dirty and crooked. Like all the best characters.

The painting itself is fair. I know my old art teacher at school would have said that the perspective isn't quite right, and the roof gives the impression of slanting backwards, but I'm happy with it nonetheless. The version of me that lives in my memory, the version of me that lives in that tiny flat, is a lot more like you than she is like me.

It starts, like all of my stories so far, in Scotland.

Glasgow to London, February 1959
Margot Docherty is Twenty-Eight Years Old

By the time I was twenty-eight, my father was the only one left. My mother had passed when I was twenty-six. And it had felt like I'd been orphaned when she went. The shellshock – they call it something else now – had eroded my father until he wouldn't even allow me to sit with him. But sit I did, when the call came. He was already dead, but I sat beside him in the hospital and I memorized his face. I whispered an apology and a good luck wish for the journey, and I felt a severing. I was looking at the final thread on my tightrope, the choking embers of my only candle, the last of the lifeboats. And he was gone – snapped, extinguished, sailed away.

It was sad, but it was also freeing. I was no longer any-body's. A childless mother and a husbandless wife, a parent-less daughter with a small inheritance and no fixed address.

I could go anywhere. I realized I was free to begin again, and I didn't lose that kernel of hope until I disembarked onto the dirty platform at Euston Station, determined that I would find my husband. The only person left.

I started with the police. It was very early in the morning; I had slept on the train but I felt dazed. My teeth had layers of fuzz when I ran my tongue along them, which, now I had felt the fuzz, I couldn't stop doing. I'd eaten half a packet of Polo mints, but my mouth was still stale.

As I came out of the station into the light, seeing the rows of cars and red buses, the people pushing past one another on their way to work, it felt as though the suitcases in my hands were the only things tethering me to the ground.

I asked a hassled man in a hat for directions to the near-est police station, and after getting lost along several identical streets, I found it. And in I went, not letting myself stop for even a moment for fear that I might turn back.

There was a secretary at a desk and a row of stained chairs. I'd been rehearsing what I would say in my head when I was on the train. *My name is Margot Docherty; I'm looking for a missing person. My husband, Johnny.*

How could you misplace your husband? would be the first question, I was sure.

I was wrong. The first question wasn't a question at all, but an instruction to take a seat and fill in a form.

I sat down. The form immediately expected more from me than I was able to give. What was my name? I knew that, but how about my address? Currently, my address was Holborn Police Station, London. But where did I live? In my recently vacated Glasgow tenement? What was my relationship to the missing person? Were we married? Really, were we still? What if he had married someone else since he left? When had I last seen him? And where? Did 'some years ago on a beach' count? Or was that as unhelpful as it felt? What did he look like? Was he still slim? Did he still wear his hair parted in the middle and combed to each side? And why was I searching for him in London?

Only this last question could I answer: because many years ago, he'd lain beside me with his hands on my stomach and said that before the baby came, he wanted to see the city. We never went.

My hands were sweating and the pen slipped out of my grasp. I picked it up and wiped my wet fingers on my skirt.

I looked to the receptionist to see if there was anyone free to talk to me, but she shook her head.

I pondered over some more questions, which were obvious facts I should have known but didn't. Things like his height, his health record, his job. With the sparse information I could tell them about Johnny, he may as well have been a stranger.

'What are you doing?' she asked. I'd had no idea anyone was beside me, but there she was. She was younger than me, though not by much. She was wearing a blue and green patterned dress and her blonde hair looked like it hadn't been washed in days. And she seemed completely comfortable exactly where she was at that moment.

'Er, I'm ...'

'What's in the bags? A body?' She laughed and wiped make-up from under her eyes, where it smeared into two dark lines below her lower lashes.

'Is it drugs?'

'No, it's ...'

'Bombs?!' she asked, and then, looking around at the people in the waiting room who were staring at us, she leant closer to me and whispered, 'Bombs?'

'No!' I said, and dropped the pen on the floor again.

'Here.' She passed it to me. Her many bracelets jangled as she tucked her hair behind her ear. 'Sorry I scared you.'

'You haven't scared me,' I said, and although she *hadn't* scared me, I was suddenly filled with the urge to cry. I was exhausted, recently bereaved, and about to file a missing person's report for a man I could barely describe. A man who wasn't really *missing*, but who I couldn't find, his mother having passed away and his brother having moved without a forwarding address. A man who had promised me his life. A man who I had missed deeply and yet had not missed in the slightest.

She leant back against her chair, folding her thin arms in on herself. She ran her fingers through the lengths of her blonde hair and twisted a piece around her finger.

I turned my attention back to the form. I knew Johnny's birthday, at least that was something. Then there was a box – 'reason for filing report'. Half the form was still blank. I filled in the box with a redundant *I don't know where he is*, and then realized that might seem flippant and crossed it out.

'What are you doing?' she whispered. She smelled of perfume and alcohol.

'I'm ...' I couldn't explain it, so I just showed her the form on the clipboard.

'*Missing Person's Report*,' she read. Her eyebrows rose. 'Who's it for?' Then, as I went to answer, she asked, 'It's not for you, is it? That would be brilliant! File your own missing person's report and then disappear ... God, that's brilliant. I want to do that one day.' Her eyes shone.

'My husband,' I said, feeling like I was speaking for the first time in days.

'Oh,' she said, and for some reason I told her the story. Most of it. With one important little person omitted.

'Do you miss your husband?' she asked when I was finished.

'I don't know,' I said. 'He's the only person I have left.'

'But you want to spend a lot of time with him when you find him?'

'No, I—'

'You want to live with him?'

'Well . . .'

'You're happy to be defined by him?'

'Defined?'

'Yes, you know, you've come all this way just for him. Your current purpose is him. He defines you.' She seemed angry about this.

'I just wanted to see a friendly face,' I told her, realizing as I said it that this was the truth.

'Put that on the form, then,' she said. 'They'll really hot up the search if they know how urgent it is that he's found.'

The blank face of the form stared back at me, unreadable.

'What will you do once it's filed?'

'I don't know,' I told her.

'Do you have somewhere to stay?'

'No.' I felt the heat rising in my face.

'That's brave,' she said, and I wondered if it was.

'I don't know,' I said again, feeling increasingly like I was about to cry.

'Do you want to know what I'm doing here?' she asked. I didn't answer but she told me three things. Firstly, she was waiting for her friend Adam who had recently been incarcerated for breaking into a university animal laboratory. Secondly, she was waiting to see if she would be arrested for the same crime. And thirdly, she was offering me a bed for the night once numbers one and two were resolved.

Then, she advised me to rip up the missing person's report and to 'liberate' myself. Which at first I thought was slang for something sexual, but was in fact, I learned much later, an invitation to stand apart from the husband who had run from me and, instead of giving chase, waving him goodbye and bidding him safe travels.

The resolution of numbers one and two took much longer than either of us anticipated, and my hand remained on the missing person's report until it was crinkled where the moisture of my palm had pressed into it. A man who'd had his bike stolen and a police officer had both tripped over my suitcases, swearing and questioning my purpose, respectively.

When Adam emerged from the cells, his hands un-cuffed, my new companion gave a cheer, and was shushed and then threatened by the policeman who handed Adam his possessions and told him, in words I shan't repeat, to leave.

'A wronged man is released,' she said. ''Tis right to celebrate.' I wondered if this was a quote from Shakespeare. 'This is Adam. Meet our Scottish runaway, Margot.'

He gave me a handshake. My hands were still wet and I noticed him subtly wipe his palms on his jeans.

We made our way onto the street in the dim sunshine.

'Oh,' she said, as though she'd forgotten, 'I'm Meena.'

We had been on the street and walking away from the police station for some time before I realized I was still holding the clipboard and the missing person's report.

'Oh, I forgot!' I hurried back towards the police station, but Meena followed me, and just outside the station she put her hand on my arm and stopped me.

'What are you doing?' she asked.

'I can't steal from the police!'

'They can have their clipboard back,' she said, 'but not this.' She unclipped the paper. 'Turn it over to fate,' she said. And then she scrunched up the missing person's report, pressed it tight into her palms and threw it, spectacularly, into the bin.

Lenni and the Rose Room

MARGOT BARRELLED TOWARDS me so fast that she was just a blur of purple. She wrapped her arms tightly around me and I breathed in her lavender smell.

'Are you okay?' I asked.

I felt her nodding.

'Careful,' New Nurse warned, but it was far too late to do anything about the fact that Margot was pressing into my newly acquired stitches.

'I've missed you so much!' she said.

The eyes of the whole class were on me. But I didn't let them swerve my attention from Margot's collection of paintings and sketches that had accumulated in my absence. They were so good that I swore. I apologized for swearing, but she didn't seem to mind. I think I could have got away with a lot that day because she was just so pleased that I wasn't dead.

Pippa came straight over to me, as soon as she had finished explaining to the class how to mix blues and greens together for the abstract pictures of the ocean they were tasked with painting.

'Lenni,' she said, 'I won't hug you,' and she gestured to the green paint splattered all over her apron. 'How are you feeling?'

'Fine, thanks,' I said.

'And everything's okay now?' she pressed. I nodded, not letting her have anything, not even a word on what had happened during my brief hiatus from the Rose Room. Even though she was only being kind, there's something irritating about people wanting to know everything, wanting to know all the surgical details. Exactly how *much* you're dying.

'Well, it's great to have you back.' Pippa smiled.

When she was gone, Margot's eyes met mine, and I sensed that at that moment she was tucking away a question about the two people with whom I used to share some very elaborate breakfasts. A question she wanted to ask but knew I wouldn't answer.

The pictures we painted that day were secondary. The stories we told were secondary too. Nothing really mattered except that I was in the Rose Room and Margot was beside me.

Lenni and the Harvest Festival

New Nurse was sitting in her favourite place on the end of my bed. Not in the way that the other nurses sometimes do, in a kind of conciliatory, uncomfortable attempt at casual that usually comes off as insincere. New Nurse wasn't pretending to be comfortable. She was comfortable. She'd helped herself to a spare pillow so she could lean against the bars at the foot of the bed without them digging into her back. Then she'd kicked off her pumps and settled herself down, legs crossed, her cardigan draped over her arms to make her cosy. She'd made sure the curtain was drawn around us so that we could be alone. Or as alone as it was possible to be.

Her hair is still the red of cherry-flavoured Tango but it's a bit longer than when we first met. *How long has it been?* I wondered. Thinking about cherry Tango made me want to taste some – the fizziness fireworking all over my tongue, the medicinal sweetness of school discos and trips to the newsagent's.

She tucked a strand of her cherry-Tango hair behind her ear. She wanted to know everything, anything. She wanted to know what I thought of her care. Really, I think she wanted to know if she was passing convincingly as a nurse. I told her that she was the only nurse in the hospital I would tell twice that she was my favourite.

'Do you think you would ever go back?' she asked.

'To Sweden?' I thought about it. 'Probably not.'

'Your mam's there, isn't she?' she asked, and I wondered what hint of a dialect New Nurse had just revealed. If I'd been born here, I'd know.

'Yep,' I told her. 'But she'd be the reason I wouldn't go back.' I noticed concern take hold of New Nurse's face, pulling her mouth into an awkward smile. 'If I went back to Sweden it wouldn't be to look for my mother, but because I know she lives there, it would be impossible *not* to look for her. If I saw a woman with dark hair pass me, I would be searching her face for my mother's. I would end up looking for her by accident. And I don't want to do that.'

New Nurse opened her mouth to ask something, but I got there first. 'Anyway,' I said, 'if I get out of here, there are so many other places that I would visit first.'

'Where would you go?'

'Paris, New York, Malaysia, Russia, Finland, Mexico, Australia, Vietnam. In that order. And then I would just keep going. On and on and on until I died.'

'Why Russia?'

'Why not?'

'I could never travel anywhere by myself,' she said. 'I'm not brave.'

'Neither am I!'

She looked at me, staring so searchingly that I looked away.

'Lenni,' she said softly, 'you're the bravest person I know.'

'Why?'

'You just are,' she said, and the moment fell between us.

'Dying isn't brave,' I said, 'it's accidental. I'm not brave, I'm just not dead yet.'

New Nurse stretched her legs out straight, so that my legs and her legs were lying side by side like rungs of a train track. Her socks matched this time; they were pink and had cupcakes printed on them. I tried to imagine what her life was like outside the hospital – her house, her car, her sock drawer.

'I still think you're brave,' she said quietly.

'If you went travelling, I would think you were brave too,' I told her.

She pulled a tiny red box of raisins out of the pocket of her dress and peeled the top off, then squeezed a finger in and popped a wrinkled raisin into her mouth.

'I bet they'll love you in Russia.'

Sometimes I deal with nurses other than New Nurse; they have names and faces but they come and go in a blur. Their non-red hair screams of conformity, and their practice of giving me as much attention as they give everyone else is grating. They never have raisin snack time on my bed late at night. I haven't checked, but I bet none of them have cupcake socks. Of course, I don't blame them – they are the wardens and we are the prisoners, and if they get too close, the lines might become blurred as to who is captive and who is free.

Anyway, after New Nurse left, it was one of the other nurses who brought around a selection of newspapers and magazines that had been donated. I went straight for *Christian Today* so I would have something to talk to Father Arthur about when I next paid him a visit. The main headline promised to tell me of 'Christ's Message at the Harvest Festival'. The front cover showed several small children smiling widely from behind a row of canned foods. It looked a lot like the

Nativity, except that the Baby Jesus had been replaced with a tin of kidney beans.

I wondered whether Father Arthur would be stacking up tins of beans on the altar of the hospital chapel. Or perhaps his donations would all be made up of hospital food, and the chapel would be filled with plastic trays of stagnant shepherd's pie, rice pudding and orange-flavoured Fortisip. Although, if Arthur was going to rely on getting a food donation from every person who visited the chapel, there wouldn't be any food at all except mine. Once again, I realized, he needed my help. I would pay him a visit and lend a hand to the Harvest Festival; perhaps I could round up a group of children for a photo opportunity with some tuna fish in brine.

Since I spent time with the octopus, some things are harder than they used to be. When I asked at the nurses' desk if I could visit the chapel, there was talk between two of them. The words 'infection' and 'immune system' were bandied about. I was sent back to my bed.

I didn't fight at first. But then, about an hour later, as I sat swinging my feet from the edge of my bed, thinking about my purple octopus and staring at the cover of *Christian Today*, I realized that I didn't have time to be quite so yielding. Having hardly any time left generates this itch inside my ribcage.

I walked up to the desk. The nurse, Jacky, whose sour face met mine, said, 'I don't want to hear it, Lenni, we are really busy today.'

'What does she want?' Sharon asked, as she folded her jacket over her arm.

'To go to church,' Jacky said.

'Tuh.' Sharon rolled her eyes, picked up her mug and her lunch bag, and made her way out. 'See you tomorrow, bab!' she called to Jacky behind her.

Once Sharon had gone, Jacky turned to me. 'You need to go back to your bed, Lenni.'

'But I'm dying.'

Jacky met my eyes.

'I'm dying,' I said again, but she didn't even acknowledge that I'd spoken.

It was daytime by then, so there were people buzzing around – porters wheeling cages of wild bed linen towards the laundry room, visitors bustling in wearing far too many layers for the tropical climes of the hospital, old people practising walking in the corridors.

'I'm dying,' I said more loudly. Jacky didn't look at me.

'I've already explained that there's nobody available to take you to church today. There are fifteen other people on this ward who need care and attention. Now stop embarrassing yourself and go back to your bed.' Her skin was wrinkled around her mouth with the early ageing of a regular smoker, but I imagined that beneath her skin was nothing but granite – hard stone that no heat could melt and no light could brighten. If you peeled back her skin, you could scratch your name into it.

I could have walked back to my bed. In theory. But in practice my feet were heavy, pulled by a force stronger than myself to stay where they were. It was beyond my control. My body was taking a stand, and I had to stand with it. We're a team. Sometimes.

'We can discuss this later,' she said. Now there were more eyes on us.

'I want to see Father Arthur,' I said.

She peered around for backup – a passing doctor or another nurse would do.

'I'm not discussing this any further. I have a lot to do.' And then she went back to the spreadsheet on her computer. Clicking and dragging and clicking and dragging and then pressing delete several times in quick succession. *Ha*, I thought, *you made a mistake.*

I think she hoped that if she ignored me for long enough, I would go away. Like a wasp. But I still couldn't. She did some more clicking and dragging, and even though she was staring at the screen, I could tell her peripheral vision was on me. I stayed there, wondering if I, with my light hair and pink pyjamas, resembled a child in a horror film. She clicked and typed and I waited.

Finally, Jacky looked back at me. This time with fire in her eyes. 'Do you know what? If you don't move from this desk right now, I will call security.'

'I don't want to be at this desk, I want to go to the chapel and see Father Arthur.'

'I've told you, you have to wait.'

'I don't have time!' I let out a growl of frustration which drew the attention of a passing set of parents.

'To be honest, Lenni, I don't have time either,' she said. 'I don't have time for your theatrics and I don't have time for this ridiculous stunt.'

'But you *do* have time.'

'What?'

'You've probably got a good forty years left. Well, maybe more like twenty-five or thirty if you keep smoking, but you've still got more time than me.'

Without my consent, a tear broke free from my eye and decided to make its own way in the world, rolling down my cheek and hitting the floor. I hoped that it would keep going, roll on and on, all the way to the chapel to find Father Arthur and tell him I was being held prisoner.

'That's it,' she said, and she picked up the telephone and dialled three numbers. She waited, and I waited. Another renegade tear made its way to the floor, in hot pursuit of its comrade.

'Security to the May Ward please,' she said when someone finally picked up on the other end, 'I have a patient who is obstructing the nurses' station.' She waited again, sternly said, 'Okay,' and then put down the receiver. I said nothing.

She shuffled some papers on the desk and clicked off the lid of a green highlighter. When she started highlighting bits of her paper, I was sure that she was just pretending to be doing something so it would seem like I wasn't annoying her in the slightest.

'Can I go to the chapel now?' I asked. 'I'll take myself if you're busy.'

'This isn't *The Lenni Show*, you know,' she said. 'I know that there are certain members of staff who give you special treatment, but you are just the same as everybody else, except you make twice as much work for everyone.'

'No I don't,' I said, but without providing any evidence to the contrary.

'Ridiculous,' she said under her breath.

Another tear broke free.

When security didn't come at once, I wondered whether the hospital security hated Jacky as much as I was starting to. It was nice. It undermined her need to swiftly deal with me, so I stayed there, refusing to wipe the tears from my eyes. Clearly thinking the same thing, Jacky picked up the telephone again. 'Yeah, it's Jacky from the May Ward,' she said, 'I called for security ...'

The door buzzer for guests, staff and other May Ward prisoners buzzed, and a tall figure emerged through the doors wearing a security uniform. He couldn't have been older than twenty-five.

The tears were out of my control now, rolling down my face and dripping onto my pyjama top. My nose decided to get in on the action too, leaking down my top lip.

'Hey,' he said. 'Are you ... okay?'

'I want to go to the chapel, to see the priest,' I said.

'Excuse me?' Jacky said to him sharply.

'Sunil. But everyone calls me Sunny.' He held out his hand, but Jacky didn't shake it.

'I'm the one who called you,' Jacky said. 'This patient is obstructing my nurses' station.'

'I want to see my friend,' I said again, as more tears slid down my face.

Sunny looked from me to Jacky and back again. 'I'll take her,' he said lightly.

Jacky looked like she was going to explode.

'No,' she said, 'she has to wait. I've told her to wait.'

Sunny seemed perplexed. 'It's really no trouble.'

'We can't have one rule for *her* and a different rule for everyone else.' She jammed the lid of her highlighter pen into the palm of her hand.

163

'Is there someone else who wants to go to the chapel too?' Sunny asked. 'Cos I can take them all, I don't mind.' He smiled.

The cruelty of strangers never usually upsets me, but the kindness of strangers is oddly devastating. As Sunny asked me if I was okay again and offered to take me wherever I wanted to go, I really started bawling.

'I called you so you could escort this patient back to her bed,' Jacky said. 'If you can't do it, I'll find someone else who will.'

Sunny glanced at me. He seemed unwilling to come and physically move me. He took a step towards me and said, 'In that case, young lady, would you mind escorting *me* to your bed?'

I nodded and sniffed. I started walking and he walked ever so slightly behind me so that anyone else on the ward would think I was leading the way.

I reached my bed, from which Jacky and the nurses' station were still visible. She had her neck craned round so that she could see if I'd made it. Like a heron searching for a worm in the grass. I sat on the end of my bed and she turned away, satisfied.

Sunny pulled the curtain so that Jacky couldn't see me any more. 'Keep your chin up,' he said.

When I'd finally gathered the energy to draw the curtain the rest of the way round my bed, I drank almost a whole jug of water. I didn't want to lie back on the bed because I didn't want to be comfortable. Being comfortable would mean giving in. I didn't want Jacky, who definitely couldn't see me, to think that I was now at peace with her decision or my detention.

And I sat there for perhaps an hour or two trying to decipher the reason for my tears – was it the fact that I had my plans thwarted? That I didn't get to see Arthur? The fact that Jacky didn't care that I am dying? Or the fact that I'm dying? Or perhaps, I realized, I was crying because I live in a place where dying doesn't make you special.

Then, a voice on the other side of my curtain whispered into the silence, '*Lenni?*'

'Father Arthur?'

'It's Father Arthur,' he whispered back.

'Father Arthur?'

'Yes.'

'Come in!'

He crept into my cubicle as though he were on some sort of parody Second World War mission.

'Sunny came to see me,' he whispered.

'You know Sunny?'

'I do. We met at the hospital's interfaith barbecue last summer. He's a lovely young man, don't you think?'

'I do.'

'Anyway, he came to see me because there was a patient from the May Ward who was upset because she wasn't allowed to visit the chaplain.' He hovered awkwardly near the edge of the bed and smiled. 'I think there's only one person in the whole hospital who would be disappointed if they didn't get to see me; and it's you, Lenni.'

'I just wanted to talk about the Harvest Festival.'

'The Harvest Festival?' His brow furrowed.

'I've been reading about it.'

'But the Harvest Festival is in September ...'

I looked down at the cover of *Christian Today*, which was on my bedside table. He must have spotted it too, because he reached over and picked it up, checking the date on the cover.

'So it's not September?' I asked.

'No,' he said slowly, looking concerned for me.

I laughed, and he laughed. But then, and without enough time to stop them, more tears began to fall.

'Lenni,' he said, 'what is it?'

'I don't even know any more.'

He held out a yellow handkerchief for me. I'd never seen anyone use a handkerchief in real life, only in films. It hung in the air between us like a springtime ghost.

'It's clean,' he said, 'I promise.'

I took it and opened it up into a perfect square, and then I buried my face in it. It was absorbent and smelled of church. It was like crying onto the hem of the pope's best dress.

'Thank you for coming,' I said, though it came out muffled.

'I do believe that's what friends are for.'

Margot and the Bottle

MEENA IS NOTHING like I imagined her. Margot found a photograph in the latest bag of things they brought over from her care home. She's ethereal. Her blonde hair is brighter than I imagined, her skin paler, her eyes rounder. There's something elfin about her ears.

Margot kept the picture on the desk between us while she painted the greenest bottle you ever did see.

London, March 1960
Margot Docherty is Twenty-Nine Years Old

My father died in the winter. It was dark and cold and cruel outside. And yet, within days of meeting Meena and sheepishly moving into her bedsit while her now ex-flatmate Lawrence furiously packed up the last of his things, it was summer. It had been summer since the day I met her.

We were getting ready for a house party. I was sitting on the carpet, trying to apply mascara in the mirror that had fallen out of its frame and was now propped up against the fireplace. This gave us a spot on the floor to do our make-up and also blocked out the draught from the broken fireplace. There was a pigeon who occasionally cooed down the chimney.

Meena was playing a record and the needle kept getting stuck. Michael Holliday could only get so far as singing, 'Every time I look at you, falling stars come into view,' before there was a scratching noise that made him fall quiet. As the track skipped, I slipped and scratched my inner eyelid with the mascara brush. As I blinked frantically and tears welled in my eyes, rivers of black mascara ran down my cheek. I sighed.

'Margot, when was the last time you had fun?'

Meena asked me that about a week into my tenancy. And I'd been unable to answer. The first memory that came to mind was running with Christabel. Just running. I couldn't remember where we were going from and I couldn't remember where we were going to, I just remembered running and laughing until I couldn't breathe. Our sandals clattering on the pavement.

'Are you having fun?' she asked me now. I turned to her and my face must have given me away. I always got nervous before the big parties. Though I knew a lot of Meena's friends, I didn't know all of them, and I had this feeling that I had wandered into someone else's life. That I was supposed to be in Glasgow in an empty church hall attending a meeting for bereaved mothers, crying into a handkerchief and clutching my Davey's bear.

'Here.' A bottle floated before my eyes. 'Have some of this,' she said.

I took it from her. It was a thin bottle with fruit modelled out of the glass, a label in Spanish, and inside was the brightest green liquid I had ever seen.

'What is it?'

'No idea,' she said.

'Then why did you buy it?'

'I didn't. The Professor gave it to me.'

The Professor was Meena's boss. She worked as a typist for a medical school. It was her fellow typist friend at the university who had recommended me for my new job at the London Library. Meena told me she worked for The Professor so she could gather information on the animal testing at the medical school. But her friend Adam told me at another party that she'd been there long enough to know everything she needed to know. And then he'd raised his eyebrows and sauntered away.

She went to fix the record player while I unscrewed the cap and took a cautious sip of the luminous green alcohol. It tasted as if all the pears in the world had been distilled into that single bottle.

She waited. I took another couple of generous swigs.

Meena climbed onto her bed and patted the quilt cover as though I were a dog she wanted to come and sit beside her. She positioned herself opposite me, both of us cross-legged so that our knees almost touched. 'Now, close your eyes,' she said. For a moment, I didn't. Meena's blue eyes had this glint in them, which with her elfin ears made her look mischievous. Like she was up to something even when she was just smiling.

She unzipped her Moomin make-up bag and I closed my eyes.

I felt her lean closer to me, so that I could feel her eyelashes on my skin.

169

She wiped the mascara from under my eyes with a tissue and something that was creamy and smelled of lavender. I felt her put shadow on my eyelids and blush on my cheeks. Her brush was so soft it made me shudder.

Then, she rattled around inside her bag for something else. She began drawing on my face. At first it felt like she was shading in my eyebrows, but then I felt her pencil looping up past my eyebrow and around my eye. Then a circle around my eye and a straight line from the top of my cheek downwards.

'What are you doing?' I asked.

'Stay still,' she said. And so I did. I felt a wet brush painting within the shapes she had drawn, but by now I had lost all idea of what she was doing. For a brief moment, she pulled me in closer and I could smell her musky perfume and the pear liqueur on her breath.

'Done!' she said. I opened my eyes and felt like I was waking up. 'What do you think?'

I clambered off the end of her bed and stared at myself in the mirror.

She'd made me a flower. My right eye was the centre in blue and around it were pink petals edged in white. A green stalk curled past my newly pinked cheeks and stopped when it reached my jaw.

'I—'

'Don't worry, I'll do one for me, too,' she said. 'Now shift it and drink some more, we have to go soon.'

We sat at the back of the bus. Both of us with our flower face paint. Meena had brought the bottle of pear liqueur with us, and she drank it as the bus swung around corners in the darkness.

A loud tutting came from an old woman sitting across the aisle. She was carrying bursting bags from the closing down sale of a department store.

'Is something the matter?' Meena asked in a voice that was pleasant, but had an edge.

The old woman fluffed up. If she had been a pigeon, her feathers would have ruffled.

'You look like an *imbecile*,' she hissed. 'Both of you. Have some self-respect.'

My stomach turned. The bus slowed to a stop. We climbed off the back of it and started walking. Meena was ahead of me so I used the privacy to pull down on my skirt, trying to get the hem to cover more of my thighs.

'Stop that,' Meena said, without turning.

'Stop what?'

'Feeling embarrassed.'

'I *am* embarrassed. I shouldn't be dressed up like this. I'm someone's—' I stopped myself from saying the M word. 'I should know better.'

She stopped then and I caught her up and she looked at me, searchingly, for what felt like just a second too long. 'You care, don't you?' she said.

I didn't know from the way she said it if it was a good thing or a bad thing.

When I didn't answer, Meena said, 'That woman was probably somewhere between sixty and sixty-five years old.'

'So?'

'So that means she was born sometime between 1895 and 1900. She was raised by Victorians. Imagine being raised by people who used mangles and couldn't show their ankles, and ending your life watching television, surrounded by women in miniskirts.' She paused. 'Are you having fun?' she asked. She appraised my face and said with a wry smile, 'Well, you will.'

Going into one of those house parties was like going underwater. My ears filled with the rush of sound, of the music and talking. And everything seemed to take on a gentle, drifting quality. The pear liqueur had numbed my edges so that I couldn't quite feel anything as I bumped around the house. I was moving slower than I ought to be and the people that passed, dancing or walking, seemed to be floating too. I could sway along quite happily around the house, looking in on the groups of people talking and dancing, but feeling as though I was looking into another world that I could observe without participating. I could float into the kitchen and watch people investigate the cupboards, opening chests and searching for pearls; I could swim to the living room and watch people dance. I was suspended and yet free.

I met Meena in the corridor. She had her fingers intertwined with those of a man in a terrible hat.

'Are you having fun?' she shouted.

'What?' I could barely hear her.

She came closer and more or less screamed in my ear, 'Are you having fun?'

'Yes!'

Several hours of swimming later and as the tides of people drained out of the front door, the house became a house again. No longer my private ocean. I went looking for Meena and I found her in the back garden, holding a cigarette a few centimetres from her mouth and watching, detached, as a man I recognized as her former flatmate Lawrence gesticulated wildly and said something that was clearly an accusation.

I stepped out into the cold garden.

'You know, the thing that really irritates me . . .' Lawrence said.

With narrowed eyes, Meena took a drag from her cigarette.

'. . . is that you don't even care,' he finished.

'You're right. I don't,' she said, exhaling smoke at the same time as smiling, so that she looked like a Chinese dragon.

Lawrence threw his hands up in a gesture of frustrated defeat and pushed past me, back inside the house. Meena sucked on her cigarette. She was so calm and still, I felt I should have left her alone.

'Can you hear that?' she asked.

I strained my ears. I could hear laughter coming from the living room where the remaining party stragglers had washed ashore.

'Listen,' she said.

Then she threw her cigarette into the grass and walked off to the end of the garden. I followed her, and as I reached the bottom of the garden where there was a line of dark trees, I could hear it too. It sounded like a baby crying.

I don't remember much until we were on the other side of the fence, in the neighbours' garden. The grass was overgrown and littered with discarded junk – there was an old iron bathtub among the weeds, and a rusted lawnmower. A baby doll without arms was lying in the grass, staring at me with its wide-open eyes.

The sound, like a child whining, had fallen quiet then. We crunched through the long grass towards the line of trees at the back of the garden. And then we saw him, behind the rotting shed, chained by his neck to the trunk of a silver elm. When he saw us, he let out a little cry.

'Oh my God,' Meena whispered. Then, to the dog, she said in a quiet, soothing voice, 'Hey there, fella.' And she half crouched and crept towards him. The dog let out a high-pitched whine.

Meena got closer while I hung back, watching. 'What if he bites?' I asked.

'He won't bite, will you, pal?' She was almost close enough to touch him. He looked up at her with doleful eyes and cried. He had a cut across his nose that was infected. A thick line of pink flesh with dark edges.

When she was close enough, Meena crouched down beside him and held her palm out flat. The dog sniffed it and gazed at her. His leather collar was attached to the chain that bound him to the tree, and all around his neck was a red ring of exposed skin where he'd tried to pull himself free.

'You're a good boy, aren't you?' she asked, and he let her stroke him on the top of his head. He closed his eyes and leant his head towards her. With each breath in, we could see the ridges of his ribs.

'Would you like to come with us?' Meena asked, continuing to stroke his head. His stumpy tail flicked once, twice. 'Roger?'

'His name is Roger?'

'Well, he needs a name,' she said, 'Why not Roger?' Then she flicked something silver in her hand.

'What is that?' I asked. 'Is that a knife?!'

'You never know when you might need one. I keep it in my boot,' she said, and then, stroking Roger's head, she said to him very seriously, 'Now stay still.' Roger looked up at her with his big brown eyes.

Carefully, Meena cut the leather collar with a sawing motion. 'It's okay, baby,' she said softly, while he cried at the pressure of the collar on his neck.

When he was loose, he turned to Meena and licked her hands. His gentle thanks.

Once we got him through the gap in the fence, we gave Roger water we poured into an empty Neapolitan ice-cream tub, and some meat from the host's fridge. Inside, the party was continuing, but now we were a party of three and we didn't care.

'We should take him to a vet,' I said as we walked, the dog alongside us, around the side of the house and to the front garden.

Meena nodded, stuffing her Swiss Army knife back into her left ankle boot.

But when I opened the front garden gate, the dog took off like a shot, his long nails scritch-scratching on the tarmac. He quickly disappeared from sight.

'Wait! Roger!' I called after him.

'Shhh,' Meena hissed. 'If his owners *are* in, we want to give him a head start.'

'But—'

'He'll be okay on his own,' she said. 'He needs to be free.'

*

As we walked home, Meena started dry heaving. Nothing was coming out though, and she stood bent over the grassy patch on the pavement not far from our house.

'We're nearly home,' I told her, stroking her hair.

We clattered up the stairs to the shared bathroom. The less said about the state of that bathroom, the better. The inside of the toilet was permanently stained brown, as though someone had been using the bowl to brew tea.

As soon as we got the door open, Meena ran for the toilet, let out a burp and heaved vomit into the bowl.

I flushed the toilet for her, ran some cold water over my hand and held it to her forehead.

'Ugh,' was all she could manage before it began again – her body tensing as she threw up.

I stayed with her, and when she was finished we both sat on the floor, leaning against the bath. It wouldn't be long before the guys from the bedsit above us would need to get ready for work.

Then she knelt up and leant her head over the loo, holding her own hair at the nape of her neck. Nothing happened and she spat into it.

After a little while, Meena, her head still over the toilet bowl, begged, 'Tell me something.'

'What?'

'Tell me something I don't know.'

I thought.

'I've never met anyone like you.'

'I knew that. Tell me something I don't know.'

'I think I love you.'

She turned. Her eyes met mine and it made my shins tingle. And we looked at one another for a moment before she heaved again, her whole body convulsing as she retched up a bright green liquid into the toilet.

Lenni and Margot and
Things You Can't Say

'LENNI, YOU CAN'T say that!' New Nurse whispered. 'Jacky'll kill me. She'll kill us all!'

'She'll also kill you for saying that she'll kill people.'

New Nurse clapped a hand over her mouth.

'How did you find out about our argument?' I asked.

'Oh, I have my ways.' New Nurse tapped her nose. Then she sat up properly. Her shoulders fell, her smile faded, and she fixed me with a searching smile that she sometimes uses when she's trying not to cry. 'Was it really that bad?'

I thought about it. Yes, I cried. Yes, I made a bit of an idiot of myself, but it wasn't *that* bad. It was mostly embarrassing.

'The security guard was very nice,' I told her.

'Jacky said you cried.'

'Yep.'

'I've never seen you cry,' she said.

'I got to see Father Arthur in the end anyway.'

'Did you?'

'He snuck in later.'

'I'll pretend I didn't hear that,' she said.

I smiled.

'Lenni,' she said, still searching, perhaps hoping I would open up. Maybe wanting to witness some of my fabled tears that she was yet to see. 'Was it really bad?'

'I was just having a down day.'

New Nurse nodded. But she wanted more. People do.

'Is Jacky going to get fired?' I asked.

She looked away, out of the gap in the curtains around my bed and into the cold lighting of the corridor.

'Is she in trouble?'

'I can't say.' She kept her eyes fixed on the nurses' station, where a porter was making one of the student nurses laugh out loud.

'Did you shout at her?'

'I can't say.'

I had a feeling that she probably *did* shout at Jacky, because there was just the hint of a smile at the corner of her lips.

'Have you booked your flights yet?' I asked.

'My flights?'

'To Russia.'

'Not yet.'

'Why not?'

She gave me a look that was apparently supposed to tell me everything, and yet it actually told me nothing. And so I pulled the poorly person upper hand and told her I was tired.

Somewhat unhappily, she climbed off my bed and shoved on her white trainers. She laced them up in silence and drew the curtain around me. I wasn't even slightly tired. Well, no more than usual. I just wanted to make her stew a bit, and to punish her for her secretive ways by forcing her to go and have

179

the rest of her break at the nurses' station. Then maybe she'd appreciate me a bit more, and realize that annoying people with the teaser trailer to a story is not the way to keep friends.

I lay down to support the facade that I was tired, and opened my eyes to find that it was somehow morning. A morning where Margot had made her way to my ward and was standing nervously by my half-open curtain. 'Lenni,' she said quietly. 'It's my heart.'

'What is?' I whispered, still blurry from sleep.

'The reason I'm here, it's my heart.'

I sat up in bed. Out of the context of the Rose Room, she seemed tiny.

'Oh. I'm sorry. I like your heart. I think you've got the nicest heart.'

'I just thought that since we tell each other everything, I should tell you what's wrong with me.'

I beckoned for her to come closer, and she crept in and sat on the bed beside me.

'Can they make it better?' I asked, relieved to see that she wasn't crying. In fact, she was calm.

'I don't think so,' she said, 'but they're trying, bless them.' She smiled, and it was like sunlight coming to rest on her face for a moment.

Lenni and the Car

'WHERE IS YOUR father, Lenni?'

'Where is your father, Lenni?'

'Where is your father, Lenni?'

Margot has asked me three times, and three times I haven't answered. So, I think she was surprised when I started talking, midway through painting a row of cars, small and like dots. Red, silver, blue, white.

'I think Meena was right,' I told Margot.

'About what?'

'About not giving chase.'

Margot furrowed her brow.

'What she said to you when you were looking for Johnny, about waving someone off into their new life but not feeling the need to follow. Letting the people who need to leave, leave. Allowing them to be free.'

Glasgow Princess Royal Hospital, November 2013
Lenni Pettersson is Sixteen Years Old

The consultant's office was very dark, but behind his desk was a wide window. In the top half you could see the grey sky and in the bottom half you could look down on the hospital car park. The cars were shining like berries. It made me feel very far away from the world, and I supposed that the consultant had had to arrange his office so his desk faced away from the window, so he didn't spend all day mesmerized by the car park.

'My apologies it's so dark in here,' he said. 'They've installed new motion sensor lights in an effort to be more environmentally friendly, but mine don't seem to be working. I've waved my hand in front of the damned sensor at least twenty times, but nothing's happened.'

The darkness made the window all the more alluring.

My father and I sat on the plastic chairs in front of the doctor's desk. My father's new girlfriend Agnieszka was outside in the waiting room, looking terrified. I liked her for my father – she was rational but soft, and she made him laugh which was something he rarely did unsupervised. I liked the idea that they could have a life together.

'So, Miss Pettersson, is it okay if I call you Linnea?' the consultant asked.

My father said, 'She goes by "Lenni",' at the exact time that I said, 'Everyone calls me "Lenni".'

'Of course,' he said. 'Lenni it is. Well, we have all of your test results back, Lenni.' He clicked a few times on his computer mouse, and as the screen sprang to life, it emitted a green glow that lit up his face.

He clicked and scrolled and then stared for a few moments at the screen, probably trying to summon up the courage to say what he said next. The doctor took a deep breath and said, 'It's as we feared.' And I tried to imagine him at home, tucked up in bed with his wife and a good book and a mug of Bovril – fearing for me, a sixteen-year-old he had met once who must have been one of hundreds of patients he saw each week. I imagined him playing squash and stopping, missing a shot, as he feared for my test results. I imagined him gnawing on his thumbnail as he drove out of the hospital car park every day for the two weeks that we had waited for the test results. Fearing for me.

He seemed unafraid now, as he began explaining terminology and procedures and limitations and time.

While all of that was happening, I was looking out of the window, watching a red car reverse backwards into a parking space. I watched the lights dim as the driver turned off the engine and I watched her get out, holding a heavy bag and something white. I watched her lock the door and walk slowly across the car park and towards the hospital. Then I watched the blue car next to hers reverse carefully and a white car stop in its path to allow the blue car the space to get out.

The doctor turned his monitor around to show some of the scan results to my father, but my father had turned grey. His eyes were fixed on the desk in front of us and he wasn't breathing.

While the doctor carried on talking about surgeries and stages and bones, the office lights flicked on.

Margot in Trouble

London, July 1964

Margot Docherty is Thirty-Three Years Old

MEENA AND I were back in the police station where we had met five years before. Except this time we were handcuffed, and Meena, for the first time since we'd met, was silent. Though she was seven years my junior, I always looked up to Meena. She was my guide through London and through life. She always knew what to do. But now I realized that she might, in fact, have no idea what she was doing.

We waited, a policeman at either side of us, to sign in for our arrest. I was trying very hard not to meet the eyes of anyone in the waiting room. I tried to catch Meena's attention, but she was staring down at the floor, biting her lip. One of the policemen escorting us had said 'Irish' to his colleague when they heard my accent. I told them I was from Scotland and he muttered, 'All the same.'

'Name and address,' the woman at the desk said.

Meena, speaking for the first time since we were arrested, murmured, 'Catherine Amelia Houghton.'

My stomach dropped. She'd given them a fake name. I couldn't believe she'd lied to the police and she'd done it so serenely, giving the name to the woman at the desk without even breaking eye contact. Meena wouldn't be getting in trouble for what we did, because someone who didn't exist, Catherine Amelia Houghton, would be in trouble instead.

I realized I was thoroughly out of my depth. It would be my turn to speak any moment. Was I supposed to lie too? What would happen when they found out that we weren't using our real names? I wanted to be sick.

The woman at the desk turned to me. 'Name?' she barked.

I decided then that I'd call myself Harriet – after an old friend of my mother's – but when I tried to speak, the sound I made was somewhere between my own name and my new alias, a kind of 'Marghaarrie'.

'Sorry?'

I tried to swallow, but my mouth was so dry.

Meena gave me a look. A look that said, *Have you lost your mind?*

'Her name is Margot,' Meena told her. She was selling me out. I tried to swallow again but I couldn't get any moisture into my mouth.

'What are we being arrested for?' Meena asked.

The policeman snorted. 'Lawyer are you, sweetheart?'

Meena didn't look like a lawyer. I remember so vividly what she was wearing that day – a paisley dress in red with flared sleeves and an old pair of leather sandals that smelled stale whenever she took them off. As we'd been waiting, she'd nervously woven little plaits into her long hair. She'd an obsession with freckles, of which she had none, and so she'd taken to drawing them on with a make-up pencil. She definitely didn't look like a lawyer.

'Ideas above your station?' the other policeman said. He was gazing at Meena like she was naked.

She, to her credit, paid him no attention and repeated her request.

'Relax,' the policeman soothed, in a slow tone that made the hairs on my arms stand up.

They put us in individual cells. I tried to make eye contact with Meena as I was led into mine, but she still wouldn't look at me. The cell smelled of urine and I didn't want to touch anything, so I paced around the room and tried to piece together what I should say, what the police would already know, and then I tried to cross-check that with what I thought Meena, or *Catherine Amelia*, would tell them.

If I told the truth completely, it would have sounded like this: at about one o'clock that morning, as I stood on lookout outside the biosciences building, Meena, Adam, Lawrence and a few more of Meena's friends broke into the medical lab at the university where Meena worked. Well, they didn't break in. They used a key procured from Meena's role as typist for The Professor, who was also the head of the medical school at said university. In they went, on a mission to free the hundreds of mice who were living in cells of their own. Unable to find or free the mice, they scrawled a demand to end the medical testing across the wall of the lab in red paint. They ransacked the office, opened the window so it wouldn't appear to be an inside job, collected me and returned to the group's unofficial

HQ at Meena's bedsit, where we toasted the mission with a bottle of warm red wine. It had bits of cork floating in it.

If I was being completely honest, I didn't do it for the mice, much as I cared about their little lives. I did it for Meena.

I didn't sit on the bed in the cell once; I kept pacing, working over and over in my mind what I would say. I knocked on the door twice and called out to ask for some water, but nobody came. What was left of my saliva had formed a slime across my tongue.

It was a Sunday morning. In another life, I would be sitting beside Johnny and Thomas within the cold echoing walls of St Augustine's Church. I would be bored and trying to amuse myself by counting all the swirling flowers painted on the stained glass windows. I would be trying to see if I could remember the hymn lyrics without looking at the hymn book. I would be giving Johnny the eye, for kicking Thomas in the shins for singing loudly and off key on purpose in Johnny's ear. I would be rubbing my gloved hands together to try to keep them from going numb. But in my current life, my new life, I stood alone in a prison cell. Alone in the cell, but alone in the trouble too, because something told me *Catherine Amelia* would never allow herself to be pinned down for long.

I tried to imagine what the people at church would think of me if they could see me now. Associating with people I had no business being lucky enough to associate with. Having the kind of fun I had no right to be enjoying when I was supposed to be in Scotland, grieving.

The slot on the door opened and I saw a pair of eyes stare in at me. 'Margot,' the police officer said, pronouncing the T. 'You're up, love.'

I was relieved to the point of tears to see that there was a glass of water waiting on the table in the interview room. I drank from it greedily and had to wipe my mouth with the back of my hand. The two policemen who'd arrested us were gone and instead there was a harried, overweight inspector in a brown suit. His shirt was straining at the buttons and I could see his hairy stomach peeping through the gaps. Beside him was a much younger uniformed officer who looked like a rabbit.

'Lydia?' the fat inspector asked.

'No,' I said, 'sorry. I'm Margot ... Docherty.'

I stood up to leave, but he waved at me. 'Sit down, sit down.' The interview room was small and smelled of feet.

'Margot, Margot, Margot,' he said under his breath, shuffling the stack of paper in front of him. 'Isn't that a song?'

'I think so,' I said, desperate to agree with him. If there is a song, I still haven't heard it.

'Right,' he said, pulling out a piece of paper covered in scribbles. 'Yes, the university break-in.' I could feel my heart thudding. He pressed 'record' on the microphoned machine.

'What do you know about the recent break-in at the medical school on Edward Street?' he asked.

'Yes,' I answered. My mouth was dry again.

'Yes?' he said, irritated.

'I'm sorry,' I said. 'What was the question?'

'Where were you last night?'

'Where you think I was.'

'And where do I think you were?' The inspector leant forward in his seat and the bare bits of his tummy touched the table.

'There. At the medical school.'

'Uh-huh,' he said. Then he waited and I waited. 'Go on.'

'I was on lookout.'

'Lookout? You didn't do a very thorough job.'

Then he laughed and the rabbit officer, noticing, joined in with a fake laugh too.

'I jest,' the inspector said, wiping his eye. 'The break-in had all the hallmarks of your lot. Shabbily done, unsuccessful, but in this case, operating on information that only someone who had insider knowledge could know.' His tone had changed into one of mock surprise. 'Which led us to the charming Miss Houghton, who I've had the pleasure of meeting several times, and what do you know? She actually *works* as a typist for the head of the medical school. And here we are.'

I didn't know if this was a question.

'So you admit that you were part of the group operating under the organization of Miss Houghton?'

'Yes.'

'And you accept that this admission implicates you in a criminal act?'

'Yes.'

'And you acknowledge that you have damaged the property of a place of education?'

'I didn't do that bit,' I said. He seemed annoyed, so I added, 'But yes.'

The inspector leant back in his chair. 'Did you enjoy your time in the cell today?'

'No.'

'Do you appreciate that if this case went to trial, you could face a jail sentence of up to seven years?'

My heart seemed to be racing faster than I could keep up with. I tried to breathe.

'Well?' he asked.

'Yes,' I said in a small voice.

He wrote something on the paper in front of him and handed it to the officer. 'Luckily for you and your band of merry men, the head of the medical school has requested we take this matter no further.'

I didn't know exactly what that meant.

'You need to sign these statements; we'll take your prints for our file and you'll be released with a caution. Understand?'

I nodded. 'Yes.'

Then he looked me square in the eye and said, 'Let this be the last time we meet, Miss Docherty.'

The rabbit officer rose to lead me out of the interview room.

'It's Mrs. I don't know if that mat—'

'Hang on,' the inspector said. 'Mrs? Who's your husband? Was he part of this?'

'No, sir.'

'Hmm,' he said. 'Why not?'

'He's . . . I don't . . .' There had to be a way of saying this that sounded less wretched. 'I don't know where he is.'

The fat inspector was intrigued. 'You mean he's a missing person?'

'No. No, he . . . left me,' I said.

'Oh.' The officer was no longer intrigued. He crossed something out on his paper. 'You're released. Thank you.'

He didn't look thankful.

When I got out of the hot police station into the still-warm day, I squinted and held my hand up to my eyes. What time was it? What had just happened? I felt that the smartly dressed man in the brown suit who passed me knew I'd been arrested. I felt it was stamped on my forehead.

'You're out!' Meena cheered, running towards me with a cigarette lolling from her bottom lip. She embraced me with her thin arms and laughed. 'It was The Professor! He dropped the charges! What a hero!'

My disorientation at the sun and the smells of the street was nothing compared to my disorientation at Meena. She'd looked so floored when we were arrested. Now she just looked flawed. How could she think this was funny?

'Never again,' I said, my voice coming out hoarse and catching in my throat.

'*Breaking rocks in the hot sun!*' she sang.

'Never. Again.'

I started walking and she loped alongside me. '*I fought the law and the law won!*'

I stayed silent, pushing my excess fury through my heels into the pavement.

'Never again,' I repeated. 'I have a caution. Meena, this isn't ... wait.' I stopped. She stopped. I stared at her. She threw her cigarette into the hedge behind her.

'What?' she asked.

'Your name. Why did you give them a fake name?'

'Fake name?'

'Amelia Catherine Houghton?'

'*Catherine Amelia* Houghton,' she corrected.

'So what is that? A name you use when you're arrested?'

'It's my name.' She stared at me like I was mad. 'You thought Meena was my real name?' She laughed again. 'You think my Irish Catholic mother named me Meena Star?'

'So *Meena* is the fake name?'

'It's my new name. I just haven't got round to changing it. Lucky I saved you from calling yourself Marjorie or whatever – they'd have done you for that.'

She started walking ahead of me and as she turned, I let out a little smile. This was so foolish. I'd lived with the girl for five years and had never known her name. I wasn't the only person reinventing myself in London. In fact, the person I most wanted to be was an invention herself.

'What else don't I know?' I called after her.

She waited while I caught her up.

'You're an idiot,' she said, laughing.

And she grabbed me by the shoulders and kissed me on the lips.

A man passed between us, using his hat to push us out of his way. Under his breath, but loud enough for us to hear, he uttered one single word: 'Dykes.'

Twenty-Five Years

TWENTY-FIVE YEARS OF our lives were laid out across the tables in the Rose Room.

A metal bucket on the floor of an air-raid shelter, a table laid for a cold but extravagant breakfast, the haunted eyes of a skeleton witnessing a first kiss, and a baby in a yellow hat. Twenty-five stories that had waited patiently within us, now ready to be hung up, admired, celebrated, destroyed. What happens to the pictures once we are finished doesn't matter that much to me.

'It's amazing,' Pippa whispered.

'It's not finished yet,' I said, standing in front of my painting of Benni the beanbag pig and judging the artist for her lack of talent. With all of them gathered, it suddenly seemed to me that filling the room, our minds, our thoughts with another seventy-five memories might be impossible. There are years of my own life that are fuzzy and there *have* to be years that Margot can't remember. And then there is the awkward looming spectre of our impending deaths.

'But look at it!' Pippa said. 'It already looks like something – you've created *something*.'

'A quarter of something.'

'*Lenni*,' Margot said gently. I caught her eye, but she looked down at the picture in front of her. It was Margot and the man

193

on the beach, captured from a memory older than my mother. What would people think, I wondered, if they saw it in a gallery? Would they guess some, or any, of the details right?

We walked around the pictures for a little longer. I passed Margot's wedding, my first day at secondary school, a bomb resting quietly on a floral quilt. Finishing felt impossible, and yet those twenty-five paintings were so deliciously real. Hopeful, even though they commemorated some of the worst moments of our lives.

Margot stroked the edge of the canvas depicting a half-drunk bottle of pear-flavoured liqueur and asked me, 'So, Lenni, what next?'

Margot and the Map

'Oh, they adored him,' Else was telling Margot as I came into the Rose Room.

Walter waved her away. 'They were just being kind.'

'What's this?' Pippa asked.

'Oh,' Walter said. 'Else was kind enough to introduce me to her sons.'

Pippa smiled knowingly. I wondered what she knew as she made her way to the front of the class and started teaching us about cross-hatching.

I spent a good twenty minutes cross-hatching the sides on the carton of apple juice to try to make it seem three-dimensional but it just made the box look hairy. Once I was finished, I told Margot the story of my tantrum in the art gallery to commemorate my fifth year on earth. I told her how I had lost my tiny mind in the middle of the quiet gallery and my mother had lost her temper with me, and then, when a security guard asked us to leave, she had lost her temper at him. He then lost his temper with his boss via a walkie talkie and his boss failed to appear. I screamed throughout, legend has it, because the straw in my carton of apple juice had split.

Then, for a little while, I just watched Margot paint. When she paints, Margot's face becomes peaceful. It's the opposite of how my face feels when I'm painting – which is crumpled and angry. But Margot is somewhere else, somewhere different entirely, and I'll wait patiently for her smile of peace to shift as the picture starts to take shape. When she's happy with it, she'll start to talk. And I could wait for Margot's stories for ever.

'Let me take you somewhere,' she said. 'To a bedsit in London where it's hot. Unbearably hot. And then your roommate decides to turn on the stove . . .'

London, August 1965
Margot Macrae is Thirty-Four Years Old

It wasn't a stove really; it was a small ring burner balanced on top of an old suitcase. But she turned it on nonetheless. It was our entire kitchen. Meena liked to light her cigarettes with it, so she'd turn it on several times a day. Then there'd be no choice but to open the window, which meant running the risk of never getting it closed again because the catch was broken.

This time, I felt compelled to ask her if she was joking, as the ring burner began to fill the room with the stink of burning fake leather as it merrily cooked the suitcase underneath. She didn't say anything, but lit her cigarette on it. It was already a baking summer day. I lay down flat on my bed and stared up at the ceiling.

'Back to the meeting,' Adam said from his position sitting under the window. 'I think it's obvious we need a lookout.'

There was a silence.

'Margot Macrae doesn't do crime any more,' Meena said, sucking on her cigarette. 'So there will be no lookout.'

I felt my insides twist. I stopped calling myself Margot Docherty after the incident in the police station. And I became Margot Macrae again. And perhaps because I was returning to myself, or perhaps because I'd made a promise to a hairy-stomached inspector, I stopped participating in Meena's activism.

Lawrence pulled a map from his bag and laid it out on the brown carpet. 'It'll take about two hours to get there,' he said, 'but my van needs petrol, so let's assume it'll take longer.'

'We don't need a map, I know the way,' Meena said, tapping the ash from her cigarette into our only saucepan.

The meeting carried on. Even with the window open, it was boiling. I felt a bead of sweat run down my stomach. Adam massaged his temples and sighed. 'Can we just get on with it?'

'Right, let's go.' Meena stood and rallied the group. They checked their bags for torches, wire cutters, tape, rope. I stayed lying on my bed. I was wearing my thinnest sundress but it was now stuck to me with sweat.

'If the police come,' Meena started.

'I'll tell them to look for Catherine Amelia Houghton.'

She laughed and blew me a kiss.

I locked the door behind them, and listened as they argued their way down the stairs about just how many animals could fit in the van if somebody volunteered to hitch-hike home.

I felt compelled to open the door and chase after them. But I had said 'never again' the day we were arrested and I had meant it.

I turned off the ring burner and picked up the map that Lawrence had left behind. Meena had a thing about maps. The wall above the fireplace was covered in them. Usually maps of places neither of us had ever been to, all stuck up with Sellotape and most of them lovingly stolen. On a whim, I stuck Lawrence's map up on the wall. It was a map of England and I'm sure it would have been no help for their route that evening. I thought of them all squashed together in the back of Lawrence's van, and I wondered how long I could continue my one-woman performance of 'I'm no longer a part of your activist group'. It wasn't a very popular play.

Now that I was no longer a part of Meena's escapades, I felt that I was slowly becoming Old Margot. The pale, self-conscious person who had experienced a sudden burst of colour courtesy of the friends she was now forsaking out of fear. I pulled a pin from the noticeboard Meena had 'borrowed' from work, closed my eyes and stuck it in the map. It pointed to a field just outside Henley-in-Arden.

When Meena came home to our bedsit that night, she was bleeding.

She forced the door open, tripped on her way in and then turned on the overhead light. She had one of Adam's T-shirts wrapped around her arm. Dried blood had formed a historical river from just above her elbow all the way down to her hand.

I sat up and stared at her.

'Little fucker bit me!' she said.

Tucked under her other arm was a thin and almost entirely featherless chicken. One of the many liberated from a battery farm on the outskirts of Sussex that night.

When I saw that chicken, I knew I wasn't ready to leave. But the pin stayed in the map, piercing the fields just beyond Henley-in-Arden, where I would go when the time came.

Lenni's Mother

WE HAVE PRACTISED for death every night. Lying down in the dark and slipping into that place of nothingness between rest and dreams where we have no consciousness, no self, and anything could befall our vulnerable bodies. We have died each night. Or at least, we have lain down to die, and let go of everything in this world, hoping for dreams and morning. Maybe that's why my mother could never sleep – it's too much like death and she wasn't ready. So she was always waking, chasing awareness, clinging to life. Too afraid to let go, and then, years later, unable to do anything else.

Glasgow, September 2012
Lenni Pettersson is Fifteen Years Old

I watched her from my bedroom window as she got out of the car and walked to my father's front door. She looked older from above – the shadows falling in strange places across her face – and I wondered if that's how God sees us. We must look so ancient to him.

I didn't hear the doorbell and I didn't hear her voice.

'Lenni?' my dad called up the stairs. 'Your mamma's here to see you.'

She had dropped me off at my father's new house after several months awake. The long purple shadows under her eyes were back. And she had that look in her eye, as she drove me to my father's house, that she wasn't entirely sure who I was. That if we passed each other on the street, she might not recognize me.

A week or so later, she brought everything I'd left behind at her house and dropped it all on the drive, with a letter saying she was moving back to Sweden. And then there she was. Taxi meter running. Ready to say goodbye and to officially tag my father in as a parent and to forever tag herself out.

I sat on the floor and wrapped my arms around my legs. Like I'd seen a child do in an NSPCC advert. Suddenly the size of an acorn, I sat and waited.

'Are you coming down?' he shouted again.

I didn't say anything. I caught sight of my own eye in the mirrored wardrobe and I looked stupid. Not at all like an acorn.

'Have you heard me?' he shouted again.

'I've heard,' I called, my voice coming out much smoother than I thought it might.

I stayed on the floor for ten, maybe twenty minutes. Because I wanted her to know how angry I was.

I thought she would wait. I thought there was no way she would leave without saying goodbye. And so it came as a surprise when I peeped out of the window to see if she was crying yet, and found that the taxi had gone and my mother had gone with it.

She left a forwarding address with my father. He taped it to the fridge. I burned it on the gas ring on the hob. The smoke set off the fire alarm and I singed my finger.

I thought she would wait.

But she had a plane to catch. And a daughter in a box room who wouldn't come out.

From her place on the driveway, the plane home must have seemed a much more appealing option than her lonely, dreamless life.

~

'Does she know?' Margot asked softly.

'My father wrote her a letter. I think.' I paused. 'I remember he had to use her parents' address, because the last place she told us she was living was a hotel near Skommarhamn – but that had been months before. I like to picture her there – looking out onto the water, surrounded by trees. Either she knows or she doesn't know. If she knows and hasn't come, I like to leave her where I imagine her – happy, free, travelling around Sweden and sleeping through the night.'

Margot seemed sad for me and maybe for my mother, too. 'And if she doesn't know?'

'I see the haunted faces of the mothers of the May Ward,' I told her. 'I like to think that my last act as a daughter will be to spare her that.'

Lenni and Margot Go for a Walk

THE CLOCK HAD ticked 1,740 times and Margot still hadn't spoken. I'd worked this out in the time that she'd been staring at the blank paper in front of her, with her pencil in hand. Margot was staring at the page as though it were a mirror and she had no understanding of the version of herself that it reflected back.

'Why don't you skip it?' I asked.

She looked at me from a faraway place.

'You know,' I said, 'move on to the next year?'

She stared down at her paper mirror. 'I can't.'

'Why not?'

'Because everything that happens next . . .' She stopped.

She seemed so small that I wanted to scoop her up and lay her down in a pile of soft toys and cushions, and cover her in a warm blanket.

'Would it help if you didn't have to tell me the story?' I asked.

'No, pet,' she said, 'I want you to know. I think.'

We sat in the quiet for a few more ticks of the clock.

Finally, I stood up. She smiled at me absently. 'Come on,' I said, helping her to her feet, 'we're going for a walk.'

Our very slow walking tour of the hospital began by taking a right out of the Rose Room and making our way to the main atrium, where the expensive WHSmith and the café that always smells of bacon reside. We mostly ignored the people in day clothes. And we shared the odd glance with those who were also in hospital wear. A man in a particularly grim brown towelling dressing gown passed us and gave a grunt. It might have been in recognition, or we might have annoyed him. It was hard to tell.

We walked down the corridor that leads to blood tests and outpatients. There were far too many normal outside people in there, so we made a U-turn and headed in the general direction of paediatrics and maternity.

When we got to a quiet bit of the corridor, when it was just me, Margot and a cage of bed linen, she said, 'You might think differently of me if I tell you the next bit.'

'Might I?' I asked.

'Yes,' she said.

'What if I promise that I won't think differently of you, no matter what you tell me?'

'You can't promise that,' she said. And I wondered if she was right.

'You told me about being arrested and I just thought it was awesome,' I offered.

She shook her head. 'It's not like that.'

We walked on a little further, both of us taking careful tiny steps.

'But you want me to know?' I asked.

'Yes. And no.' She seemed frustrated at her own answer. 'I've never told anybody this story,' she said.

'So, it's a secret?' I asked.

'Yes. And no,' she said again.

A Healthcare Assistant carrying a tray full of cereal bowls made her way swiftly past us, and then the corridor was silent.

'Come on.' I took Margot's hand.

'Where are we going now?' she asked, but she held on to my hand anyway. And she didn't let go as we wove around the corridors. When we got to the May Ward, I gave the nurses at the station a wave and then took Margot to my bed.

'Lenni?' she asked.

I positioned Margot on my visitor's chair and drew the curtain around the bed so that nobody on the ward could see.

I lifted up the mattress of my hospital bed and underneath was my secret. I pulled him out. He's a paler pink than he used to be, and his snout is a little fuzzed because of our way of saying hello to each other by touching noses. He wasn't like the others – not a bear or a lamb or a rag blanket. But I loved him anyway. I liked that in a room full of dolls and bears, he was a pig.

'Nobody knows he's here,' I said.

I gave him to Margot and she looked like I'd just handed her a priceless jewel. She held him as you'd hold a newborn, his head resting in the crook of her arm. His beanbag body well supported.

'Well, you must be Benni,' she said, shaking his beanbag trotter.

She smiled and went to hand him back to me.

'No,' I said, 'keep him. For a while.'

'Why?'

I just shrugged, but I hoped she'd know that I was giving him to her because he's the only secret I've got. And I trusted her with him completely.

A few days later, Margot appeared in the May Ward. I took a break from my busy schedule of napping to make room for her at the end of my bed. She had Benni in her pocket and she brought him out, gave him a kiss on the head, and then she held on to my secret while she told me hers.

London, July 1966
Margot Macrae is Thirty-Five Years Old

Somewhere down in the bottom of my brain, it lives.

Sometimes, it will flick its shimmering tail above the water and sprinkle glittering water particles across my vision. Other times, I forget it's down there, and when I'm feeling heavy and sinking down, ready to drown, there'll be a thud and we'll collide, my memory and me.

A memory of her.

After eleven happy months as our flatmate, Jeremy the chicken had gone missing. It was a silly sentence and explaining it to the neighbours seemed sillier. One, I remember, opened their door with the safety chain still on.

'Excuse me, I'm looking for my chicken.'

'No Irish.'

He started to close the door and I caught the glimpse of a goatee.

'I'm not Irish.'

I didn't catch any word except 'potato' as the door shut in my face.

I stood in the dark hallway of our building. Inside it was cool, but outside the summer was raging. Meena was already in the street, asking people to stop and look at the Polaroid photograph of our chicken. She was heading in the direction of the park, based on the idea that Jeremy might have remembered the time we took him there for a picnic. He might have had a craving for fresh grass, she said.

I stood in the dark hallway feeling lost.

I studied the back of the front door: the crack in the glass from a failed attempt at a break-in, the cage on the letterbox that only the landlord held the key for – holding all of our letters prisoner until he trundled around on a Sunday to dish them out, and, we suspected, intercept anything that felt like it had money in it.

The latch on the door was so high that I could only reach it by standing on my tiptoes. There was no way a chicken could have got through this door without help.

When Meena first brought Jeremy home, I thought he was a house guest. An unusual one, but a guest all the same. I didn't know he was a tenant and so when, several days into his stay, Meena bought several sheets of wire to build him a 'run' around the bedsit that would keep him away from the electrical sockets, I didn't understand.

'Aren't we going to take him to the RSPCA?' I asked.

'You want to take our *son* to the RSPCA? What kind of mother are you?' I knew she meant it as a joke, but it stilled my heart. I still had not introduced Meena to Davey.

'So he's staying?'

'As long as we're staying, he's staying,' she said.

I pretended to react to this normally, and then I made an unnecessary trip to the corner shop so that I could cry without her seeing me. I had never had pets as a child. The first living thing I'd been accountable for was Davey. The immense responsibility of caring for a living, breathing creature seemed impossible when I had failed so spectacularly the last time.

I went out into the burning sun. Meena would already be at the park now. It seemed that all the houses opposite us had become smaller and larger at once. I walked down the steps from our house and crossed the road, almost being hit by a boy on a bike.

I knocked quietly at the front door of the house opposite, which, like ours, had been purchased by an industrious landlord and turned into several bedsits. When nobody came to the door following my almost inaudible knocking, I was relieved that I could honestly tell Meena I had tried. I repeated the pattern on the houses to its left and right, until I came to a door and was about to knock, only for a tall man in a camel-coloured suit to appear. He held the door open for me, and I thanked him and went in.

The hallway smelled of other people's cooking – of onions and peppers and toast. Everything was quiet, and I just stood for a moment, wondering what it would be like to live in this building instead of my own. I could be a person who lived here, instead of across the road. I could walk across this floor and unlock the door to 2A and call it home. If I lived here,

Meena would just be a woman from across the road I saw occasionally. I'd see her float by in one of her long dresses and I'd wonder about her, but I'd never know.

~

About three days after we brought Davey home, Johnny went back to work. Up until that point, I hadn't felt any great sense of dread or fear over the little pink thing in a bundle of blankets in my arms, but as I watched Johnny trudge through the darkness from the living-room window, I felt this incredible sense of weight. I looked at Davey who was sleeping, a bubble of saliva on his lip, and I saw this deep dark space. How could I have had a baby, I wondered, when I didn't know how to drive a car? When I didn't know how to pay any kind of tax? When I didn't know how to roast a chicken? How could I have a baby when I didn't know how to be a mother?

~

A woman in an orange sundress came down the stairs.

'Have you seen a chicken?' I asked her. She gave me a baffled smile, put her sunglasses over her eyes, and said nothing as she opened the door and went out into the world. She left behind her a sweet powdery perfume scent. I followed her out into the sunshine.

I wandered down the road.

~

When Davey first got ill, Johnny didn't want to take him to the doctor.

~

I walked for about ten minutes, and then dipped out of the sunshine of the chicken-less day and into the newsagent's on the corner of our road. The newsagent was watching cricket on the grainy black and white television that stood on a chair – its antenna being given a boost by a wire coat hanger.

He groaned at a caught ball and then turned.

'Margot, my dear,' he said, 'what can I do for you?'

'Have' – I cleared my throat, but my voice still came out strangled – 'have you seen a chicken?'

'Sorry, dear. We can't sell meat until we get the fridge unit fixed.'

'No,' I said, 'our chicken. Me and Meena have a pet chicken and he's gone missing.'

'You have a pet chicken?'

I nodded.

He gave me a bemused smile and wrinkled up his nose. 'If he comes in trying to buy seed, I'll let you know.' And then he wheezed out a laugh.

~

Two days after Davey passed, I woke up in the middle of the night, hit with the sudden feeling that he had just been crying and then suddenly fallen silent. I raced to his cot but he wasn't

209

there – where had he gone? He was too young to be able to climb out of his cot. I could hear the echo of his cry in my ears. I ran back to our bedroom. Johnny was sleeping, one arm hanging out of the bed, his knuckles on the carpet.

'Johnny, Johnny, wake up!'

He stirred.

'The baby's gone!' I cried.

'I know,' he murmured, thick with sleep.

'Someone's taken him!' I looked at the closed window. 'We have to call the police!' I pulled the telephone in from the living room, the cord straining and eventually pulling out of the wall altogether. I held the phone in my hands out to him. 'We have to call the police!'

Johnny sat up then, staring at me with such contempt that I could feel it in my stomach. '*What?*'

The veil of sleep lifted and I put the telephone down on the end of the bed.

~

Beside the newsagent's was a hair parlour, with a row of those whole-head driers used for setting perms. I couldn't go in there, I couldn't face the embarrassment. I walked onwards to the end of the road, but when I reached the junction it felt like I'd found the junction at the end of the world.

~

We arrived at the headstone shop at the time Johnny's mother had set, but she was already inside. 'I got here early,' she told us. The mason had sketched out on tracing paper the wording that is still scratched in stone on Davey's grave to this day.

May the Lord have mercy on the loving soul of David George Docherty.

I hated the wording – the implication that God might be anything but merciful to my baby boy – and when I started to cry, Johnny's mother told him that I was overwhelmed and to take me home so she could deal with this for us.

~

Meena was sitting on the steps that led up to the front door of our house. She had the Polaroid of Jeremy in her hands. Her shoulders were pink from the sun.

'No luck,' she said as I approached. 'I don't understand how he got out.'

'It wasn't me,' I said.

She gave me an odd look. 'I know it wasn't.'

I tried to squeeze some air through my throat, but it felt like it had closed.

Meena stared at me then. 'What is it?' she asked.

I sat beside her, and I sobbed so hard that I was struggling to breathe and the hot tears were smeared down my face.

I'd never seen Meena so serious. 'What happened?' she asked.

I had to introduce them, I knew, and I couldn't wait any longer.

'My son.' I drew in breath. 'My son.'

She was very still.

A breeze moved between us and I caught some of the air. She said nothing while I introduced her, at last, to my Davey,

211

whose name I hadn't even whispered in seven long years. I showed her the picture from my purse, of the little bundle in my arms wearing a yellow hat that just wouldn't stay on his head, and in the background the flowers from my mother.

When I fell quiet, Meena took me by the hand and led me up the steps. She unlocked the front door without letting go of my hand and led me up the two sets of stairs to our flat, where she sat me on my bed.

I watched as she slipped my shoes off my feet and paired them neatly by the bed. She did the same with her own. Then she took a glass from the cupboard and walked out of the flat. From the bed, I could hear the tap in the shared bathroom hissing. She always waited for the water to get really cold. When she returned to me, the water inside the glass was swirling with the white particles that looked like a snowstorm. I drank from it as though it were the first water to touch my lips.

As I drank, she locked the door, closed the curtains, and then I heard the squeaking of her divan bed's wheels as she pushed her bed up against mine.

The still-bright sun worked its way through our blue curtains in waves, and the room became the ocean.

She took the glass from my hand and placed it on the dresser. Then she sat beside me, so close that I was sure I could hear her heartbeat, though in hindsight it must have been mine. And in between her eyes, a freckle that I'd never noticed caught my attention and held it as her lips gently touched mine.

And she laid me down on my bed and kissed me.

*

When I woke, I was surprised to see that the sun was shining.
I thought the world might have tipped on its axis.
Meena's bed was back on the other side of the room and Meena was gone.

Chickens and Stars

'DID YOU LOVE Meena?' I asked Margot.

We were sitting in the corridor outside the Rose Room, both of us having forgotten that this week's class was cancelled on account of Pippa being on a half-term trip with her nephew. She was taking him to see the dinosaurs at the Natural History Museum.

The corridor was quiet; only the occasional porter went by. Nobody seemed too interested in the girl in pink pyjamas and the old lady in purple, sitting side by side on the shiny floor.

'Of course,' Margot said.

Then she looked up to the ceiling and thought.

'She was always moving, always up to something. Fidgeting, talking, smoking. She was never still. And when I first met her, it was her constant evolution that thrilled me, because I wanted it for myself. I wanted to be able to change out of Margot and become someone better. Someone happier. Or at the very least, someone new. But for all the good things about her, she was headstrong and unpredictable and flighty. And the more I found things I didn't like about her, the more I hated myself because those things didn't matter to me in the least and I loved her anyway. But I decided that they *should* have mattered and I couldn't love her. So I searched

214

for more reasons, hoping I'd finally pile them high enough that they *would* matter, and then I could leave London and by doing so escape the unanswered question of the gap between our beds.'

Margot and The Professor

London, August 1966

Margot Macrae is Thirty-Five Years Old

I hadn't ironed a thing since 1957, so when I returned home from work one afternoon, I was surprised to find a man sitting on the end of Meena's bed whose suit was so well pressed it appeared that he could simply be snapped in half.

'Oh,' we both said.

He was older than me. Late forties, perhaps. He was holding a wedding ring in the palm of his hand.

'Are you a policeman?' I asked.

His brow furrowed. 'No,' he said.

'TV licence?'

'We don't have a television, Margot.' Meena's voice was behind me. She came into the room wearing a very short pair of pyjama shorts and an almost see-through teddy top.

'Where have you been?' I asked. Meena smiled at me blankly, as though she couldn't hear me. 'I haven't seen you since ... I thought—' I wanted to end my sentences but I was aware of the man's eyes upon me.

'Are you back?' I asked.

'Back?' she scoffed. 'I never left.'

While she'd been gone, I'd taken apart Jeremy's run and thrown away his stash of seeds. I'd made her bed and I bought us a new mirror in a green frame and I'd hung it on the wall. If she noticed, she didn't say anything. She sat beside the man and gave me a smile I couldn't read. The dressed-ness of the suited man and me only served to make Meena seem more naked.

'I need to teach you about self-incrimination,' she said.

'What?'

'You find a strange man in your flat and the first thing you do is assume you're being arrested?'

'I didn't think I was being arrested,' I snapped, 'I thought he might have been here to tell me you were dead.'

'God, Margot, I go on holiday for one week—'

'Three weeks.'

'And you think I'm a missing person?'

'So, who is he, then?' I asked.

'This man is your saviour.'

I looked at him. He tucked the wedding ring into the inside pocket of his jacket.

'Did you join a cult?'

Meena laughed so hard that she snorted. 'Do you know, my mother is always asking me that. This man, my dear Margot,' she said, 'is . . .' She started on an H sound, but then the man's eyes flared and an expression that was briefly frightening passed across his face. 'The Professor,' Meena finished. 'The very man to whom you owe your freedom from your twenty minutes of incarceration.'

'Oh,' I said, and for the first time The Professor smiled. He didn't look at all how I'd pictured him – as a young, bearded fellow with knitted tops and tinted brown glasses. This man was smart, with grey ripples along the sides of his neatly combed hair. He looked like a politician, not a professor.

'The Professor,' I said, trying out his name against him.

'Anyway, do you mind?' Meena asked, and because I thought she was talking to him, I didn't look at her, instead going over to my bed and kicking off my shoes. They were red leather sandals that developed a hot, muggy smell whenever I wore them without socks. I wondered if the smell of my feet had made it across the room to the suited man and my nearly naked roommate.

'Margot?' Meena said. Her voice had an edge to it that caught me by surprise.

'What?'

'*Do you mind?*' she asked again.

'You want me to leave?'

I walked to the park and sat on the grass, getting green stains on my white work dress. And I wondered about the wedding ring nestled in his pocket, and the woman he was married to and the woman I loved, and I wondered when I could go home.

Lenni and the Man at the End

NEW NURSE CAME to me with a confession. At least, it seemed like she was going to confess something. She scuttled towards my bed looking embarrassed. I sat up, channelling Father Arthur. 'May God forgive you, my child,' I said, sweeping my hands outwards dramatically, so she could admire my long (imaginary) priest-like robes.

'What?'

'You have come to confess something, my lamb?'

'What?' She was breathless. 'No, I need to ask you a favour.'

I was a bit disappointed by her, to be honest; I was ready for secrets and admissions of large-scale wrongdoings. I was ready to pray to Jesus that he might forgive her, while giving her a knowing look that would say, *I know all your secrets now and I'm not likely to forget them.*

When I didn't reply, she carried on anyway. 'It's Swedish that you can speak, isn't it?'

'The Lord speaks in all tongues.'

'Can you translate? You know, from Swedish into English?'

'I can. In fact, I was the official translator for my parents' divorce.'

'We can't get hold of our Swedish translator, and there's a man who's in a bad way. I know the doctor treating him, I said you might be able to help. Would you mind? As a favour to me?'

219

I shrugged. I couldn't understand why she was so nervous. Even when I told her I would do it, the guilt didn't release her face. I shuffled to the edge of the bed and put on my slippers.

The source of her guilt made itself apparent then. Black, wide, consuming. It came before her, stealthy and silent. I understood why she couldn't meet my eye as she made her way to my bed. And there I was thinking her a friend. When this whole time she had been Judas – a slithering traitor in waiting, her weapon of choice sliding across the floor to the end of my bed.

'I thought it would be quicker,' she said quietly, evidently now wishing that she had chosen tardiness over betrayal.

I didn't say anything. Sometimes it's better not to. Silence can be more powerful than speech when trying to convey abject treachery and disappointment. Anything I said would only make her feel better.

I slipped on my slippers and stood. I kept my pace slow and dignified, making sure our eye contact never wavered.

'I'm sorry,' she said, sweating under the heat of my fury. 'You don't have to use it, we can walk!' Her voice was strained. But it was already there, waiting for me.

'I just thought,' she said, faltering, 'it's a long way. The other side of the hospital, you know . . .'

I raised myself up with dignity and turned, letting her help me down into it – black and wide, not built for one so slender as me, but wonderfully impersonal, one size fits all. It had the hospital name and a reference code written on the seat in case anyone should want to steal it. Why anyone would want to do that, I don't know. I lowered myself down and was surprised to find how much it gave way to me. I rested my hands on the arm rails.

'Are you sure?' New Nurse asked.

I lifted my feet up onto the foot rests.

'Okay, here we go,' she said with false cheer. I wondered if she would start crying. She pulled it back so that she could swing me round and get us on our way. I knew without asking that it had come from the May Ward, meaning it had been waiting for me this whole time. Destined to be mine when I, or in this case, a friend, deemed me too broken to even walk. When my final shred of independence was torn from me like a septic limb. When they finally admitted that all they could do now was make me as comfortable as possible.

There's nothing worse than being made comfortable.

Not even my most ardent supporter still believed that I could make it to the other side of the hospital without dying.

As New Nurse wheeled me out of the May Ward and I avoided making eye contact with Jacky as she sat eating crisps behind the nurses' desk, I thought about a story I once heard. Maybe I didn't hear it, maybe I read it, but however I came to know about it, it's a good story. There were two men in hospital. Both of them were ill. One man was told that his condition was going to improve, that he had a life expectancy of many years, and that with time he would recover. The other man was told that he was going to die within a year.

One year later, the man whose death had been predicted was dead, and the man who was told he would survive had survived and reported feeling well. It was then that the hospital realized there had been an error and the two men had been given the wrong information, each hearing the other's fate. The man who passed away had in fact been healthy, and the man who had lived was the one with the fatal illness.

If I am the only one left who still believes I might live, then it is only a matter of time before I accept my doom and I end up dying. If *I* had had my test results swapped, would I be out there somewhere now, at college or working, or wandering the streets of Sweden searching for my mother, feeling well and looking rosy? If the mind is so powerful that it can kill a man with no illness and save a man who's dying, I would never want to give my brain the opportunity to kill me by not believing that I might get better.

When I've passed people in wheelchairs in the hospital before, I have never really considered that they are low down. Very low down. I never realized how small it could make you feel to be half the height of everyone and not even strong enough to generate your own motion. Everything looked bigger from the chair, like I was a child again.

The shiny floor underneath my wheels changed from blue to orangey-red to a grey with coloured lines as we passed the different wards and made our way to wherever we were going. I didn't speak and neither did she. I was glad. And not because I was trying to use the silence to make her feel bad, but because the way I felt, I didn't know if I would crack a joke or burst into tears. I didn't know if I was going to laugh along with life, or if this was it, proof that the only way was down and then down once more, into the earth, to wait in the dark for the coming of Vishnu, or the Buddha, or Jesus, depending on who's the better at timekeeping.

When we got closer, New Nurse slowed down, checking the numbers on doors until she took me into an emergency ward. There were beeps and machines and the white sunlight was cutting into the room, slicing the beds into slivers of light and shade. In one of the beds, there lay a man. His beard was coarse and dirty, and his hospital gown was dirty too, spotted with blood at the neck. Standing beside the bed was a doctor. New Nurse stopped the wheelchair and I looked up at them.

The doctor leant down to my level and shook my hand. 'You must be Ellie,' he said, 'thanks so much for helping us out with this.'

'It's Lenni, actually.'

'Oh, sorry. Lenni ... Gosh, that's an unusual name.' He was posh and embarrassed. He ran a hand through his hair.

'It's Swedish. Obviously ...' I gestured to the situation we were in at that moment.

'Right,' he said. 'Swedish. Splendid.'

I accidentally laughed at his awkwardness. He put a hand up to his chin.

'Anyway, Lenni,' the doctor said, 'this is Mr Eklund. He came in about a week ago. He's of no fixed address and we've had a nightmare trying to get a Swedish translator, with it being the bank holiday. We need to tell him that he's booked in for surgery tomorrow. I also need to find out if he's in pain. This is, er' – he ran his hand through his floppy hair again – 'it's, um, a completely unorthodox situation, so you must let us know if you feel unable to do it.'

The doctor was fairly attractive and his blue eyes made me shiver. *If I can use my mind powers to survive another ten years,* I thought, *we could get married.* I told him I was fine, but that my Swedish hadn't been used for a while, so I might need to warm up.

Mr Eklund looked tired. His silvery beard needed to be washed. His face was cut, and he looked like he hadn't eaten properly in months, but his eyes were bright and observing me from under his bed covers.

The doctor gestured to the seat beside Mr Eklund. I got up out of the wheelchair quickly, trying to prove how incredibly healthy I am. I shuffled over and sat beside Mr Eklund.

'So to start, Lenni, if you could just introduce yourself and ask him how he is, and then we'll take it from there,' the doctor said.

'*Hej, jag heter Lenni Pettersson.*'

Mr Eklund turned, and in complete astonishment asked, '*Svensk?*'

I nodded.

He sat up in his bed, regarding me with grateful surprise. He scratched at his beard. The backs of his hands were covered in purple bruises. It looked like someone had stamped on them.

I asked him how he was.

He laughed and looked down to his feet, where New Nurse stood guarding my empty wheelchair at the end of the bed. I'll tell you as though he said it in English.

'I'm dying,' he said.

'You would think that would get you more places, but actually it doesn't.'

He leant forward in the bed. 'What?'

'I thought it would get me more things. I thought people would be nicer.'

'You're dying?' he asked, folding his hands across his chest.

I nodded. Mr Eklund looked pained at my fate.

'They want to know,' I said, 'how you're feeling.'

'I feel like I'm dying,' he said, and he laughed.

'They want to operate on you tomorrow.'

'It will be a waste of their time,' he said, 'I know it's going to take me.'

'Do you want me to tell them not to?'

He thought about this, a bruised hand going up to scratch his eyebrow. 'We might as well let them try.'

I nodded, and translated his sentiment to the doctor who watched with interest.

'It's nice to hear someone speaking Swedish,' Mr Eklund said. 'How did you end up here?'

'Oh, it's a long story,' I told him, 'I won't bore you with it now.'

'Do you miss Sweden?'

'Sometimes. But I can't go back.'

'No,' he said, as though the realization that he would never go back were just touching him now.

'Where in Glasgow do you live?' I asked.

He smiled. 'Anywhere.'

'The doctor said you're homeless.'

He nodded.

'Why don't you have a home?'

'I have lived terribly. I deserve nothing more.'

I thought about reaching out and touching his hand, but those purple bruises looked sore.

'Can I do anything to help?' I asked.

'Thank them for me, for trying to save a bad old man. Tell the doctor I came to Glasgow to find my girl and ask them to find her for me, if they can, once I'm dead.' He gestured to a blue holdall bag sitting on the table beside a bloodstained pair of jeans. Mr Eklund leant forward and said the next part quietly, even though nobody else had a clue what we were saying anyway. 'I have her birth certificate in my bag. Tell them when they find her, to say that I am sorry for everything I did. I missed her daily. Give her everything else that is in the bag, it is hers. If they can't find her, give the bag to the first homeless person you can find.'

I nodded and stared briefly at the bag. It had clearly started life a very different colour to the one it was now.

'They want me to ask you if you're in pain.'

'Yes. But I deserve it.'

I wondered what the man had done to deserve all that he had decided he did.

'Tell them I want to sleep,' he said.

'Do you?'

'No. I want to die.'

'The operation might make you better,' I said. 'You might find your daughter yourself.'

He smiled at me like a grandfather might smile at his granddaughter – warm, caring, but conveying that he had seen much more of the world than me and knew many more of its secrets.

'I'm ready,' he said.

'How do you know?'

He rested a bruised hand on mine. 'I know,' he said.

I wanted to save him. In that room I was the only person who could speak to him and he was going to give up.

'But *how* do you know?' I asked again.

'I can feel it, that's all.'

'Aren't you scared?'

He inhaled a laboured breath and fixed me with another soft smile. 'Don't be afraid to die, sweet nose.'

'But I am,' I whispered.

'But you have no reason to be!' He laughed, and the next part he said in English: 'It will be like sleeping.'

At his use of English, the doctor looked up.

Mr Eklund switched back into Swedish. 'You just close your eyes.'

'How do you know?'

'Well, it is true that I haven't died yet, but that is how it will be.'

Another laboured breath rattled through his lungs.

I translated to the doctor that Mr Eklund wasn't in pain, which felt like a lie.

'You can trust yourself, you know,' Mr Eklund said. 'Trust yourself that you will know. In the same way you know when you have hunger and thirst, you will know when it is time. I hope for you, sweet nose, that it isn't for a long time yet.'

'I've already been alive for a hundred years,' I said. He didn't ask me how.

'Also, please tell them that when they think I have been asking for water, I have been asking for wine. It's too late for alcohol to kill me, but it's not too late for it to make me feel better,' he said. 'If I wake up again, I'd like a glass of red – Merlot if they have it, although I'm not fussy, I'll take a Shiraz or even a Zinfandel.'

I laughed and he did too. 'I'll tell them,' I promised.

'Thank you, Lenni Pettersson,' he said. 'Now tell them I'm going to sleep.'

He closed his eyes, and his eyebrows and lined forehead relaxed into a blank face of peace. But he didn't look dead. If anything, it looked like he was pretending to be dead.

'Well?' the doctor asked.

I reverted back to English. 'Operate away, find his daughter, and give her his bag and her birth certificate. Let me know when you find her,' I said, rising and walking carefully to the wheelchair. 'I'll tell her the rest.'

I sat in the chair and began to wheel myself away. It was harder than it looks. 'And he wants red wine when he wakes up. A Merlot, if possible, but he'll take whatever you've got.'

Meena and Margot and Things You Can't Say

London, September 1966

Margot Macrae is Thirty-Five Years Old

It was the middle of the night and there was a hand touching my hand.

Had there always been a hand touching my hand? I wondered in my sleep.

When I opened my eyes she was there, in my bed, her cold toes touching mine.

She whispered something, but I couldn't hear her.

'What?'

'Don't you remember what you said?' she asked. I didn't then, but it came to me afterwards. The night of the pear liqueur. Sitting in the bathroom. I had told her I loved her.

She looked at me, staring for so long, unblinking in the dark. And then she blinked and the tears fell.

And I willed her to say it.

And she willed herself to say it.

But she couldn't. And before I could speak, she was gone.

Lenni and Little Surprises

THE TEMP HAD not had much luck since she was unceremoniously ejected from her position at the Glasgow Princess Royal Hospital. She had started out with aspirations – applying only for the jobs that made her feel excited, or inspired. If the responses came at all, they were rejections. So, The Temp set her sights lower – applying for typing, data entry, reception work . . . and still nothing. The rejections were as impersonal and as unrelenting as the ones from her dream jobs. Only this time it was worse, because she was being rejected for jobs she didn't even want. While waiting outside the twenty-four-hour supermarket manager's office with the other candidates for 'seasonal sales assistant: zero-hour contract', The Temp learned she was in the company of a qualified mechanic, a PhD student, and three other graduates with degrees in History, Mathematics and English respectively.

To her surprise, the manager phoned her that afternoon and offered her a role on the deli counter. When she was at university, The Temp had imagined herself working as an artist in a gallery after graduation. At no point had she envisaged herself reporting to work in the middle of the night to help insomniacs decide which honey-glazed ham to buy. But she resolved to carry on, and arrived at work the following evening with her hair net on and her pride tucked away.

Several months later, when The Temp came home from the deli, her mother asked her to sit in the living room and fiddled anxiously with the sofa cushions, unable to make eye contact with her. In a small voice, The Temp's mother told her that the father she had met just once in infancy had been found, and that he was in possession of the birth certificate which had gone missing some twenty-two years earlier. The Temp struggled to identify what emotion, if any, she felt upon hearing this news, and it was perhaps a good thing that she hadn't identified what she felt, because if it had been happiness, it would have been even harder when her mother went on to say that her father was not in a good way, and that the doctors hadn't given him long to live.

The Temp and her mother discussed at length that night what The Temp would do; whether she would visit or write, whether she would go alone or with her mother, whether she would ask for the birth certificate that had been replaced long ago, or allow him to keep it. She wondered whether she was angry at his abandonment or pleased at his return, whether she wanted to say goodbye or whether he even deserved a hello. Before their decision was made, however, another call came. The Temp's father had died. The Temp had cried then. It was equivalent to hearing of the death of a stranger, and hearing of the death of an irretrievable part of herself, all at the same time. A great loss, and yet no loss at all.

The nurse on the phone added in a conciliatory tone that the family might take comfort in knowing that he managed to fulfil a dying wish. The Temp's mother enquired what he had stolen, knowing his proclivity for taking things that didn't belong to him. After a long pause, the nurse confirmed that he had stolen a bottle of wine from the hospital chapel. Though, the nurse added hastily, it was not the wine that killed him, and the hospital chaplain had posthumously forgiven his actions.

Though The Temp's mother tried to end the conversation, the nurse on the line added that there was an item in the deceased man's possession that he had intended to be passed on to his daughter, should she be found.

The next morning, The Temp drove to the hospital. It was surreal that a father she never knew had been in the very place she had once worked. The nurse had told her mother that he'd been in the area looking for them both when he fell ill. Making her way from the car park, everything she saw became significant – had he been through these doors? Had he come to this wing of the hospital? Had he walked across this floor? It was the closest The Temp had ever felt to her father. In life, they had met once. Her mother kept a battered copy of a photograph of The Temp with her father, she dressed in a stripy dungaree suit and holding herself up on the side of the sofa, having, her mother recalled, just learned to stand. Her father was sitting on the sofa looking down at her, his face half hidden in shadow.

The nurse she spoke to at the nurses' desk knew nothing of her father, or the item he'd bequeathed her.

'What was the name? Reckland?'

'Eklund,' The Temp said, 'it's Swedish.'

The nurse shook her head and went to get another nurse, who also didn't recognize the name or the story. In the end, it was a porter with some wonky tattoos on his forearms who came to her aid.

'Mr Eklund?' he asked, coming to the desk to appraise The Temp.

'Yes.'

'Old guy? Grey hair?'

'I don't know.'

'Swedish? Stole some wine?'

'Yes. I think so.'

'You're the daughter?'

'Yes.'

'Of course you are, you look just like him.'

The sentence hit The Temp as though she had just walked into an invisible wall.

The porter said, 'I'm sorry for your loss, darlin'.'

She nodded, knowing that if she tried to speak now, she would cry.

The nurse behind the desk spoke up. 'Do you know where the Recklund guy left this stuff for his daughter, Paul?'

'Course I do,' he said brightly, exiting the ward and leaving The Temp alone with the nurse.

The nurse was dipping a chocolate digestive biscuit into a cup of tea. Her mug was adorned with coloured cartoon cats who were cartwheeling. The Temp focused on the mug. Right now, she reminded herself, people are having normal days. Drinking tea, owning mugs with cats on them.

'I don't know what's in it,' the porter said, as he reappeared through the automatic doors and handed it to her. It was a stained blue duffel bag. It came with its own smell. Ammonia. Damp. Earth. The straps were orange, or they were on the sides of the bag. By the handle, the orange had worn to a brown.

The Temp was unable to find a word to appraise it.

'Was you expecting anything?' the porter asked. The Temp shook her head. The bag was lighter than she'd expected. 'Have they given you the birth certificate?' he asked.

The Temp shook her head again.

The porter went behind the desk.

'Paul! What are you doing?' the nurse said, as he started opening the top drawer of her desk and ruffling through papers. Half of her recently dipped digestive biscuit crumbled and fell into her tea.

'Birth certificate,' he said. 'This young lady's father had her birth certificate.'

The nurse was uninterested. 'Haven't seen one. I'm on my break.' She picked up a teaspoon and started trying to scoop out the wet bits of biscuit that were now floating on the surface of her tea.

'Gotcha,' he said, pulling the pink square from the drawer. Paul read the full name on the certificate. 'This you?' he asked.

The Temp nodded.

The missing birth certificate had always been a mystery to The Temp and her mother. It had disappeared from the drawer in the kitchen on the day of the stripy dungarees picture. What purpose could an absent father have with his daughter's birth certificate? Looking down at it then, The Temp saw that he had managed to keep the certificate in perfect condition, except for the creases that formed a cross in the centre where it had been folded in half and in half once again.

He'd taken care of it.

The Temp had always associated her father's stealing with negativity. When her mother told stories from their courtship of his thieving, it was always bad. It always ended with embarrassment or police or fighting, or trouble of some kind. But this wasn't like that. It was an act of love, a keepsake, a sign that she had meant something to him.

'The girl that translated the Swedish for him,' Paul told her, 'she said that he wanted to tell you he was sorry for what he did and that he wanted you to keep what's in the bag.'

'What's in it?'

'Not a clue, haven't looked.'

The Temp nodded. 'Thank you.' But before she reached the door, she turned and asked, 'A girl translated for him?'

'She certainly did.'

And with a smile, The Temp asked, 'Which way is it from here to the May Ward?'

The Temp didn't know this part of the hospital well and, having immediately forgotten the porter's directions from her father's ward to the May Ward, she wandered directionless for a while, the bag in one hand, her birth certificate in the other. Eventually she stopped.

The corridor was empty and had long windows all along it, the sills of which reached just above the floor and so made a perfect place to sit. The Temp crouched down onto the windowsill. She placed the bag in front of her.

The zip that ran along the top of the bag was the same faded orange of the straps. For a moment, The Temp wondered if she was actually capable of opening the bag. If maybe it would be better never to open the bag at all. That way her father's endowment could be both wonderful and terrible, both meaningful and meaningless. But she had to find out.

The black jumper was the first thing she pulled out. It was the source of much of the smell. It was, The Temp couldn't ignore, the smell of urine. Nevertheless, she took the jumper out and put it on the windowsill beside her.

Also in the bag was a straggle of blue rope, and several empty cans of corner shop own-brand energy drink. They cost 19p a can. The Temp and her friends used to mix them with vodka on nights out.

As she moved an old newspaper to the side, she saw the first banknote. In trying to pull it from the bottom of the bag, she almost tore it, as it was weighed down and tied with a woman's hair band to a stack of notes of the same design. They were unfamiliar – a man with a long beard and a floppy hat staring glumly at her. Whatever currency it was, there were a thousand in one note alone. And in the stack she held at least two hundred notes. The second stack was the same size, also held together with a woman's hair band.

Ett Tusen Kronor was printed at the top of each note.

There was only one person The Temp wanted to speak to in that moment, and fortunately she was already on her way to see her.

And that's how The Temp came to be standing at the end of my bed holding a duffel bag full of Swedish money.

Margot and the Birthday

London, 11ᵗʰ May 1967

Margot Macrae is Thirty-Six Years Old

DAVEY'S BIRTHDAY IS more of a ghost than he has ever been. It haunts me. Stalking the calendar.

But on what would have been his fourteenth birthday, I opened the door to mine and Meena's bedsit to find it filled with yellow balloons. Hundreds of them.

When I found Meena in the pub in town later, The Professor was nowhere to be seen, and it made me breathe out a breath I didn't know I was holding. Sometimes, when he wasn't around, Meena was her own person again. And a little bit mine.

I tried to thank her, but she couldn't hear me over the music. So instead, I just hugged her tight.

As soon as I introduced Meena to Davey, she loved him.

And it made me love her more.

Lenni and the Mass

THERE WERE ONLY a few weeks left until Father Arthur would be a Father no more. I decided, as I imagine people did in black and white days when an actress announced her retirement, to go and see him as often as I could. I'd attend every one of his last performances before he retired to rest his ankle or wed his true love or move to Los Angeles to try his luck in the movies. Then one day I would wave a battered programme in front of my grandchildren's eyes and say, 'I was there way back when,' before boring them with stories of Arthur in his sequin-encrusted finery wowing the audience in a way that only he knew how.

My resentment for New Nurse, Harbinger of the Wheelchair, hadn't completely evaporated. The evaporation of resentment had been slowed considerably by the fact that the wheelchair remained. She'd used it to take me to the Rose Room and everywhere else since then. She may as well have carved the first half of my tombstone: *Lenni Pettersson, January 1997–Any Day Now.*

I asked Suzie to take me to the chapel. She's a May Ward nurse but I never see her doing nurse things. I knew she wouldn't bring a wheelchair and I wanted to walk.

'A Catholic mass, is it?' she asked.

'Maybe,' I said, taking her hand as she helped me up from my bed.

'You don't know?' She gave me a look.

'I can't remember.'

'Huh, a mystery,' she said. 'I like a mystery. My dad won't play Cluedo with me any more because he says I get too aggressive.' And then she laughed. 'I read at least one mystery book a week, I can't get enough of them. My dad says he doesn't like them, says they give me ideas.'

As we walked together out of the May Ward, a rush of nausea crept up from my toes to my throat. I was hot and I was going to be sick.

'I love all the Miss Marples too, and my friend got me a Poirot for my birthday. I love how he talks about himself in the third person.' When I didn't say anything, she carried on, 'I want to start doing that, you know, say things like, *Suzie has her suspicions about the corporal.*'

She led me away from the May Ward and down the corridor, and all I could think of was that we were leaving behind all the places where I could be sick without ruining the floor. As we left, I yearned for the cardboard hospital sick buckets that as a child I mistook for disposable top hats. I will forever want to live in the world of my ten-year-old self, where I believed hospitals were prepared for any temporary black-tie emergency with cardboard top hats for every patient.

Unfortunately for me, the corridor that leads to the corridor that leads to the hallway that leads to the corridor where the hospital chapel is, is devoid of any kind of vomit receptacle. They should know by now, I thought. There should be sick buckets on every corner. It would save so much money on mops. Suzie kept her arm in mine and I focused on her words, trying to ignore the rising nausea crashing through me, pulling on the back of my tongue, willing it down, encouraging me to gag.

'... I read this one that was so good ...'

I felt the pins and needles pricking the ends of my fingers. It would go. It would go as quickly as it came. I just had to get through this next bit.

'... so there's this murder on a harbour and this fisherman has been stabbed, and they can't match the wound to any kind of weapon. Sorry' – she stopped – 'is that too graphic? You're not squeamish, are you?'

I just smiled and shook my head. We walked slowly onwards.

'Anyway, the next murder is this man on a car park roof in a rainstorm, and he's been stabbed, but nobody knows where the weapon is. But the next murder is in this school, but that's where they get the crucial clue – when they test the third victim's blood, they find that it's been diluted with water.'

We went through the final set of doors and I could see the chapel ahead of us. It became symbolic – if I could fight every natural instinct in my body that was telling me to bend over and heave for all I was worth, then I would be okay.

'And so they realize that because the car park of the second murder had been wet and the harbour had obviously been wet, they had missed the clues – that the weapon was made of ice, and that rather than hide the weapon, the killer just left the ice dagger in his victims and it melted before they arrived. Isn't that cool?'

I nodded.

'Anyway, it ends with the woman detective and the man detective getting together, and then they go ice skating and they make this joke about being careful because ice can be very dangerous. I think it would make a great film, I read it all in two days!'

I don't think anyone has ever described a book plot to me that I've actually wanted to read.

Suzie was walking more slowly as we got closer to the chapel, so she could tell me more. I let myself free of her grip.

'Thank you for taking me,' I said. My voice sounded weird. Tight. Not mine.

'No trouble,' she said. 'I hope I didn't bore you!'

I waved my hand at her to tell her she didn't.

'I'll come and get you in an hour, then?'

'Thanks.' I pushed open the heavy door of the chapel before she could say anything else, not sure if I was going to vomit or fall on my knees and pray. I barrelled into Father Arthur's sizeable stomach and we both rebounded, not quite sure what had happened.

'Lenni?' he said, unable to conceal his joy.

'I came for mass.'

'You're just in time,' he said, and I looked into the chapel to spot the only other member of the congregation – an elderly man in striped pyjamas with a suit jacket over the top. I looked from the single congregant to Father Arthur, who just shrugged. I like that he doesn't pretend any more.

Father Arthur was dressed for the occasion in his black trousers and shirt, with a long scarf thing around his neck that had grapes sewn onto it.

I seated myself on the third row. I didn't want to be on the front row in case there was audience participation. The nausea was fading now that I was sitting down, and I watched Father Arthur light the final candles in the corner and turn on the hymn music on the CD player.

The old man on the front row sniffed loudly, and then pulled a handkerchief out of the pocket of his suit jacket and blew his nose into it. Then he opened the handkerchief and inspected the contents before folding it back up and putting it into his top pocket.

Father Arthur moved smartly to the front of the church and paused for a moment to take us both in. His flock. His sheep. Just waiting to be welcomed into the woolly fold of Jesus' love.

'Welcome,' he said.

And I took it in. The words, the music, everything. And I didn't even laugh when the old man on the front row's head bobbed forward as he fell asleep. But then he snored, loudly. A rasping inhalation that was suddenly broken when his head shot up and he shouted 'Theodore?!' And then, I did laugh. And Father Arthur laughed too.

Margot and President
Ho Chi Minh

MARGOT WAS WEARING lilac. The sunlight hit the tops of the desks around her and made her look like she was shining.

'You'll like this one,' she said, sharpening her pencil and blowing the shavings from her canvas.

Without really appearing to think about it, she started drawing ovals on the page, rows and rows of them. Slowly, the ovals were gifted with shoulders, and two tall buildings rose up on either side of them. Then they were given clothes and faces and signs. And then they were given a story.

London, 18th March 1968, 1 a.m.
Margot Macrae is Thirty-Seven Years Old

I sat on the steps that led up to the front door of our house, bleeding scratches like tallies on my arms, the skin on my left knee having flapped back and revealed something raw and bloody underneath, my right kneecap swelling into a dark, lumpy bruise. My palms were encrusted with tiny pieces of gravel that I tried to unpick with my fingernails, but that only tore at the skin and made it bleed.

It was dark. And cold. But still I waited.

I hadn't eaten since breakfast the previous morning and my stomach reminded me. For a moment, it felt like it had when Davey was swimming within me and almost ready to meet the world, and he had turned the right side up to begin the journey.

I had been sitting on the cold stone steps for so long that my bottom had gone completely numb. My hair was dirty. My clothes were dirty too, and I was tired in a way that I hadn't been since Davey passed.

I supposed, though, that the steps were as good a place as any to wait. The next train out of London wouldn't be until 6 a.m.

Two suitcases waited beside me. I pulled a jumper from inside one of them and draped it around my shoulders. I wouldn't put it on until later because I didn't want the blood to stain the sleeves.

I had promised myself there would be no more protests, no more law breaking, no more activism, and yet I'd found myself standing in Trafalgar Square on 17th March 1968, with my heartbeat humming in my ears and my hands shaking. Hoping it would make Meena notice me.

The Professor was there again. In fact, The Professor had become a staple in our lives. He had got much better at remembering to take off his wedding ring. From our flat window, I would watch him. He would pull at it, twisting and twisting (he was obviously a thinner man when he got married) until it came off, and then he would tuck it into his left blazer pocket for safekeeping.

That day in March was their first trip out together in public. Meena was excited. The Professor was smoking and trying to affect an attitude of calm, but he was clearly as nervous as I was. He had on a pair of rounded silver sunglasses, presumably hoping he wouldn't be recognized by anybody while he held on to the hand of a woman who wasn't his wife.

We were standing in what was once Trafalgar Square. Only, it wasn't Trafalgar Square any more; it was a hive of people. The crowd buzzed and jostled and pushed. Two men held a wooden sign with a picture of a smiling President Ho Chi Minh, and underneath a message to the American army: *Go home!* They shoved past me and forced their way forwards to get closer to the action. Adam and Lawrence were somewhere in the crowd too, wearing T-shirts that said in messy black marker: *You can tell Uncle Sam we won't go to Vietnam.*

In the darkness, on the steps, I waited.

I patted my bloodied knee with the flannel I'd brought from upstairs. It stung so much that I pulled it back off quickly, and the last wet bit of skin tore off too. The flesh underneath was pink and shining. But much as it hurt, I didn't move.

In the half-light of the lamp posts at the end of the road, I saw a figure walking along the pavement. I strained my eyes, but it wasn't her.

The noise was impossible. It was time to move to Grosvenor Square for the actress to deliver the letter. It was immediate – the tide of people turning.

'I'm going,' The Professor said, dropping his cigarette on the ground and not bothering to extinguish it.

Meena stared at him. 'What?' she said. 'You can't go now, it's just about to get good.' But he gave her a smart kiss on the cheek and then elbowed his way through the crowd, telling a woman to back off as she waved a sign in his shaded eyes.

Meena stopped. So did I. She looked like she might cry. Her petulant face set something in me on fire.

She turned to me and she must have seen it, because she asked me, 'What?'

The crowd was getting louder and swelling around us. There was no way out.

'Stop it, Meena,' I shouted. 'Just stop it.'

The people flowed around us on either side. In the middle of the chaos, it felt like it was just loud enough that I could shout it and not be heard by anyone but her.

'Stop pretending it's him that you want!'

As more of the crowd, impatient to get to Grosvenor Square and see the letter delivered, pushed forwards, it was as though we were standing in the middle of the sea against a strong current that was pulling us all in great waves. But she didn't move and neither did I.

I reached out and took her hand.

The noisy couple who lived in the bedsit below us clattered down the street under the light of the lamp posts. He was only wearing one shoe, but she had both her high heels on and they clacked along the path as they ran, hand in hand.

When they got to the bottom of the stairs, they saw me but said nothing. They picked their way carefully up the steps, but her ankle gave way and she stumbled, falling into my suitcases, which rattled down the steps. The smaller case sprang open, vomiting everything inside it onto the pavement. 'Oops!' she said, and as they let themselves inside and shut the front door, I heard them both laugh.

Meena looked at me and while the chaos surged around us, neither of us moved.

'Let go,' she said. And I didn't understand fast enough, so she pulled her hand from mine and ran into the crowd.

'Meena!'

I went after her.

I scrabbled down the steps and picked up my open suitcase. I bundled skirts and dresses and shoes back inside. And I stopped at the balloon on the bottom step. The yellow one. We had had as much fun popping all of the yellow balloons as we did living with them buttercupping our bedsit for a week. I'd kept one of the deflated balloons, with its string still attached to it. Because I didn't want to forget that she had remembered.

The chaos was getting worse. I passed a man who was bleeding from his nose in great rivers down to his lips, so that he had to spit the blood pooling into his mouth onto the floor.

She was quick, darting between people and under signs.

'Meena!'

A policeman brought his truncheon down on the shoulder of a protester who disappeared out of sight. His friends launched at the officer, grabbing his jacket and pulling him to the ground.

On the Pathé news later, the reporter would call it the most violent protest ever seen in London.

The photographs had slid out of the suitcase and fallen face-down on the pavement. I had only packed two. A photograph of me in a green dress, dancing with Meena at a cèilidh her friend Sally had thrown on my first New Year's Eve in London. Meena's laughing and we're dancing, arms crossed and held together while we spin. It was one of the nights when I had marvelled at how happy it was possible to be. And my favourite photograph: Meena and I, our faces painted with flowers, at the house party of someone or other. The night we had saved the dog. And she had shown me that I wasn't the only soul she was teaching to set themselves free.

I picked them both up and sat back down on the steps. I guessed it was probably around three in the morning. But still I waited.

A horse bayed and whinnied with fright as his police rider tried to control him. More smoke bombs were set off as officers and protesters were carried away on stretchers.

'Meena!' I tried shouting, though I couldn't hear my own voice. She must have been so far ahead now. And probably still running.

Someone cracked into my head with a heavy sign, and for a moment everything went blurry. White smoke was rising up and I had the feeling I wasn't really there at all. Then I felt the full force of someone falling onto me and I remember hitting the ground.

I didn't hear her footsteps, but there she was at the bottom of the steps, draped in a stranger's coat and carrying a sign that said *Peace*. Not a scratch on her.

I wondered at how she could be none the worse for the experience.

Her eyes journeyed up my bruised shins to my bloodied knee, to the scratches on my arms, and then, finally, to the suitcases beside me.

There were so many things I wanted to say to her. I wanted to ask her why she could be so free in so many ways but one. Tell her that she needn't be afraid of me. Explain that I felt for her in a way that I never felt for Johnny, because the way I felt for her wasn't born of obligation. It was completely and wholly voluntary. And that I could love her for ever, if only she would let me.

But no words came out.

I could taste metal and blood, but I kept walking on and on, in the opposite direction of the protest. I found a side street and then another. As I kept walking down the road, now littered with missiles that had been thrown – rocks, shoes and discarded signs – I saw the smiling face of President Ho Chi Minh once more, now lying on the ground and marked with brown where disrespectful shoes had trampled over him. *Go*, he told me, *go home!*

But I didn't have a home.

So, I would have to find one.

*

Meena sat beside me on the cold step and rested her head on my shoulder and we didn't say anything. I didn't have the bravery to say it again. And I didn't have the bravery not to hear it back.

At some point I must have slipped into sleep, because when I opened my eyes, the sky had turned from darkness to a hopeful grey. The sun was coming. She was still there, her head resting on my shoulder, dreaming.

I went to stretch out my legs to get the feeling back into them, and my movement must have woken her. Her sleepy face as she opened her eyes made me want to keep her.

But I couldn't.

So I handed her an envelope with the next month's rent in it. And the photograph from the cèilidh. So she wouldn't forget me.

And then I picked up my bags and, in the grey morning light, I made my way down the road.

Looking for home.

An Exchange of Riches

'About £35,000.'

'You're kidding!'

'Nope.'

'Oh my God. Trust me to miss the one day when something exciting happens. What's she going to do with it?' New Nurse had completely forgotten she was meant to be giving me my anti-DVT injection, and was standing with one hand on her hip and the needle absently held aloft in her other hand, like a needle catalogue model (if there are such things).

'She said she would put some aside to make sure her father had a decent funeral, and then she said she didn't know, perhaps go back to university or travel or put it towards a house, give some to her mother. She had a lot of ideas.'

'Wow.'

'I know. She tried to give me one.'

'One what?'

'One of the notes. After she asked me to work out how much was in the bag, she offered me one, so that I would have something Swedish with me in hospital. She said she hadn't forgotten meeting me in all the time since she left the hospital, and she smiled when she saw that the yellow roses are still on my bedside table.'

'Did you take it?'

'No, I couldn't. She's the one who came up with the idea for the Rose Room – she's the reason I met Margot.'

'Isn't it amazing to think that her dad carried that money around with him and even though he was homeless, he didn't spend it. And now she knows – her father had been thinking about her the whole time he was gone.'

'It was an exchange of riches. She gave the hospital a gift and it gave one back.'

Lenni and the Man Who Used to Be Her Moon

'OH, I REMEMBER your dad,' Paul the Porter said. 'Tall fella? Glasses?'

'That's him.' Paul was walking me to the Rose Room because he had to go that way anyway and, in his words, we hadn't had a natter for a while. He was walking beside me as I wheeled along. He'd asked me if I wanted a push and when I said no, he let me get on with it and I liked that. I mentally awarded him some Porter Points. He's beating the other porters by miles.

'Used to come round a lot?' Paul said.

'That's him,' I said again, as we reached a flat part of the corridor which I could wheel across like a dream.

'Quiet guy,' he said, thinking. I wondered if he was picturing my father correctly, with all the colour drained out of him, which is how he always was when he came to the May Ward. As though he'd had to leave his coat and any fresh flowers and all the colour in his face at the nurses' station before he could come into the ward.

'He doesn't come around so much,' Paul said, holding open a set of doors for me.

'Nope,' I said, sliding through. 'Margot's been asking me about him. I don't know why she's worried about me. I don't want him to come back.'

'Maybe she's not worried about you,' Paul said thoughtful-ly, 'maybe she's worried about him.'

If Paul hadn't just won himself an extra fifteen hundred Porter Points for insight, I might have felt nervous coming into the Rose Room to tell her the rest.

Margot had pinned her hair up into a bun, and for a moment she looked like the brown-haired girl I'd seen on the beach in Glasgow.

'What do you think?' she asked.

'Love it,' I told her, wheeling up to my seat. 'If we go back to visit my father,' I said, 'can we go somewhere fun after?'

She nodded.

Glasgow Princess Royal Hospital, December 2013
Lenni Pettersson is Sixteen Years Old

The first Big Surgery happened a few weeks after the meeting with the fearful consultant.

The dream I had while I was under the general anaesthetic was so orange I could taste it.

When I left the orange dream, I found my father.

I watched him sitting by my bedside and he looked hag-gard. His face was grey and his jaw was set into stone.

'I can't do this, Len,' he said, and his voice cracked. 'I can't sit here and watch you *die.*'

'Then don't.'

He looked at me then, for a long time. Like he was trying to find something in my face that would tell him what he didn't already know.

*

At first he still came, between the visiting hours of three and six, and he continued his slow transition into a gargoyle – all stony and grey. Agnieszka had had to return to Poland for work and I knew that he had stopped laughing.

The visits became shorter, and he would miss a day or two, or a week. He became quieter and greyer, and I would watch the clock until the end of visiting hours and be relieved if he didn't appear in the doorway, all hunched and mourning.

'I meant it,' I told him one afternoon as, through my eyelashes, I watched him watch me pretend to sleep, with the same expression of despair with which he had watched my mother stand in the kitchen staring into the garden wearing only a T-shirt and knickers. He wanted to row out to me, to pull me back to shore. But, like my mother, I was underwater already, where it gets dark.

I knew it was time. 'Papa,' I said. I hadn't called him that in years. I was pulling out all the stops. 'I want you to do something for me.'

He looked at me.

'I want you to promise me you won't come back.'

There was a really long pause.

'I can't do that, Lenni,' he said, 'I can't leave you here on your own.'

'I'm not alone, I have all these nice nurses and doctors and all these tubes. Look at them all! I'm out of my mind with all the tubes!' I pointed to the tubes burrowing into me, across the bed, attached to the various machines.

'Lenni,' he said softly.

And then I couldn't be soft any more. 'I don't want you here.'

He didn't speak.

'I want you to go to Poland. Take a holiday and see Agnieszka, meet her family. Then come back and start your life together and let her make you laugh.'

'No, Lenni.'

'You can't say no to a dying child.'

'You're not supposed to make jokes about this,' he said, but he smiled a little.

'I want you gone.'

A few tears fell from his eyes and he had to take off his glasses to wipe them away.

'It will be a promise. Promise that you'll go away and you won't come back.'

'But I—'

'And if I get to the end, the nurses will tell you. They will call you and they will tell you to come. And then you can come and say goodbye. But that won't be our real goodbye. This will. While I'm still Lenni. When I'm flush for tubes and looking forward to when they bring dinner because I like the strawberry yoghurts they have here.'

He shook his head and more tears fell, so he just took off his glasses and rested them in his lap. Then he took my tubed hand in his wet one.

'If—'

'If I change my mind, I will get them to call you and you will come,' I said. 'I know. But you have to promise.'

'Why?' he asked.

'Because I'm setting you free.'

He sat with me for hours and when they brought my dinner, he asked the nurse to swap my lemon yoghurt for a strawberry one.

I woke up the next morning and found Benni the beanbag pig sitting in the visitor's chair where my father had been, and there was a picture resting in Benni's lap – a folded photograph of my father and me on my first birthday. I am in his arms and holding one hand up to my own eye and smushing it with the palm of my hand, and he is laughing. I have cake icing all over my cheeks and on my dungarees. The photo was worn at the centre in a cross from having made a home in his wallet for fifteen years.

And on the back, in green highlighter pen borrowed from the nurses' station, he'd written: *I will love you forever, pickle.*

~

Margot gave me a smile that looked like she understood. And that maybe, although I might be wrong, she was proud of me.

'Can we go to London now?' I asked.

'Well we *could*,' she said, 'but today we're going somewhere new.'

Margot and the Road

Warwickshire, February 1971
Margot Macrae is Forty Years Old

The A4189 between Redditch and Henley-in-Arden is winding, long and lonely. It's worse in the dark. The winters in London were never as cold as those I experienced in the countryside. In London there are all those tall buildings and bright lights to protect you, whereas out in the country you are exposed and vulnerable. If the pin in the map on the wall of Meena's bedsit was still there, it pierced a spot just a few miles from where I was now driving, where I had found myself a job in a local library and settled into a small, quiet life.

I caught my own eye in the rear-view mirror and surprised myself with the fact that I now looked like a grown-up. I didn't feel twelve years older than the Margot who had stepped off the train at Euston, alone and grieving, but I was.

And there I was, on the road, completely alone and in darkness. There were no cars ahead to follow and no cars behind to reassure. I went up a steep hill where leafless trees clawed up to the sky like grasping hands. I followed my headlights around another corner, and noticed briefly that the grass

258

either side of the road was being blown about by the wind. A leaf flew past my window and I wondered for a moment if it were a bird, thrown out of control by the heavy winds. Spots of rain announced themselves on my windscreen and I turned on my wipers. Wipe, wipe. I kept my eyes on the road; I wasn't far from Henley now. There was nothing to be afraid of. Wipe, wipe. I drove on, curling around another corner and past the old church. In the night, the place looked haunted.

The darkness rose up around my little car, and anything not illuminated by my headlights waited in the black unknown.

Around another corner – the empty hedgerows shivered against the wind and I leant closer to the steering wheel. I reached a straight section – the last part of the journey before Henley would be in sight. I was just starting to relax when my headlights lit up the dark figure of a man standing in the middle of the road. A man I was about to hit with my car. He didn't move and for the briefest of seconds, neither did I. The shock of seeing him arrested my brain, but then my foot took over, pushing the brake with all my strength. My car swerved to the left. I jabbed at the horn, trying to gain control of the wheel. He turned then, and took a large step onto the grassy embankment by the side of the road. My engine stalled, or cut out, and I stopped, my front left wheel joining him at the edge of the road.

It must not have taken more than a few seconds for all that to happen, but it felt like it happened very, very slowly. I sat motionless for a moment. On this empty, seemingly endless stretch of road, he was standing dressed entirely in black. Apparently unafraid.

I tried to re-start my engine, but my hands were shaking so much that I couldn't get a grip on my keys.

He knocked on my passenger-side window and I screamed.

I grabbed at the ignition for my keys again, and this time I got them. The engine made a whining sound, but nothing happened. I pressed the accelerator and turned the key again, but nothing happened.

Then he was bending over and smiling at me. He knocked again. His face was not the face I thought it would have been. He was probably around fifty, with a ruddy nose, and a fisherman's hat on. His hair was greying at the sides and sticking out in tufts from underneath.

'Hallo!' he shouted. 'Terribly sorry to have scared you!'

I didn't say anything. I turned my key hard, and a dry grunting came out of the bonnet.

'I think you might have flooded the engine!' he shouted at me through the window.

I still didn't speak.

'Try letting go of the keys a minute – the engine needs to rest before you try again.'

I did as he said. I was so full of adrenalin I probably could have abandoned the car and run home.

'Are you all right?' he asked, peering through the glass and smiling inanely at me as though I were a zoo animal.

I nodded, hoping he would go away.

'The name's Humphrey!' he cried, pointing to himself. 'Humphrey James!'

'What were you doing in the road?' I shouted from the driver's seat, finding my voice at last.

'Sorry?'

'The road, what were you doing in the road?'

He beckoned for me to get out of the car and join him.

I must have looked unsure.

'There's nothing to be afraid of, I don't bite!' he said. And then he laughed.

'What were you doing in the road?' I asked again.

He pointed up. I glanced at the ceiling of my car.

'Not that,' he said with a chuckle. 'The stars!'

I leant forward in my seat to peer through my windscreen, but it was so fogged with my own breath that I couldn't make anything out.

He knocked on my window again.

'What?' I snapped.

'Come and have a look!'

I shook my head. 'No, thanks, I'm fine!'

I tried to start my engine again, but the whining noise continued.

'What's your name?' he shouted.

I sighed. 'Margot.'

'Margot, I think you've flooded your engine!'

'Yes, you said!'

'Well, I can't fix it while the engine's hot. If we wait twenty minutes or so, I can have you back on the road.'

'You can fix my car?'

'I can indeed! We have to wait for the engine to cool, though!'

'Oh.'

'Would you like to see the stars, Margot?'

'I don't know.'

'It's a once-in-a-lifetime astral event!' His face was so wide with excitement and his enthusiasm so earnest that I put my hazard lights on, checked my wing mirror and got out of the car. The February air was freezing; it stung my cheeks.

'Come with me,' he said, and he walked back into the middle of the road, illuminated now by the headlights of my car and the dancing rays of my hazards. 'Look' – he pointed – 'look.'

I followed him down the embankment, but I didn't go onto the road. I looked up and I couldn't believe it. There were stars. More stars than I thought possible.

A Van Gogh sky hung above us. It seemed to wrap right around the earth.

'It's beautiful,' I said.

'See how the trident there and the bow are almost on top of one another?' he said. 'This almost never happens. It's to do with the axis of the earth.'

'So this is why you were standing in the middle of the road?' I asked.

'Of course. It's once in a millennium that you get to see something like this.'

'I might've hit you. You were just . . . right there, no torch, nothing. You might've been killed.'

'Oh no,' he said, 'I find that people always stop.'

We stood watching the stars in silence. I almost expected them to start moving, as though we might be able to actually see the earth rotating. All that time in London with the smog and the light pollution had knocked the idea of stars right out of my head; I couldn't quite believe that what I was seeing was real and not in fact a series of bright bulbs shining through dark blue velvet.

'I'm awfully sorry about your car,' he said, not taking his eyes off the sky. 'Please know I will pay for any damage.'

I thanked him.

'And I'm sorry to have scared you,' he said. 'I don't meet many drivers on this road, but I must say, I am out earlier than usual.'

'Why's that?'

'Margot,' he said, 'it is, as I told you, a once-in-a-lifetime astral event!'

The night was still, and the fear and dread from nearly hitting him had been drained out of me by the mere sight of the sky.

'I can see how you got carried away looking at it,' I said.

'Oh, I could watch the stars for ever,' he said. 'I didn't even bring my telescope. I just wanted to see it. As it is for me to see.'

My car waited behind us. The battery was probably being run down by the headlights.

'What if another car comes?' I asked.

'Then it will be an expensive evening of repairs for me!' He laughed as though this were the funniest thing anyone had ever said.

'Do you do this every night?'

'Often my roof will suffice, but this deserved proper attention. It was worth it, don't you think?'

'But don't you feel scared out here all alone in the dark?'

He smiled at me then. 'Not at all, Margot. *I have loved the stars too fondly to be fearful of the night.*'

*

He didn't fix my car. After twenty minutes of quiet stargazing, he lifted the bonnet and tinkered, umm-ing and ahh-ing while I shivered and stared at him and at the sky.

In the end, he took off the handbrake and wheeled my poor car up onto the grassy embankment, promising he would have it towed in the morning by a mechanic friend who owed him a favour. So we walked towards Henley-in-Arden through the darkness. I kept to the grassy knoll at the side of the road, but Humphrey James, stargazer, strolled right in the centre, straight down the white line of the middle of the road like a tightrope walker, one foot in front of the other. I kept turning to check behind us, to make sure that a car wasn't silently approaching.

'So, Margot, what brings you here?'

'You were standing in the middle of the road and I broke my car trying not to kill you.'

'No, what brings you to Henley-in-Arden?'

I didn't say anything.

'The country life?'

'No.'

'The isolation?'

I laughed. 'No.'

'The Bard?'

'I never cared much for Shakespeare.'

'*Never cared much for Shakespeare?*' he repeated.

'No.'

At this Humphrey James roared with laughter, and in between gasps for breath he said, 'That is the greatest thing I've ever heard!'

We continued walking. The night was bitterly cold, but I didn't mind it.

'And what do you do?' I asked. 'When you're not stargazing on the road?'

'Oh, this and that. Mostly stars.'

'Mostly stars?'

'Exactly.'

He stopped, so I stopped too. He pointed to the sky. 'Every star you see up there,' he said, 'is bigger than the sun.'

'Is that so?'

'Oh yes, and brighter too. The faint ones might be the same size as the sun, but the brighter ones are bigger. People don't realize that – they think that because they seem small and twinkling they *are* small, but they are large, massive, and so very powerful.'

'Gosh.'

'You, Margot, you can see approximately twenty quadrillion miles tonight.'

'Can I? I sometimes have trouble making out road signs without my glasses on.'

'You can see the stars, can't you?'

'I can.'

'Then you can see twenty quadrillion miles.'

I smiled at him. He smiled at me.

We carried on walking until we reached the railway bridge that announced the beginning of Henley-in-Arden and the end of the wildness.

'Which way is home?' he asked, and I pointed.

'I have to visit a friend that way,' he said. 'Would you mind the company?'

'Not at all,' I said.

So we took up walking again, this time both of us on the pavement. He pulled a white handkerchief from his pocket and wiped his nose with it.

'So, Scotland, of course,' he said. 'But also, perhaps London?'

'I'm sorry?'

'London? You've got a twinge to your accent.'

'Oh, yes. I've been living in London.'

'For how long?'

'Oh, about twelve years.'

'Wonderful city,' he said. 'Incredible libraries, and the universities are really first rate.'

'Have you lived there too?'

'No, but I visit occasionally. I could never live there, I couldn't bear the visibility.'

We turned onto the high street, and the town seemed to be waiting in a calm, quiet glow.

'Which way are you?' he asked.

'Just along here,' I gestured.

'And what do you do now?' he asked.

'I work at the Redditch library,' I said.

'Ah, so it's words, then?'

'Sorry?'

'It's words that you do.'

'I suppose ...'

'Yet not a fan of Shakespeare,' he said, as though he were piecing together clues in a mystery and this one didn't fit. I think he was impressed. Incredulous, at least, that I could be one and not the other.

'It's not a requirement ...'

'You're controversial, aren't you, Margot?' he asked. 'A rebel?'

'Um, I don't—'

'Nothing wrong with that!' he shouted. 'All the best people are.'

Then he paused and we walked in silence for a moment. I pulled my keys from my handbag.

'This is where I leave you, then,' he concluded, as I selected my door key with freezing fingers.

'Yes,' I told him.

'I will have your car collected first thing in the morning,' he said. 'What time do you leave for work?'

'Eight.'

'In that case, your car will be back here by seven, in full working order.'

'Will it?'

'Oh, ye of little faith.' He laughed.

I opened my door and felt the need to thank him, although I couldn't work out what I would thank him for. The interruption to my evening and the damage to my car were all his fault, and yet I felt as though I were in some way in his debt, perhaps for the company, for the first non-transactional conversation I'd had in months . . . or perhaps for the promise of a mended car.

'Thank you,' I said.

He smiled and bobbed his head. 'Goodnight.' As I let myself into the flat, I heard him shout, 'Never cared much for Shakespeare!' as he walked away down the street, laughing.

The next morning, I opened my front door to find that my car had not only been delivered to the parking space outside my flat, but that the engine had been repaired and started

267

like a dream. On the passenger seat sat an envelope. The letter addressed me as 'the kind-hearted woman who went out of her way not to kill me', and asked if it would not be too forward to invite me to share in some tapas and stargazing at my earliest convenience. And then, 'because you are a woman who likes words, Margot,' he wrote, 'a poem from my world to yours'.

And in his arachnid writing, he had copied out the first verses of a poem:

Reach me down my Tycho Brahe, I would know him when we meet,
When I share my later science, sitting humbly at his feet;
He may know the law of all things, yet be ignorant of how
We are working to completion, working on from then to now.

Pray, remember, that I leave you all my theory complete,
Lacking only certain data for your adding, as is meet;
And remember, men will scorn it, 'tis original and true,
And the obloquy of newness may fall bitterly on you.

But, my pupil, as my pupil, you have learned the worth of scorn;
You have laughed with me at pity, we have joyed to be forlorn;
What, for us, are all distractions of men's fellowship and smiles?
What, for us, the goddess Pleasure with her meretricious wiles?

You may tell that German college that their honour comes too late.
But they must not waste repentance on the grizzly savant's fate;
Though my soul may set in darkness, it will rise in perfect light;
I have loved the stars too fondly to be fearful of the night.

PART THREE

Lenni

'I DON'T WANT to die.'

As I say it, I feel the goose bumps shivering their way onto the surface of my skin. I like that. Whenever my body announces a part of itself that's working normally, I feel proud. My skin's reaction to temperature? Fine, it turns out. Never better.

The man turns to look at me with disdain and confusion. His cigarette hovers somewhere between his shoulder and his mouth, outstretched as though he's offering me a drag.

He has no hair on the top of his head, but it's gathered in dark and grey tufts on the sides and I wonder if it's keeping his ears warm out here. He's wearing a beige dressing gown that goes down to his bare knees. The skin on his legs is pale but the hairs are really dark and long. So long you could brush them . . . if you wanted to.

He watches me, completely suspended in animation.

It seems an obvious sort of thing to say, but he doesn't light up with recognition or agreement.

'Did you know, the best place to scavenge for discarded cigarettes is the bus stop?' I ask. 'The chances are that someone will have lit up only to have to stub their cigarette out when the bus arrives. And that's where they'll be. Plenty of barely smoked cigarettes.'

271

'You know, if you wanted to get some for free,' I add, when I'm not sure if he's understood me. 'A homeless friend of mine told me that,' I carry on. 'He said I wasn't likely to find a use for it, but I've passed it on. And maybe now that you know, you'll pass it on and it'll keep on going for ever.'

He holds the cigarette still, and I watch the snake of smoke curling left and right as it winds on up to the sky.

'He's already dead, that friend of mine,' I say, though he still doesn't respond. A breeze drifts through us both and I wonder if the man feels something.

'I'm not ready,' I tell him, and he turns away, looking out at the hospital car park and taking the cigarette almost to his mouth.

'I'm not,' I tell him. He looks back at me. The confusion has ebbed away and there's just disdain now. I'm ruining his cigarette break and he wants me gone. But I am grateful for it. Hostility is fine. It's the sympathy that kills you.

The roar of the outside is all around us – the road in the distance, the wind in the trees, the murmur of people, and the clink on the ground as pound coins miss the slot on the parking ticket machine. The noise should be oppressive, but it isn't, it's freeing. The hospital is so quiet. But out here, sounds can get lost.

'How can I possibly die when I'm this afraid of dying?' I ask him.

He wants me to go, but I can't just yet. The grey stubble around his mouth twitches and he very briefly bares a yellow tooth. I wonder if this is an innate response. A jungle cat baring its teeth to a bird who just won't go away. He throws the cigarette to the floor with a forward arc that makes it skitter and roll along the paving slabs and underneath one of the benches.

Then, with another look that tells me in no uncertain terms that I have ruined his cigarette break, he turns and hunches, with a slight limp on the left side, back through the revolving doors into the hospital. The doors stop with him halfway in, halfway out. They do that whenever the sensor thinks someone is too close to the pane of glass in front.

I follow the cigarette and pick it up. It's still lit, but the light is fading. I've never held a cigarette before and I'm surprised at two things – one, it's very light, and two, it's very smooth. I roll it forwards and backwards between my finger and thumb, and hope I don't see anyone I know.

When I am just beginning to entertain the question of what would happen if I smoked it, I take the option off the table and throw it into the bin. That's my good deed for the day sorted.

I know I should go back inside before New Nurse notices I'm gone, but I linger for a moment or two, watching the cars perform their merry dance. A reverse into a space, a pause, giving way, a do-si-do around the mini roundabout.

When the smoke starts gently snaking its way up from inside the little green bin, I think that it might be time to go. By the time the flames appear, spilling out above the symbol on the bin with the three arrows all going in the same direction (I'm not sure what they stand for. Health, wealth, happiness? Father, Son, Holy Ghost? There are so many great threesomes to celebrate), it's definitely time to go.

Margot and the Astronomer

'Pippa, have you got any glitter?'

'Glitter, Lenni?' Margot asked sceptically.

'Yes, glitter – of course glitter!' I told her.

'But won't it end up looking like a Christmas card?' Margot asked.

'Of course not. So . . . glitter?'

'I don't think so, Lenni,' Pippa said, pulling out each of the drawers in her desk in turn, 'but I can certainly add it to The List.'

I nodded, authorizing the addition of glitter to The List. 'Gold, please.'

Margot looked down at the piece in front of her that she was adding the finishing touches to – a dark blue sky studded with tiny stars, and a little cottage sitting patiently underneath.

'I bet you fell in love with him. You did, didn't you?'

'That would ruin the story.'

'Telling me would ruin the story or falling in love would ruin the story?'

Margot only laughed.

'Can I hear it?'

'Of course.'

Warwickshire, 1971
Margot Macrae is Forty Years Old

His house was chaotic. The main building used to be a farm-house – it was tall and made of crumbling stone. He'd bought it from an heir-less farmer with the intention of converting it completely into a modern home, but had given up as soon as he'd installed water, electricity, and an attic observatory with windows nested in the roof. The windows whistled when the wind blew and the radiators didn't work.

There were several other buildings; one in which he kept a gaggle of chickens, in the other his car. In the third, he was in the process of creating a larger observatory. He had already had the good fortune that some of the roof tiles had fallen in the previous winter. He told me, as he walked me around, that he was going to set up a clear glass roof so that he could see the stars without, as he put it, 'getting as cold as a witch's tit'.

The chickens were many and he delighted in feeding them, picking them up and talking to them as though they under-stood. He had named them all after old Hollywood film stars: Marilyn, Lauren, Bette, Judy . . . When I asked him why, he told me that partly it was because he liked the idea that they were stars, but that mostly he was getting a bit sick of naming things after the constellations. He didn't believe me at first when I told him that I, too, had once been a proud parent of a chicken. And I immediately wanted to call Meena. I often wondered what became of Jeremy. Whether he was still out there somewhere, pecking his way around London, living the life of a free-range chicken.

We stood in the field that spread out behind his house, and we looked up at the sky. Originally home to many cows, the field was now home to an extraordinarily overgrown garden. It was a night so cold that our breath danced away from us in ghostly patterns, but it didn't bother me. The best way I can describe it would be to say that with him, I felt sanctuary. I felt we had all the time in the world to talk, and so much more to see. There was no hurry to speak, to impress him, to make him laugh. I felt so calm in his presence.

We sat and ate spicy tapas on his unstable kitchen table, which was propped up on one side by the Yellow Pages and on the other side with a Monopoly box. Humphrey was like nobody else I knew. He was both connected to and disconnected from the world. Connected to the intricate movements of the stars, the nowness of where each satellite, constellation and moon was in relation to the earth, but disconnected from everything else – his fridge contained a block of butter that had expired two years earlier, and the calendar that hung on his wall claimed that it was still 1964. He had tickets and flyers for events long passed, remembered sentences from Radio 2 programmes he'd loved at university, but often couldn't recall if he had fed the chickens that day or when his sister's birthday was.

'I'll just go and check the chickens aren't hungry,' he said, and I chose not to remind him that he had fed them twice in the two hours that I had been there. Instead, I was happy to stand alone in his kitchen among the bric-a-brac and just read. There were notes all over the place from Humphrey to Humphrey, and labels stuck on things that shouldn't have needed labelling, like 'The Big Spoon'. One of the saucepans was labelled 'good' and one 'bad'. Why he kept both, I'll never know.

He came back in, stamping his wellies on the mud-marinated doormat. 'They've plenty of food, too much if anything!' And he laughed as though it were another excellent joke. He took me by the hand, eyes bright, and asked, 'Shall we go and observe them properly?' And he led me up the stairs to the attic, where his homemade observatory let us mere mortals glimpse the heavens.

My Friend, My Friend

'THERE ARE SILVERFISH living in the corner of my bathroom.'

Father Arthur sat down in the pew beside me.

'At first sight,' he said, 'on an early morning visit to the lavatory, I thought they were slugs, but they're not – they're silverfish. There was just one, a dark thing that slithered into the gap between the floor tile and the skirting board.

'You might think that I would want to get rid of them, that I might fear they are greater in number than me, that they might be living in the wall in their disgusting thousands, but I quite like them. They remind me that life is possible in even the most inhospitable conditions. They're such funny things – little slips of silver that move like water and are so unlike any other life we know.

'When I take a bath – and please stop me if you find this an inappropriate topic – I no longer read. Instead I watch and wait, hoping the absence of movement on the floor might bring one of them out – coax it into an adventure into the unknown lands of my bathroom floor. Often, they don't come out. I have two theories. The first is that they don't like the light – on my many night-time lavatory trips, they always scurry away. My second theory is that they are nocturnal. Though I confess I know nothing about the sleeping patterns of our invertebrate friends, I often wonder if they don't like the day and prefer to explore by night.

'In an effort not to kill them, I have asked Mrs Hill to refrain from using bleach on the bathroom floor. She told me I will get germs and that those germs will make me ill, and that at some point she will have to do it, but I begged her not to, at least for now. I think of them as my tenants, my tiny immigrants, and I am their protector, their observer and their friend.'

'How many are there?' I asked.

'At least two, but I hope for more.'

'You could take down the skirting board and have a look.'

'But what would I do then?'

'Count them.'

'And then what? I don't think I'd feel good about destroying their home.'

'So you will just have to drink a lot before bed.'

'Why's that?'

'So you need the toilet in the night.'

He laughed. Quietly at first, but then it got louder. 'Oh, Lenni,' he said, 'that's simply wonderful.'

'Is it?'

'Yes.'

'Why?'

'Because I never would have thought of it.'

And then the smile faded from his face and he was sad again, just as he had been when I'd come into the chapel and New Nurse had gone off in the direction of the main entrance, telling me she was getting chocolate and a magazine, and if I wanted anything I should tell her now or forever hold my peace.

He stared up at the brown stained glass cross. 'I've been looking at this window for so many years and now I'm worried I've been taking it for granted.'

'Taking it for granted?'

'I've only got a week left as hospital chaplain.'

'What? A week? When did that happen?'

'Lenni?' He was concerned, worried that I didn't know the date. But nobody who spends their days in nightwear has much need to concern themselves with the date.

'I thought you had four months left.'

'I did.'

'It's been four months?'

'It will be, at the end of next week.'

I watched him breathing, pulling the air in through his nose slowly, his eyes still on the stained glass cross.

'What's wrong?' I asked in the gentlest voice I have.

'What if nobody comes?' he said, finally looking at me.

'To what?'

'My final chapel service. I fear it might be rather poorly attended.'

'What about the old man? The sleeping one.'

'He was discharged.' He took a sharp breath in. 'I'm sorry, Lenni,' he said, 'it's my job to help *you*, not the other way round.'

'You help me, I help you. That's just how it is,' I told him.

'Thank you.'

'Hey, you'll always be my friend, my friend.'

New Nurse chose that moment to push open the heavy chapel door and then stumble as the door gave way and let her in. Although I suppose she didn't really *choose* the moment – how could she know what was happening on the other side of those doors? But I wish she'd waited. I wanted to stay.

Margot's Getting Married

MARGOT AND I sat side by side as rain battered the Rose Room windows. It wasn't so much like the rain was falling from the sky as it was being thrown. I managed to get acrylic paint all along my pyjama sleeve as I painted a characteristically terrible picture of myself, aged three, crying at the nursery school gates. But it was very cosy, sitting in the warm room while the rain fell outside. Margot drew with such delicacy that you could almost hear their crunchy leaves, see their skeletal structure – a small posy of dried flowers, browned and curled at the edges and tied together with a ribbon.

West Midlands, September 1979
Margot Macrae is Forty-Eight Years Old

The sunlight had crept all the way across the half-laid carpet of Humphrey's sitting room and still I hadn't written a word. There was a patch where the carpet wasn't fixed to the floor so it was very easy to catch your toe under it and trip. We often did. I'd tried Sellotape, but it didn't stick to the flagstone beneath. The stones were icy in the winter mornings, such that we would each try to convince the other to be the one to go downstairs and put the kettle on. That room was everything – kitchen, living room, dining room – and then the stone staircase led up to the bedroom/observatory. I was sitting at the writing desk Humphrey had built for me, and I stretched out a leg and tucked my toe under the gap between the carpet and the floor.

'Are you finished?' Humphrey asked with a smile, the bucket of chicken feed in his hand shaking and spilling a few crumbs onto the floor. The girls would be in soon enough, pecking away at the flagstone for their unplanned second helping. Along with the writing desk, Humphrey had also built a chicken flap into the kitchen door. The less said about that the better. ('Why should cats have all the fun?' he'd said.)

I shook my head.

'Mine's on the side,' he said, and I took it up – the list of invitees to our 'little do', as he called it. His brother, his sister, various aunts and uncles, a number of colleagues from the university, some from the observatory in London, one or two of the locals at the pub; his arachnid writing building a web of friends and family. A safety net spinning out around him.

My page was blank.

And so I wrote a name, just one. And putting it down in black ink was like carving open my chest and giving Humphrey a glimpse of my heart.

I didn't have the right address, I was sure of it, so I wrote to the last one I'd held.

And I placed my one white envelope into the bag of invitations and I held my breath.

Of course, no reply came. The aunts and the uncles and the colleagues sent back their slips of paper with the box ticked according to their attendance and their preference for the meal.

I checked the bottom of the bag to make sure my one invitation wasn't still with us, and I imagined it out there in London, vulnerable on top of the scratchy doormat of strangers, frowned at, murmured at, and then eventually thrown into the rubbish bin on top of an egg shell and some still-steaming teabags.

I sensed that Humphrey felt sorry for me, that he wanted to cheer me up, so we went for a drive to Coventry and, splitting up inside Rackhams, he went to buy his first morning suit, and I went to buy my second wedding dress.

The women's department was empty and without any windows. It felt like I'd wandered into the gently lit night with only racks and rails of quiet clothing for company. A saleswoman spotted me browsing and came over. Feeling instantly like I was under suspicion of stealing, I tried to act very normally.

'Can I help?' She smiled.

'I'm going to a wedding,' I said. I don't know why I said it like that.

'Oh, lovely,' she said, 'when is it?'

'Next weekend.'

She made an 'ooh' face and sucked air into her mouth. Clearly it was far too late to be shopping for a dress for an event happening so soon. I decided I'd made the right choice in not telling her that it was my own wedding I'd be attending.

'Well, let's see,' she said, looking me up and down. 'Do you have any preferred colours?'

'Not white,' I said.

And she laughed as though I'd just admitted to being quite partial to oxygen. 'Well, of course!' she said, putting her hand to her head at the mere suggestion that I, as a wedding guest, might wear white to someone else's wedding.

'Do you mind?' she asked.

'No, not at all,' I said, not knowing what I was consenting to. But it became clear when she started picking up dresses from the various rails, and in a matter of minutes she was holding at least ten coat hangers with dresses in reds, greens, blues. My own hands were empty.

'Shall we?' she asked, and I followed her into the dressing room.

I got the sense I might have been the first person she'd spoken to that day.

The first few dresses I tried on were terrible – a pillar-box red thing that hung in all the wrong places, a shiny green satin tube. I felt uncomfortable that now we'd started this sartorial journey together, the sales assistant was loath to leave my side. She kept knocking on the curtain while singing 'knock knock!' and asking to see. The fourth, or perhaps fifth dress was the only one which I felt I could show her. It was navy blue with sleeves to the elbow, and it flared out ever so slightly at the knee. When I moved, it swished.

The saleswoman kindly got me a blue fascinator to clip in my hair, and a fuzzy blue cardigan that fell to the same place on my arm as the dress.

'Perfect,' she said as I looked at myself in the mirror. I wanted to thank her for helping me find my wedding dress, but I couldn't break the artifice, so I just thanked her as she put the dress into a bag for me.

I told her, 'The bride will love it.'

I found Humphrey in the shopping centre café, sipping some tea and craning his neck up at the ceiling, to see the cold blue sky through the high glass roof.

'Well?' he asked.

'Success!' I said, pointing to my bag.

'Mm,' he said, swallowing some tea, 'me too. If it's not too taboo to tell you, I decided to go for blue.'

The night before the wedding, Humphrey stayed the night with his friend Al. 'The suspense!' he said with mock drama as we kissed goodbye at the door. 'See you at the end of the aisle!' he shouted as he got into Al's car, clutching his suit bag.

The morning of my second wedding, I made myself toast and marmalade and a cup of tea. The house felt curiously still without Humphrey trampling around, moving things about and generally making a mess. I curled my hair and carefully applied my make-up. I picked the pale pink lipstick that had once lived on a pile of books in a bedsit in London, and fortunately it still worked.

I walked myself to the church, and the vicar gave me a handshake and a warm smile. He invited me to wait in the little room to the side. He asked if there would be anyone else coming who might want to wait with me. I tried not to feel sad as I told him it was just me.

And so, I waited. I'd arrived far too early, and all I had in the side room for company were some detached pews and some Bibles.

And then the door opened and there she stood.

I tried to breathe in and swallow at the same time and I started to choke. I was wearing the white lace gloves my mother had made me for my first wedding. I didn't want to cough into them so I tried to pull them off, but they were too tight. Meena stepped forward and held her order of service pamphlet out, just in time for me to cough a lump of mint green phlegm onto the *Wedding of Margot Macrae and Humphrey James.*

I was apologizing while she was laughing.

I regained my breath; I took her in properly. Her hair, which was still blonde and wavy, was pinned to the back of her neck. Her face was much the same as I remembered, though a little fuller. And her pink dress hung just past her knees, effortlessly skimming her considerable bump.

For what felt like just long enough to make it real, I had the thought that I could take her hand and we could run – go to a life somewhere far away where she could be mine.

And then she smiled and the thought fell away and was replaced with the image of Humphrey's hand on mine as we lay in bed and watched the stars.

Despite being old enough to have been a mother for many years, she looked like a teenager in trouble. She gave me a shrug and a smile, and I remembered how looking into her eyes would sometimes make my stomach twist.

I took an incredibly deep breath in, as though I was about to go underwater, and then I crashed into her. I held her tightly and wondered if this was what reunions with the dead felt like. I'd spent so long remembering her, thinking of her, imagining her, that I'd forgotten she was a real living human, and now here she was.

'Congratulations,' she said to me.

'Congratulations,' I said to her.

A sound from several miles away echoed in my ears and it took some time for me to realize that it was the organ, playing the music that would come before my entrance. Originally we wanted piano music, but the priest had offered the parish church's organist, and I had felt unable to tell him that the music of the sweet hunched lady named Elspeth set my teeth on edge.

On the windowsill that looked out onto the church car park was a bouquet of dried flowers in a milk bottle vase, tied with a ribbon. The pink bud in the middle had been a carnation once. I pulled the stems from the vase and, though I was as careful as I could be, several of the leaves shivered in their skeletal way and disintegrated to the floor.

'Here,' I said, handing Meena the posy, 'be my bridesmaid.'

Over a cold cup of tea, I held her long enough to hear the details. She told me as carefully as possible, but pieces of me still broke and fluttered to the ground.

His (the father's) name was not important because he wasn't going to be involved, she'd said. He'd been a colleague and then a friend and then a lover and then a father and then nothing at all. Of course, I knew it was The Professor. His (the baby's) surname was going to be her own – Star – which, she said, she had finally made legal several years before.

'If I can help . . . If *we* can help . . .' I started, but she shook her head.

The cannonball inside her rolled around, and she grabbed my hand and pressed it to the line where her tights met her tummy.

And I was aware, as I sometimes am, of the earth moving. That the earth was rotating and pulling us forwards, and millions of milliseconds were flying by, and that this moment was precious. More precious than my time with Humphrey, which was unlimited and so of much lower value. Time with Meena always passed faster than it should have and it was always more fleeting.

As our eyes caught, she pulled herself up, resting her hand on the back of her chair.

'You could stay,' I said, knowing that she wouldn't.

She kissed me on the cheek.

And then she was gone.

A few weeks later, an envelope addressed to 'Mrs James' settled on the doormat. And in that envelope was a photograph of a baby. On the back of the picture, familiar looping handwriting told me that this baby was *Jeremy Davey Star, 6lbs 10oz.*

Lenni and the First Goodbye

I MET A priest a little while ago. An old man with an empty chapel. I shook his hand and we became friends by accident. I learned nothing about Jesus from him. If anything, I think I've made him more confused about God. But that's not really important.

That same priest emerged from his office today ready to conduct his final Sunday service. Expecting his average audience of two people, he barely raised his head until he got to the altar. And then he did. And his already red eyes widened at the sea of smiling faces sitting before him. Two of Pippa's art classes made about forty people. Some of us in pyjamas, some in Sunday Best. All of us waiting and listening for Arthur's last mass. I was in the front row with Margot, Else and Walter.

'Well, goodness,' he said, putting on his reading glasses. His voice cracked as he said, 'Welcome!'

I gave him a wave and he smiled at me, giving a nod. Everyone was holding the playbills I'd made. Nobody was too certain that church services needed playbills, but we have to have *something* to show our grandchildren. The final great performance of Father Arthur.

'How wonderful of you all to come,' Father Arthur said. 'As some of you may know, this will be my last service at the hospital chapel.'

'We know,' Else said. She was dressed all in black and wearing a sequinned black hat. I have no idea what ward she's in, but I can only imagine she has a large amount of storage by her hospital bed – I don't think I've ever seen her wearing the same outfit twice.

'So please forgive me,' he continued, 'if I get emotional. However, I should add that I' – he sneezed, excused himself, then laughed and continued – 'I also have a cold.'

Father Arthur moved behind the altar and took a moment to collect himself. The pinks and reds and purples of the stained glass window gave his white robes a pink hue. I breathed in the familiar scent and took a mental picture of the moment. Of Arthur in the chapel where he belongs. After a moment or two, we all fell silent and he lifted his arms.

'Our Father, who art in heaven, hallowed be Thy name ...'

There are some words in the Lord's Prayer that I don't know. But I do know the word *art*. It's a necessary inclusion, I think. We should all be artists. Especially if God is doing art in heaven; we should follow his example.

'Our lives are rich with blessings. Sometimes we stop to count them and sometimes we don't. Having worked at this hospital for many years, I have often pondered whether I have made any difference to the hospital, and in the end, all I can really know for certain is that the hospital has made a difference to me. I count myself blessed to have spent my days here, worked here and prayed here. And I will be forever changed by the people I have met and their bravery, their courage and their light.' He looked at me then and took a deep breath. 'And with that in mind, we will offer up our thanks to God ...'

This time, nobody fell asleep and I didn't feel like laughing. I wanted to stop the clocks. I wanted Arthur to stay. And I was worried for Arthur – what would happen to him? Did he have a pension? Would Mrs Hill still make him those egg and cress sandwiches when he was no longer a priest? And what in God's name was he going to do all day?

All too soon, it was over.

'Go in peace to love and serve the Lord,' he said. And I didn't realize I was clapping until I was already doing it. From further down the pew, Margot joined in and the clap grew, until a ripple of applause was emanating from the various artists of the Rose Room.

Arthur blushed and nodded. 'Thank you.'

As we made our way, oh so slowly, to the door, Arthur asked Pippa, 'Can I have a word with Lenni? It won't take a second.'

Pippa agreed and shuffled out with the others.

'You know,' Margot said to Else as they made their way to the door, 'Father Arthur looks very familiar, but I can't quite put my finger on it. Do you think he's been on the television?'

'Well, it *was* a very unusual service,' I heard Else saying from the corridor. 'My first husband was an Anglican, my second a Methodist and my third a Catholic, and it seemed like a mix of all three.' I didn't get to hear whether anyone agreed with her or not, because the heavy door closed behind them.

I walked back down the aisle to see Father Arthur with a sad smile.

'Thank you,' he said.

'For what?'

'I'm going to miss you, Lenni.'

I reached out and gave him a hug. His robes smelled of fabric conditioner, which was an absurdly homely smell for sacred robes. 'Thanks for everything, Father Arthur,' I said into his shoulder.

He drew back.

'Can I come and visit?' he asked.

'If you don't, I'll never forgive you,' I said. I reached out a hand to lean on the pew beside me because everything was hurting. I had (on pain of death) forced Pippa to leave 'my' wheelchair outside the chapel.

'I promise I will visit,' he said, and then he stopped. 'You asked me, Lenni, to tell you something true, when we'd only just met. Do you remember?'

'I do.'

'Well, this is my final truth: if I had a granddaughter, I would want her to be exactly like you.'

And because he was about to cry, I held out my right hand. He looked confused.

'It started with a handshake.' I smiled.

Understanding, he put his hand in mine.

'Until the next time, Lenni,' he said, shaking me by the hand.

And when I had taken back my hand from his, he said, 'Take care,' with such force that it was as though he thought the more emphatically he said it, the more likely it was to happen. That if only I could just bloody *take care* of myself, I might not die.

I was putting a lot of work into not crying, so I left him standing in the chapel and managed to make it to the wheelchair without stumbling. Taking care, as he hoped I would.

And then it was over. Pippa very kindly wheeled my chair for me, and we occupants of the Rose Room made our way back to our art supplies. 'Thank you,' I said to them, and when they told me it had been no trouble, I had to stare up at the bright lights on the ceiling of the corridor to keep from crying.

Sixty

New Nurse wheeled me to the Rose Room to celebrate the latest of our landmark numbers. We forgot to celebrate fifty, the half-century, so sixty would have to suffice.

'I'm having trouble knowing where to store them,' Pippa said to nobody in particular, as she pulled the bigger pieces down from one of the shelves over the sink and laid them on the table. She placed them carefully around the room, seeming to have some preferred order. The colours were what struck me most. A night sky over a cottage in Henley-in-Arden, a chicken with most of its feathers missing, my terrible rendering of my sparsely attended tenth birthday party.

'Is this one of yours, Lenni?' New Nurse said, pointing to Margot's painting of the green park where she'd sat and waited for The Professor to leave.

'Well, now you're just being mean.'

'What?'

'Of course it isn't mine!'

I got up out of the wheelchair and waited for New Nurse to try and stop me. When she didn't, I wanted to push my luck, to try running, or skipping, or sitting on one of the tables swinging my legs. I stood by my painting of my mother and a waiting taxi, as viewed from a great height.

'It's amazing,' New Nurse said.

'What is?'

'All of it,' New Nurse replied, a serious look clouding her face. 'You've done something amazing here. And Margot too, of course.'

'It was all Lenni's idea,' Margot said.

'She's a bright one.' Pippa smiled.

I realized then that but for sixty pictures, some art supplies and my still-beating heart, they could have been at my funeral, discussing me, talking of my achievements with a sentimental over-exaggeration of my good qualities, nursing stale sandwiches on their plates and wondering what I might have done with my life if only I'd lived.

That was all I could think. Not, *Hey, we've painted sixty pictures*, but, *This is it. This mothering, sombre way that they'll talk about me when I'm . . . wherever I end up.* I wanted there to be more. I wanted there to be so much more. But maybe everyone wants that.

I wanted them to be able to say, *Lenni Pettersson? Yes, I remember Lenni. The one who miraculously healed and then joined the circus?*

I sat back down in my wheelchair. It's almost impossible to make a bid for freedom in a manual wheelchair when you have the upper body strength of a mosquito, so I couldn't escape without all three of them noticing. To their credit, they let me go out of the door without trying to stop me.

Halfway down the corridor, I heard the familiar squeak of white canvas trainers behind me.

'Len,' she said, and I was impressed that she didn't hold the handles of the wheelchair and push me herself, but let me struggle on.

'I'm just going somewhere.'

'Oh, are you?' She sounded concerned.

'Yep.'

'Anywhere in particular?'

'Just away from here.'

'Father Arthur?'

I wheeled on down the corridor. 'No, remember. He's gone.'

'Well, then where are you going?'

'I just wanted to get away from it.'

'From your paintings?'

'From the little funeral you're having for me in there.'

She didn't say anything as I reached the end of the corridor and rounded the corner. I got to a set of double doors. New Nurse held them open for me and let me go.

I wheeled around several corners, trying to lose myself. Because if I got legitimately lost, I could stay away from the May Ward for as long as it took me to be found. Just past the phlebotomy lab, I spotted Walter and Else. Side by side in their dressing gowns, walking along very slowly. He had a walker which I hadn't seen him use before and I wondered if perhaps he had had his surgery on his knee. He said something that made her laugh. So hard that she put her hand on his arm. She looked different laughing. Like she might not be the composed woman she seemed. That she might not be the chic editor of a French magazine, but something else. A mechanic maybe. Someone messier.

They rounded a corner, Walter taking tiny careful steps, without noticing me.

And I thanked the hospital for letting me see them.

Margot and the Sun

MARGOT WAS WEARING a fuzzy purple jumper, and when I came into the Rose Room she wrapped me up in a big hug. Which was exactly what I'd hoped she'd do. She cleared a space on our table and began to paint. Using the thinnest watercolours, she layered orange and red and yellow on top of each other inside a long-stemmed cocktail glass until they were almost bright enough to drink.

Majorca, August 1980

Margot James is Forty-Nine Years Old

I'd never been on a proper holiday and neither had Humphrey. We'd eschewed the idea of a honeymoon until his sister had recommended a hotel in Majorca – telling us both it was time we got some sun.

We didn't fit in at all. The people by the pool knew what they were doing – they had towels on sunbeds before we'd even made our way down to the restaurant for breakfast. They knew to order three drinks at a time to make the most of the 'all-inclusive' system. They knew when to drag their sunbeds to the other side of the pool to get the best of the afternoon sun.

Watching Humphrey try to deal with the cognitive challenge of being in no way cognitively challenged – with just a spy novel I'd bought him in a charity shop and hours of relaxation ahead of him – was wonderfully amusing. As I lay in the sun, feeling that something inside me that had become concrete was beginning to soften, he struggled to get comfortable, to keep himself entertained.

He asked a complete stranger what he thought of the Wellington Observatory while we were waiting in line for our first dinner.

'Dunno, mate,' the man had said. 'Don't really wear wellies.'

On the first night, we decided to try out the hotel bar. The heat from the day had dissipated with the evening breeze, and if the outdoor bar hadn't been so full of people, and if there hadn't been a shaky rendition of 'Don't Cry For Me Argentina' being performed by a hotel rep on the harshly lit stage, we'd have been able to hear the grasshoppers and the sway of the sea.

A sweet-natured couple came to ask if the two empty seats at our table were free. I can't remember their names now, but we'll call them Tom and Sue. Humphrey had gestured for them to take the seats, but rather than carry them away, they sat down and joined us. Much to our collective horror.

'So, do you have kids?' Sue asked, several questions in to the ice-breaking chit-chat we'd been making over the top of 'Born To Be Alive', which was being admirably belted out by a very sunburnt holidaymaker.

I'd opened my mouth to tell Sue the stranger-friendly version of why no, Humphrey and I had no children, but he got there first.

'Oh, yes,' Humphrey said. My mouth fell open.

'Girls,' he added, 'two girls.' And Tom and Sue made the requisite ooh-ing and ahh-ing noises.

I took a sip of my drink so that they'd know not to expect me to speak any time soon.

'What are their names?'

'Bette and Marilyn,' Humphrey said, and I nearly dropped the brightly coloured cocktail I'd accidentally ordered when I'd tried to use Spanish to ask for an orange juice.

'What unusual names,' Sue said.

'We're both really big film fans,' Humphrey said, holding his hands up as though he'd just been caught midway through a crime.

Though I tried my best to communicate to him the sentiment *Stop pretending our chickens are our children*, Humphrey put his hand on my knee and smiled as Tom asked how old our daughters Bette and Marilyn were.

'They're both eight,' Humphrey said.

'So they're twins?' Sue said excitedly.

'Well, they came together!' Humphrey laughed.

'I love twins,' she said. 'My grandmother had twins. They say it skips a generation, so if we had kids, they might be twins.' Sue looked at Tom with such hope that it almost hurt to witness.

'That must have been a handful,' Tom said, downing his watery pint.

'Well, we got very lucky with them,' Humphrey said. He had that twinkle in his eye that only appeared when he was really enjoying himself. 'As long as they're fed and watered, they're happy.'

I took another big sip of my cocktail.

'Girls, though, lots of pink,' Tom said.

'Not for us. Marilyn and Bette are both very outdoorsy,' Humphrey said. 'Although they are quite incorrigible at times – they're always sticking their beaks in, aren't they, Margot?'

Fruity alcohol exploded out of my mouth and across the table, settling in a number of little pools on the white plastic tabletop. Tom looked on in alarm as I apologized and Sue patted at the puddles of my regurgitated cocktail with her small paper napkin.

'Went down the wrong way, did it?' Humphrey asked, his eyes gleaming.

P

'ARE YOU IN pain, Lenni?'

Derek's eyes betrayed his fear of an honest answer. But luckily for him, I wasn't going to be honest.

'No,' I said, and I did my best not to wince as I sat down.

'I was talking to a woman the other day,' he said, 'who lost her daughter to ...' He struggled for the words and eventually settled with gesturing towards me with an open palm. The Lenni Thing. Whatever it is that I have. I liked that he feared naming it in front of me.

'She said that her daughter was in a lot of pain, towards the ...' Derek gestured again, and then let his hand fall to his lap with a sad slapping sound. Even *he* had realized that my presence being used as a conversational placeholder for the notion of death was probably not the most comforting thing that had happened to me that day.

'Anyway,' he said brightly, as though all things were now forgiven, 'it made me think of you and I wanted to ask. Arthur doesn't like to talk about pain, but I do. I think it's important to be honest about our symptoms.'

'Do you have a background in medicine?'

'Well ... no.'

His cheeks flushed and I remembered what Father Arthur had said to me when he heard I was going to visit Derek in the chapel: *Be nice.*

It was easier said than done.

Derek ran his hands across his completely smooth chin. 'Perhaps we could hold a prayer session.'

'You mean you're not already praying for me?'

'I—'

'Because that seems a little harsh, Derek.'

'I've asked you not to call me that. I'd prefer you to call me "Pastor Woods".'

'But it doesn't rhyme.'

'What doesn't?'

I sighed and looked up at the stained glass window. *Give me strength, beautiful purple glass.*

'Father Arthur has the good sense to rhyme.'

Derek clearly didn't know what to do with this, and I had the feeling that not only had he rehearsed this conversation in his mind, but that I had now made us stray so far from the script that he had no idea how to rescue us.

'Do you ever wish you had retrained?' I asked.

'As what?' Derek tried to mask the frustration in his voice.

'A doctor,' I said, 'or a nurse. You know, so you could do something practical about people's pain.'

'Lenni, what are you trying to imply?'

'I'm trying to imply that putting a church inside a hospital is like looking at an oil painting to see what the weather will be like.'

He stiffened, opened his mouth to speak, paused and took a sharp breath in. 'Hospital chaplaincies provide support to those in need. Sometimes that is all we provide; other times, we also spread the love of Jesus Christ. We are respectful to all cultures and religions and, if you can permit me to be so bold, I might suggest that respect is an area in which you are lacking.'

'Like butter?'

'What?'

'You said you spread Jesus' love. When people say that, I think of them spreading Jesus' love like they spread butter.'

'Lenni, it's not *butter*—'

'Jam, then.'

'Jesus' love is not jam.'

'Why not? He can be bread and grapes and a sheep and a lion and a ghost, but he can't be jam?'

Derek inhaled loudly and then stood up from his place in the pew beside me, navigated past my empty wheelchair and disappeared into the chaplaincy office. I interpreted this as his sign of surrender, but he reappeared moments later carrying a book.

He came back and crouched in the aisle beside me, a position not befitting someone so stiff. Derek belongs on the vertical axis only.

'Here,' he said, passing it to me. The book was called *Questions About Jesus*. On the front were three friends of different races all smiling around a copy of the Bible. 'Obviously something about the church calls to you,' he said. 'Why else would you keep coming back?' He gave me a shark smile. 'I put it to you that the thing making you come back over and over isn't that you like to challenge people, or your fondness for Father Arthur, but that you are searching for something to believe in.'

He stood up from his crouching position and I heard all the bones in his knees click. 'And now,' he said, 'I take my leave of this conversation.'

'Aren't you going to give me any answers?'

'I'm going to make my scheduled visit to the Scovell Ward.'

'But you can't leave. I have *Questions About Jesus*!'

Lenni and Margot in Trouble

I WOKE UP in the night and I couldn't breathe. It felt like I'd swallowed thick PVA glue which had sealed my throat closed. No matter how hard I tried to pull the air in, I couldn't pierce the glue to make a gap. I could cough out a little, but not enough to clear it, so I was stuck, not able to suck in enough air to breathe and not able to cough enough of the glue out. I got up and pulled my curtain back. Everyone else in the ward had their curtains pulled around them. It was dark, but the light through the open door from the corridor shone on the floor in one large square. If I could just get someone's attention. My chest was burning and my eyes were tearing up. *Not now*, I thought, *not now. We're not finished. I still have stories to tell.*

I must have fallen over because the next thing I knew, I had both of my hands out on the smooth plastic floor of the May Ward.

'Shit!' Jacky ran towards me. 'What is it?'

I shook my head and tried to breathe in. She heard my breath get so far and then stop.

'You need to calm down,' she said.

I tried to breathe again and it got stuck. I was in trouble, I knew it.

'Lenni, you have to calm down!' she said.

I felt a tear run down my cheek, and all I could think of was the fact that I couldn't remember how many minutes without oxygen it takes for people to die. Was it two and a half? I was sure I must be well into my second minute.

Jacky, cruel mistress of the May Ward, knelt beside me. 'Have you swallowed anything?' I shook my head.

She placed both arms on my shoulders. 'Look at me,' she said. I tried another scuppered breath that got stuck. 'You're going to be okay,' she said. 'You just need to clear your airways. Try to cough.' I did, but I couldn't cut the glue and it made me gag, lurching forwards.

Jacky got up and disappeared for a moment.

'Here. Swallow.' She shoved a plastic cup in my hand. I filled my mouth with water, closed my eyes and swallowed. It went down and the glue moved. I could breathe. I gasped in the air, but the glue moved back in place. 'Again,' she said. I swallowed more of the water; the glue lessened and I could breathe again.

'Now breathe in gently,' she said. I did – a gasp of air was mine, and another and another. The glue was still clinging to my throat. I breathed in again, thinking about my brain cells. They die without oxygen. Perhaps I had just killed several thousand of them. 'Good girl,' Jacky said, coming to sit on the floor with me. She put her hand on my shaking knee.

'When you feel ready, you need to do a big cough,' she said. 'You have to clear that phlegm out.'

I was enjoying breathing far too much to do that.

'Lenni, you need to cough now,' she said. I hated her for it, but I coughed as hard as I could. At first it blocked my throat again and my breath stopped, shuddering at the closed border of my larynx.

'Swallow again,' she said. And I did.

I coughed hard, and some of the glue rose up into my mouth. I spat it out.

Jacky wiped the phlegm and blood from my hot hand.

I took another sip of water and tasted metal.

Trouble.

For the crime of coughing up blood, Lenni Pettersson was sentenced to bed rest lest that pesky larynx of hers tried to close again. She was blacklisted from going to the Rose Room, the chapel, or anywhere that might bring her happiness. And all she was invited to do was sleep.

While she tried to sleep, she thought about all the other people in the world who were, at that moment, on that evening, trying to sleep. People in waiting rooms, at boarding gates, sitting all crooked on an overnight train. Clutching newborn babies. All just trying to slip into nothingness.

'Lenni?' came a little whisper.

The curtains round my bed opened just a peep, and in the gap was Margot's face. I beckoned her and she scuttled in, pulling the curtain closed behind her. She was wearing a lilac quilted dressing gown and a pair of purple slippers. I'd never noticed how tiny Margot's feet are before. A child could have worn those slippers. And it made her seem even more precious.

'Are you all right, Lenni?' Margot whispered. I nodded. She came up to me and gave me a kiss on the top of my head. Then she pulled back and regarded me with a look of mischief. 'Lenni,' she asked, 'shall we get ourselves in trouble?'

Like the most vulnerable, least conspicuous bandits, we escaped from the May Ward, creeping past my wheelchair because Margot still believes.

Margot didn't tell me where we were going but I enjoyed the mystery. *Maybe she's kidnapping me*, I thought, as we wound our way through the hospital corridors. Although it would be a mostly voluntary kidnapping, as there is no way she could possibly overpower me. For starters, she only comes up to my shoulders. I wondered what picture they would use on the news. *Swedish-born terminally ill teenager kidnapped by older, also terminally ill Scottish woman.* They probably wouldn't be able to get a picture of the two of us together. *Instead we are using a file photograph of some geese on a pond. It is likely they will both die before they are found.*

'We need to take a photograph,' I said as we walked along.

'Now?'

'No, just soon. Of the two of us.'

She led me into the main entrance atrium, with its huge overhead lights and high glass ceiling. There were hardly any people around, but there was a cleaner with a big round floor polisher.

Margot took my hand and led me through the first set of automatic doors and then the second, and then we were out in the fresh air and into the night.

I've never run away before. I mean, I've run around the hospital a bit, but I've never actually gone out of the main doors and walked away from the hospital. I thought it would be harder. Margot, I realized, was wearing her dressing gown and slippers for a reason.

It was cold and the bright pitch lights that illuminate the front of the hospital were shining. I saw them all, the other people in their pyjamas: one with a colostomy bag, one in a wheelchair, the rest standing hunched against the cold, and I saw their smoke snaking upwards towards the dark sky. They were like statues, cold, marble statues, their only movement the taking of their cigarettes in and out of their mouths.

'You've not taken me out here to smoke, have you, Margot?'

'Lenni!' She nudged me in the ribs with her elbow and it made me laugh.

A man who was leaning against a lamp post smoking caught my eye, and I wondered for a moment how we looked. Like a girl and her grandma on a late-night pyjama party stroll around the hospital. He looked down and I thought I saw a hint of a smile. *I don't have time to care what you think*, I thought.

Margot pulled me further, past the smokers and towards the car park. 'Are you all right, Lenni?' she asked. 'Not too cold?'

'I'm fine,' I said. Although it was freezing, it was a nice freezing, like when you leave a hot country to come home to the cold and you feel like you can finally catch your breath.

'We need to get away from the light,' she said, and she took me to the left, past a building signposted as the haematology lab and another entrance, until we reached a quiet fire exit door. From there, we were invisible. The lamp post above our heads was broken, so it was a good patch of darkness.

After several moments of standing there, I began to feel a creeping sense of disappointment. What did Margot think was happening? We stood holding hands in the darkened spot.

'Margot?' I said slowly. 'I—'

'Look up, Lenni,' she said.

And I did, and then I saw the stars. Remembering the words of an eccentric astronomer spoken to a woman on a dark road in Warwickshire sometime in 1971, I knew I could see for millions of miles.

I couldn't remember the last time I'd seen the stars. If we'd been on that dark road in Warwickshire we might have seen more, but those we could see were like the whole galaxy to me. They made the world seem big again. It's been just the hospital for so long.

It felt like the first time I had breathed in years, the air cold and crisp and wonderful. I could feel it in my lungs. Unlike the warm, medicinal hospital air, it was fresh and real and new. And when I exhaled, my breath danced away, up to the stars.

'This is a very clear night,' she said. 'It's supposed to be the best visibility in weeks.'

I gave her a look. 'How long have you been planning this?'

She didn't say anything and kept her eyes on the stars.

'*Though my soul may set in darkness, it will rise in perfect light. I have loved the stars too fondly to be fearful of the night,*' I said.

'You remembered.' She smiled.

And we stayed there, watching the stars.

'I find it so peaceful,' Margot told me after a while.

'Me too.'

'Do you know,' she said slowly, 'that the stars that we see the clearest are already dead?'

'Well, that's depressing.' I took my hand from hers.

'No,' she said gently, linking her arm through mine, 'it's not depressing, it's beautiful. They've been gone for who knows how long, but we can still see them. They live on.'

They live on.

Verboten

'You're just not up to it.'

'Not up to it?'

'Not well enough.' New Nurse looked at her shoes.

'I'm fine,' I told her.

'This isn't working.'

'What?'

'Pretending to be fine.'

'I *am* fine.'

'You're ...'

'What?'

I watched New Nurse out of the corner of my eye as she pretended to check one of the charts above my head.

She didn't say anything for a long time.

'What?' I asked.

'Lenni, your temperature is high, you've not responded well to this new drug, and I know you've not been sleeping.'

'How do you know that?'

'Linda told me.'

'How sneaky. Obviously, *Linda* can't be trusted.'

'Lenni, she's the night shift nurse, it's her job to—'

'She's lying. I sleep with my eyes open.'

'You do not.'

'Like Frankenstein's monster.'

'What?'

'Or a bat.'

'They're blind.'

'Yeah, so why would they bother closing their eyes?'

'Lenni, this is serious.'

'It is. You are stopping me from going to the Rose Room because I happen to sleep with my eyes open.'

'That's—'

'Aside from *Linda*'s version of events, what other reason do you have to think that I haven't been sleeping?'

'Those.' She pointed.

'My eyes?'

'No, the bags under them.'

'Don't you know it's rude to make personal remarks?'

'I wasn't being rude. I was simply saying that you've got—'

'Bags under my eyes, I know.'

'Lenni, will you calm down a bit? I can't think. I'm just saying that maybe this week you could use this time to rest, your body needs a break—'

'My body doesn't need any breaks. It's my mind that needs the break.'

She looked at me for a moment like a little girl about to cry, and I felt like a parent telling her that summer was over, that her favourite teddy bear had been left behind in the hotel and that school was starting early in the morning.

'Lenni, please.'

'Fine!' I shouted louder than I needed to, and folded my arms because now I was committed to being furious.

She leant in closer and whispered, 'This is the first time they've let me make a decision like this.'

'Fine,' I said again and unfolded my arms, because maybe the hotel maid would find her teddy bear and post it home.

And then she left.

And nobody came.

No Father Arthur, no Margot, no Pippa.

Not even a friendly smile from Paul the Porter.

Even an evil stare from Jacky wouldn't have gone amiss. But nobody came. And in the end, I slept. I slept for days.

When the Planets Align

'HELLO, PET.' MARGOT peeped around my bed curtain.

I tried to give her a smile, but I'm not sure if it worked.

She came in and gave me a kiss on the top of my head. 'If Lenni can't come to the Rose Room,' she said, 'the Rose Room will come to Lenni.'

On my bedside table she placed a plastic cup full of coloured markers, a tray of charcoals and a clutch of pencils, and she put a white canvas on my lap, and as she sat down on the visitor's chair, she rested a canvas of her own on her knees.

Using a black pencil, what she drew was so simple – a line of planets in a sky of stars.

West Midlands, 16th August 1987
Margot James is Fifty-Six Years Old

It had been marked in our calendar for three years: 16th August 1987. It was the equivalent of Humphrey's Christmas. All his Christmases and a birthday thrown in too. Harmonic Convergence. The day that the sun, the moon and six planets from our solar system would perfectly align.

Of course, he didn't buy the 'twaddle' that this day would spark the beginning of an age of enlightenment (an idea that was generating worldwide celebrations), but he did want to enjoy the 'once-in-a-lifetime astral event'. I told him we'd already experienced one of those and he gave me an arched eyebrow in response.

I was much more interested in the two planets that wouldn't be joining the line. I liked the idea that they were refusing to do what all the others were doing. They were being pulled by a different force – governed by a different law.

Like those two errant planets, I had been invited to the party but had declined. The party was being held by some of Humphrey's friends in the London observatory. It was to include several hours of looking at the sky and recording what they saw, and then a party with food and drinks and dancing. The observatory team could enjoy an astral event like the best of them.

I couldn't tell him why I didn't want to go, I just knew that I didn't. And so I offered to babysit the girls, rather than having to send them to his friend's farm. After Bette and Marilyn had flown to the big chicken coop in the sky, we had taken on two older ladies – Doris and Audrey. They were to turn eleven that year. 'Quite an achievement for a chicken,' as Humphrey had put it.

So Doris and Audrey and I had stayed and watched as Humphrey packed up his best telescope and put on his 'party cords', and went on his way.

The bathroom was always the coldest room in Humphrey's house, so it was only possible to have baths in the summer. Taking advantage of the warm weather, I took a bath, read several chapters of my book and shaved my legs. Then I came out, with the idea that I would watch a film on our newly acquired VHS player.

But there was something lying on the doormat. And it hadn't been there when Humphrey left. It was addressed to Mrs James. It often took me a little time to remember that that was me. And I knew it was from her.

She always called me 'Mrs James'. It was her way of reminding me of the permanence of my decisions, of reminding me she'd never change her name for a man. But my taking Humphrey's name had been unconscious. Accidental, almost.

I picked up the envelope and laid it on the sofa cushion. I sat beside it. It could contain something good or something bad, but it was from her so it would probably be both.

It took me an hour or two before I could open it. In that time, I reasoned, Humphrey would almost be off the motorway and at the observatory. Probably having spilt some coffee from his car thermos on his party cords. The sun had rolled its way across the carpet and now a sliver of light lay warming my toes. Doris came into the kitchen, pecking at the gaps between the stone tiles in the hopes of finding some corn.

I should have known when I pulled at the envelope and the triangle flap came away easily, the adhesive still gummy.

Peeping at me from inside the open envelope were Meena and Jeremy. His eighth birthday wasn't far away, but in the photograph he was a toddler still, his arms up in celebration, wearing only a striped T-shirt and a nappy. Meena had her arms around his middle and she was laughing.

The last time I saw her, she'd looked exactly as she did in the picture.

*

Meena and baby Jeremy were living in Acton, in a houseshare with an older couple who were both musicians in a London orchestra. Jeremy was somewhere between one and two. It was the middle of July and the sun had been relentless for weeks. As I'd passed signs for London along the motorway, my palms had started to sweat. I had this light-headed feeling that I wasn't really in the car at all, but that it was one of the many dreams I'd had where I tried to drive to Meena only to discover I was lost, or that my car was broken or that she wasn't where I was driving to. I felt like I was watching my car navigate the busy motorway, rather than being in control of it. I wondered if I'd die on the way to see her, and then fretted over why I felt that I would be okay with dying in a car accident as long as I was on my way to see her.

When I pulled up outside the house with the mint green door, I tried to turn off the engine without putting the gear into neutral, and then I couldn't remember how to put the handbrake on.

I was sweating. Not just in the usual places but everywhere – in my hairline, on my thighs, on my bottom cheeks. My hands had left a wet pair of prints on the steering wheel. There were dark patches under the armpits of my striped sundress. I opened the glovebox. Tissues, wet wipes, even a map would have done to at least try to dry myself down. All that was in the glovebox was a single dessert spoon. I cursed myself for letting Humphrey borrow my car.

I'd spent so long wondering what I would wear to meet Jeremy, and to meet Meena as a mother. I'd fixed my hair – only to sweat my way down the M25 until I was an unrecognizable mess. I cursed myself for wanting to look nice for her.

Sitting in the boiling car, it was only getting worse. I pulled the keys from the ignition and got out. The street was quiet, the houses merrily baking in the hot sun.

I noticed a small hand at the warped flowered glass of the front door before I'd even walked down the path. It disappeared and then came back. He was real. And he was waving to me.

And then she opened the door.

'Hello, Mrs James.' It took me a while to take her in. She'd cut her hair and now it brushed against her collar bone. She was wearing an overall dress, and on her hip she held her child. Though she was at least forty-two by then, she seemed so much younger. And the child. He was ethereal, like his mother. He had blond hair that was curled in tight ringlets and her blue eyes. He reached out for me, unafraid, wanting me to hold him. Meena passed him to me. I was surprised by the weight of him on my hip as he struggled, trying to grab my earring in his tiny fist.

I followed her into a blue kitchen with a high ceiling. The walls were covered in sheet music. There was a cello in the corner and an open but empty violin case on the kitchen table.

Meena cleared one corner of the table of plates and papers and sat down. I sat beside her and transferred Jeremy to my lap. Now he was really struggling, trying to get at my earring. This little squirming thing was named after two lost boys, but he was very much real. Ruddy cheeked and angel haired. I opened my mouth to say something, though I wasn't sure what it was going to be, and at the same moment she jumped up. 'Do you want some lemonade?'

'You made lemonade?'

'Of course not. Geoff made it. It's kind of his one redeeming feature. There's lemon drizzle cake, too.'

I accepted both and, as I watched her move about the kitchen, I felt my heart break for all the time that had passed. I'd been absent when Meena became just another normal person. A person who had plates and responsibilities. Granted her son was named after a chicken, but he was *hers*. Her child. His finger paintings had been made into a collage on the wall. He had a high chair; he had a home. And she had a job now, something in a theatre box office. She was no longer the version of herself I had preserved in my memory. She was no longer wild.

I bounced Jeremy on my knee. The weight of him was astonishing. Not because he was particularly heavy but because he was a human. Created out of nothing.

She sat down and handed me a plate of lemon drizzle cake. It had a black hair just peeping out of the corner of the sponge. I pulled it out. It was thick. I wondered if it was Geoff's. The glasses of lemonade stood on the kitchen counter, forgotten, but my mouth was dry. Meena pulled her own plate onto her lap and broke a corner off. She held it out to Jeremy's mouth and he ate it.

'I can't—'

'What?'

'I can't believe you made a human,' I said.

She beamed. 'I know, it's weird isn't it?' She pulled him onto her lap and used the corner of her top to wipe the dribble off his lips.

'You're not so bad, are you?' she asked him. 'Are you?' She lifted him high in the air, narrowly missing dropping her plate on the floor, and Jeremy shrieked with delight.

And I wanted to fall into the hole in the ground that was opening up for me.

In the quiet of Humphrey's living room, I ran my hand across the photo. I could still hear that shriek of pure happiness from Jeremy. He'd be older now, wiser, more careful. I wondered if his hair was still blond, if his ears had grown to look elfin like Meena's. There was nothing else inside the envelope, but there was something written on the back of the photograph.

In her unsteady writing were the words *We're moving!* and then an address. The alphabet was English, but the letters were all marked with accents and shapes I didn't recognize.

It had the effect of being familiar and unfamiliar at the same time.

Meena and Jeremy Star
32 Nguyễn Hữu Huân
Lý Thái Tổ, Hoàn Kiếm,
Hà Nội, Vietnam

She was moving to Vietnam. Of course she was. She needed an adventure. She'd been unwild for far too long.

On my way to pin the photograph onto the corkboard in the kitchen, I picked up the envelope to put it in the bin and the absence made itself known. The lack of colour where there should have been. A missing monarch. The envelope was without sovereign rule. A republican. It made my already short breath catch in my throat. I don't remember but I must have dropped the envelope and the photograph, and in my bath towel, with my hair still wet on my shoulders, I ran out of the house.

Humphrey's house was in the middle of a field. The road that led to it was a gravel path that turned into grass the closer you got to the house. And the whole field was hidden from the main road by a line of tall dark trees.

There were tyre marks that didn't run up to the patch where Humphrey usually parked the car. They led around to the left.

She'd been here.

Sometime between Humphrey leaving and me getting out of the bath, Meena had hand delivered the envelope. I stood in the August sun with the water rolling down my shoulders and I wondered if I was going to throw up. Into the silence, I wanted to scream.

I rushed to the back of the house in case she and Jeremy had gone to see the chickens.

Audrey was alone, sitting in the grass with her eyes closed against the sun, her feathers tucked neatly beneath her.

Meena had gone. I had missed her. It was her cruellest trick.

Above us in the unending skies the planets were aligning, but we could never quite align, Meena and I.

I took the photograph from the kitchen floor. I didn't want her to mock me from the corkboard so I slipped the photograph in between the pages of one of Humphrey's big books, the *Fifth Annual Astronomy Conference, Calgary, 1972*. It slid in between the thin white pages effortlessly. So effortlessly you wouldn't even know it was there.

She could stay there among the stars.

Let Us Celebrate the
Happy Accident of Your Birth

'SHARP SCRATCH,' THE nurse said. But I knew it wasn't a scratch
– it was a needle and it was going into my skin.

It felt like lightning.

'Good girl, stay really still,' the doctor said.

I felt some sneaky tears slither down my cheeks.

'I used to be tough,' I told no one in particular.

Margot placed a hand on my hand.

'Look at me, Lenni,' Margot said.

'Another sharp scratch,' the nurse said.

'Lenni,' Margot said, 'do you want to go somewhere?'

I nodded.

'You can't go—' the doctor started to caution, but then
Margot began her story, and she took me back. To a farm-
house somewhere in the Midlands, where I've been before.
And where I sometimes visit in my dreams.

West Midlands, March 1997
Margot James is Sixty-Six Years Old

The note was resting on the pillow where Humphrey's head
should have been. In ink that had smeared across the page

were the words: *Let us celebrate the happy accident of your birth.*

I read it several times. Was it a quote from something? Quite possibly. He was often trying to convince me, though I know he'd have been disappointed if I'd relented, that I should really try to get into Shakespeare.

It was a bright March morning. There was a light frost in the corner of the window that had caught the light and was twinkling. Clinks and clanks in the kitchen made me smile. He was down there, tinkering away at something.

I pulled the quilt from me and slipped on my dressing gown and one of my many pairs of slippers – the flagstone floor was forever freezing. If I ever stood in the gap between the bits of carpet that covered the living room, it was like a shot of ice in the tips of my toes.

The smell of bacon and cake rose up to meet me.

I stood at the bottom of the stairs and watched Humphrey in the kitchen. The egg timer was going off as he pulled the cake from the oven. While he flapped at it with a tea towel, he stirred something in a saucepan. Whatever it was, it was creating a lot of steam. The radio jazzed in the background and then he dropped a spoon and swore. This should have been nice. But it was something other than that.

On the table were three balloons, a messily wrapped pink present, and a card addressed to me.

I went quietly into the kitchen.

'Humphrey?'

'Ah,' he said, turning round with a smile, 'the woman of the hour!'

I searched his face for something, but I couldn't find it.

'What's all this?'

'It's not every day your young lady turns sixty-six!' He laughed at this as though it were particularly funny. He started whistling along with the radio.

'You know when my birthday is, don't you?' I asked gently.

'Of course,' he said, tapping me on the nose.

'When is it?'

'The eighteenth of January.' He gave me a baffled smile as though I were behaving rather oddly.

I was lost for words.

'I made you rum and raisin,' he said, flapping the oven mitt at the cake resting on the kitchen counter.

The thing in the saucepan looked like it was in the early stages of becoming jam. He pushed at the raspberries with the wooden spoon.

'But we already celebrated my birthday,' I said, going to turn off the oven for him. 'We went to the botanical gardens. We had lunch with your sister. In January.'

'We did?' he asked.

I started crying.

The doctor had a stain on his corduroy trousers. It was just above his knee and it was distracting me. It was yellow against the green. Curry sauce, perhaps. Or lemon jelly.

His hands were moving as he explained something. I dragged my eyes up from his trousers and tried to concentrate.

'I just got confused,' Humphrey said. 'It can happen to anyone.' He'd said this several times every day since the birthday party. The gift was a soft silk scarf with butterflies on it. 'There's no need for a fuss, I really am fine.'

The doctor nodded, but I don't think he agreed.

'These things can happen,' the doctor said, and he glanced briefly at me. 'However, based on what your wife has told me, I think it makes sense to do a few tests just to be on the safe side.'

Humphrey nodded. And he looked small. And old. And scared.

'It'll be a blood test first,' the doctor said, as my attention journeyed back to the stain. I wondered if some white wine would work in getting it out. 'Then some simple memory tests.' Perhaps bicarbonate of soda would do it. I could take a dry toothbrush and scratch the stain off. 'And we'll go from there.' The doctor was holding out his hand to Humphrey, who shook it. And then to me. As we stood, he brushed briefly at his green corduroys and I had to look away.

'I really am fine,' Humphrey said in the corridor, 'I just got old by accident.'

Silver

'THE SILVERFISH ARE back.'

I thought I'd fallen out of bed. I felt a rush of sudden descent and an imminent ground swooping up to hit me.

I sat up, gasping for breath.

'Sorry, I didn't realize. I thought—'

It took me a moment to see the man standing in front of me. He was wearing jeans and a shirt underneath a smart blue jumper.

'Father Arthur?' I whispered.

'Hello, Lenni,' he whispered, because I was whispering.

'You're wearing jeans.'

'I know.'

'You look so . . .'

He smiled. 'Yes?'

'Different. It's like a dog walking on its hind legs.'

He laughed. 'It's good to see you, Lenni.' He took a seat at my bedside and tried not to disturb the new equipment I was attached to.

'How long has it been?' I asked.

'A few weeks.' He seemed embarrassed. 'I've been at a conference. I, er, told some of my colleagues about you. I hope that's okay?'

'What did they say?'

'They were very interested. I told them about your one hundred paintings. They thought it was a very meaningful endeavour.'

'So I'm famous now?'

'Among a group of recently retired priests, yes.'

'That's always been the dream.'

He laughed.

'You know, I finished my seventeenth painting.'

'You did?'

'I did.'

'So what did you paint to commemorate your seventeenth year?'

'I think it might be my best one. I did one hundred hearts on a white canvas. Eighty-three of them in purple, seventeen in pink.'

'To represent you and Margot?'

'Exactly.'

'It's good to see you, Lenni,' he said again.

I took a coughing break then. Father Arthur poured some water into my cup and handed it to me. The first sip went down smoothly, but then some of it got caught, and I coughed harder and had to catch the water dribbling out of my mouth in the cup.

Arthur was doing a terrible job of not looking at me like I was terrifying him.

'Do I look ill?'

'I, um.'

'That's a yes, then.'

'I was taught a long time ago never to remark on a lady's appearance.' He smiled, but it was a sad smile.

'So, the silverfish?' I asked, once I'd swallowed some of the watery glue.

'Ah, yes. I was dusting the bathroom and—'

'Dusting?'

'Sorry?'

'It's just . . . how dusty can a bathroom get?'

'Well, mine's never dusty. Because I dust it.'

When I laughed, he leant back in the plastic visitor's chair as though it were a deep, cushioned armchair – comfortable, absorbing. I almost expected it to absorb him into its folds. Or to create some folds and then welcome him in.

'Shall I tell you the story?' he asked.

I nodded and he began, giving me an eye not to interrupt when he started again with 'I was dusting the bathroom'.

I said nothing and he carried on. 'I promised Mrs Hill that, as she isn't allowed to bleach the floor, I would take over all cleaning responsibilities for the bathroom. "Unhealthy," she kept calling it, "it's unhealthy to have the floor covered in germs." I asked her how she could be certain that the germs were even there, and she told me that she just knew. I told her I was worried about what the bleach might do to the silver-fish. She asked me how I could even know they were there, and I told her I just knew. She laughed and let me be.

'So I was dusting the bathroom, making sure not to dis-turb the part of the skirting board where the silverfish like to come in, and I saw one – underneath the sink, if you can believe it! The sink is a fair way away from the door, especial-ly for something of a silverfish's size. I watched him slither under the bin for safety and I retreated, whispering that I meant no harm, turning off the light and closing the door, and hoping that he would make it home to tell his friends that I come in peace.'

I smiled.

'I'm not going mad,' he said.

'Of course not.'

'I just feel I ought to protect them.'

I nodded. He sighed.

'Would you like the truth?' he asked.

'Always.'

He leant forwards in his chair, resting his elbows on his denimed knees.

'I haven't known what to do with myself since I retired. I feel like I'm . . .' He paused. 'Lost.'

'Did you like working here?' I asked.

'I loved it.'

'Then come back.'

'I can't. My job has gone to Derek and he's a nice young man, it wouldn't be right. I'm far too old anyway. Oh Lenni, please forgive me for being so self-involved when it's you who's the patient and I'm meant to be the visitor.'

'Come back,' I said again.

'I can't.'

'You can. Maybe not as *Chief Priest*, but as something else – you could volunteer, you could read to people, you could help Pippa in the art room.'

'Perhaps.'

'Not *perhaps*, definitely.'

'Do you really think?'

'It's like you're my silverfish.'

'Sorry?'

'I'm just dusting the bathroom and you're already over by the sink! You should come back to the skirting board by the door, come back where you belong.'

I Have Loved the Stars Too Fondly

West Midlands, February 1998
Margot James is Sixty-Seven Years Old

We made a deal, Humphrey and I, shortly after he was diagnosed with Alzheimer's disease. And the deal was this: on the occasion that Humphrey forgot who I was, I was to bid him goodnight, give him an unreasonably large kiss, and never return. At first, I'd resisted. I told him I'd never leave him and I'd stay until the very end, no matter if we were strangers by then.

But he'd persisted. He made me sign a contract. He wrote it up himself, so of course it was barely legible. 'It would mean the world to me, Margot,' he said, 'to know you won't spend months, or years, toiling with me when I'm already up somewhere with the stars.'

And I'd cried. And he'd cried. And I signed it.

We were lucky, in the end: there were eleven good months where memories and certain things eluded him but I did not. Only at the end of those good months did he start to slip. Sometimes he was Humphrey, sometimes he was not.

The contract also stipulated at what point he was to be moved into a care home. And the day came far too soon. I wasn't allowed to go with him when he moved. I was to help them pack up his things and let him go on ahead. I stood in the house surrounded by him and yet without him and I didn't know what to do with myself, so I went to the attic and I stared up at the sky through his biggest telescope – the one that the care home said was far too big to fit into his new single bedroom.

He'd been there for three days when he permitted me to visit.

'My window looks onto the courtyard,' he said as I was buzzed into the centre. He was sitting on a waiting chair with his cane in his hand, seeming out of place.

I signed the visitors' log and went to him. I was expecting a hug, but he didn't give me one.

'The *courtyard*!' he said again, as though I hadn't heard.

'Shall we sit somewhere?' I asked, and he led me down a long corridor. We'd viewed the place together when we were deliberating which care home would be for him, but it felt completely different then, like we'd sneaked into school after it was closed – like neither of us should have been there.

'This is the best room in the place,' he said, taking me into a small day room called 'The Field'. 'The main day room stinks,' he said, 'I don't know why people pretend it doesn't. It's like rotting cabbage – it's full of farts and cups of tea that have been forgotten about. No matter where you go in this damn place, you can't escape the smell of shepherd's pie, even though we are yet' – he sat down in one of the high-backed armchairs – 'to actually be *served* shepherd's pie.'

I couldn't help laughing. I had known, or at least hoped, he'd be out of place here.

'Everyone is so old,' he said.

'We're old!'

'We're not *that* old. We'll never be *that* old. We're never going to give up,' he said, 'that's the difference.'

We were alone in The Field – there were six or seven armchairs and a few coffee tables scattered about. Everything was yellow or green – the walls, the chairs, the carpet. And it had one big window that looked out, unlike the rest of the windows, onto the field next to the care home – which was wide and bordered by a long line of trees.

'So that's why you like this room,' I said. 'Have you seen anything good?'

'Not yet,' he said. 'If I'm to get my telescope down the corridor without being ushered back to bed like a schoolboy, I'll need to know their night staff rotations.'

'You know, you could just ask if they'll let you take it in.'

'And have them need to fill in a health and safety form? No chance.'

'Have you met anyone nice?' I asked.

'Of course not.'

'I'm sure that's not true.' I gave his knee a squeeze.

He looked into my eyes and there was a moment that I couldn't identify or define, but I know that it didn't feel good. His beard was neater than it was when he left. I wanted to ask if they'd done that for him, but I knew that if they had, it would be the last thing he'd want to talk about.

'So,' I said, 'your bedroom faces the courtyard?'

'There are two floodlights that light it up from six p.m. to six a.m. I can't see a bloody thing.'

'Could you ask to be moved?'

'I did. Not for three months, they said. Three months without seeing the stars. I'm going to go mad.'

'Come home, then,' I said, before I had time to think about whether it was a good idea. This, I thought, must be how parents who send their children to boarding school feel when they visit. Guilty and sad, and like each time you see your child they've become someone else, and the next time you visit they'll be another someone else entirely.

I waited for him to reply, but he didn't.

'It's fine. Shall we play dominoes?' he asked, and I wanted to cry.

'What if,' I said, once he'd finished gloating about winning at dominoes, 'I watched the stars for you?'

'Hm.'

I pushed on, regardless. 'I've got the big telescope still set up. You tell me what to look for and I'll do it, and then I'll—'

'Telephone me,' he said. 'Describe what you see.'

'Shall we try?'

'Yes. I'll be like an alcoholic getting calls from his sommelier.'

So every evening, I sat down and telephoned Humphrey's bedroom and reported as carefully and accurately as I could everything I saw in the sky. He would ask me questions, tell me to move the telescope a degree here or there, or remind him if something had been in the same place in one of our last calls. I could always hear the scratching of his pencil as he wrote. Even once he'd been moved to a room with a much better view of the sky, at seven thirty on the dot I'd call him and tell him what I could see, and he would tell me if he could see it too. We were connected because we were looking at the same point, millions of miles away.

And then, on a Tuesday in February, I called and he didn't answer. So I called again.

'Hello?' a young woman answered.

'Yes, I'm trying to speak to Humphrey. Humphrey James?'

'Oh, who am I speaking to?'

'Margot ... I'm his wife.'

'Margot, Mrs James, I was just about to call you. Humphrey had a bit of a fall when he was getting out of the bath. He's with the doctor now; we'll update you as soon as we can.'

'Should I come and see him? Do you need me to come over?'

'I'm sorry, Mrs James, visiting hours are over for today, but if the doctor alerts us to anything serious, we'll make an exception. Please hold off until we know more.'

The next morning, I drove over to the care home. 'Just bruising' was the verdict. But I felt betrayed. He'd promised me we would never get that old. And now he needed help bathing, he needed to have a bath with a door in it.

The nurse, who seemed far too young to be a nurse and had covered her cardigan in badges for various charities, led me to The Field. 'This is his favourite space,' she said.

'I know.' I tried to smile, but it felt like my face was trying to do something it had never done.

'So, just to warn you, his leg has a bandage and we are keeping it elevated to bring down the swelling, but other than that he's fit as a flea.' She smiled and held the door open for me.

He was looking out of the window, his leg, as promised, elevated on three cushions, and his shin bandaged up.

I sat beside him.

'Darling. How are you? They told me about the fall,' I said.

He turned to me. 'Everyone saw my penis!'

And then he burst out laughing and I laughed too.

Following three rounds of dominoes, in which he was almost certainly cheating, I felt the need to lean forward and kiss his cheek. It had lost some of its sponginess, but it was still him.

'You won't forget, will you?' he asked. 'Our promise?'

I pulled my chair closer to him and put my hand on his.

'I won't.'

'I'm serious, Margot, I don't want you here when I'm gone. Why should you have to sit here when I'm not here any more?'

'I know. I remember.'

'And you promise?'

'I signed the contract, didn't I?'

'I'm serious.'

'I promise.'

'You know I love you,' he said. 'You're my stars, Margot.'

'I love you too.'

Then he leant back, stretching out his toes in the socks that I'd bought him the Christmas before.

'Have you heard from her, from ...?'

'From who?'

'Your friend from London, Jeremy's mother? Oh, what's her name!'

'Oh, Meena?'

'Yes, yes, have you heard from Meena?'

'The last I heard was this Christmas. She sent me a letter – Jeremy's eighteenth birthday was a success. He's started going to university classes run by an international school.'

'And is she well?'

'I think so.'

'You should write to her,' he said.

Try as I might, I have no memory of what we did the rest of the day, or even of saying goodbye, because it's blended in with all my other visits and all the other goodbyes. Sometimes I try to trick myself into remembering, to observe the day casually from the side, trying to get it to roll itself around and reveal to me what we did or said when the visit came to an end. But I can't.

That night I had seen a shooting star and I had to tell him about it to his face.

As a treat, the next day I made him some carrot cake. I rarely visited two days in a row, so I hoped to surprise him.

The nurse was wearing the same cardigan as the day before.

'You'll never guess where he is,' she said with a smile.

'The Field?'

He was sitting in the same spot as the day before, a new pair of socks on show and his leg still elevated on cushions. It was quiet and calm and the sun was warming the carpet. He was staring out of the window across the field.

I sat beside him.

'Hello,' I said.

He started.

'Hallo!' he said warmly.

'I'm sorry I scared you,' I said.

'Not at all.'

'I thought you might like some carrot cake.' I pulled the cake box out of my bag.

'Thank you,' he said, 'carrot cake is one of my favourites.'

'I know.'

'How did you know that?'

'You told me.'

'I did?' He frowned.

'Here,' I said, as I cut a slice and placed it on the picnic plate I'd brought. I was playing for time.

He took it, looking at me quizzically.

'How's your leg?'

He peered down at it, as though he had never seen the bandage before.

'Do you know, I haven't the foggiest!'

'I . . .'

'And, if you don't mind my asking, I'm having the hardest time placing you.'

I fell about a thousand feet. But somehow remained sitting.

'I'm Margot,' I said.

'Margot.' He toyed with my name in his mouth, no light of recognition to lead him home. 'What a great name.'

'Thank you,' I said. My heart was beating so fast my chest was shaking.

'How do I know you, Margot?' he asked.

'Oh, we're old friends.'

'We are? I'm terribly sorry,' he said. 'How rude of me not to remember!'

'It's okay,' I said, 'it was a long time ago that we met.' That part, at least, was true. 'But it's okay, I was looking for someone else.'

'Anyone special?'

'My other half,' I said.

I could feel the tears forming in my eyes so I put down the carrot cake and I stood in front of him. I took his beloved cheeks in my hands and I looked him in the eye.

'I made you a promise,' I told him.

He smiled kindly, though there was a hint of confusion there. And I made a memory of those bright eyes and the feeling of his warm face between my hands. And I kissed him, on the lips, for quite some time, and to my surprise I felt him kiss me back. Even when lost, he was still the kind of man to seize a chance when it came to him. And then I told him.

'Goodbye, Humphrey James. It was truly wonderful to meet you.'

And he smiled at me oddly.

'Oh,' he said, as I reached the door, 'who was it you were looking for?'

'My love,' I said, trying to wipe the tears from my cheeks so he wouldn't notice I was crying.

'Well,' he said, 'I'm sure you'll find him . . . or her.'

'Thank you.'

'Keep an eye on the skies tonight,' he said. 'It's a once-in-a-lifetime astral event.'

I had to leave right in that moment or I'd never go, and in doing so I'd break the last promise I'd made to him.

'I have to go,' I said, barely above a whisper.

'Well, goodbye then, Margot,' he said, 'and thank you for the kiss.' And he winked.

Several months later, Humphrey James passed away peacefully in his sleep, sitting beside his telescope in his armchair by the window.

Morning

West Midlands, May 1998
Margot James is still Sixty-Seven Years Old

purple is the colour of morning
the moment
when the sullen sphere rolls around
and there's a shift
from black to biro blue

light,
                dawn,
                        day.

the space of sunlight
that we predict will last a few minutes longer than the one
                                            before

and we'll call it wednesday

344

but it isn't wednesday, not one in seven,
but new,
a gap of light between
the darkness

and who can say for certain
that it will come again?

in this light, they carry the coffin
on this wednesday, we say goodbye
our sadness a gap of darkness between
                    the light

and a priest in robes of violet and white
informs us,
'purple is the colour of mourning'

Humphrey's funeral was very well attended – all the staff from the observatory and several from overseas were there; his side of the family came in great numbers, led by his sister, who stayed with me for the week before to help with the preparations. Even the nurse with the cardigan from the care home came to say goodbye.

At the funeral, I read the Sarah Williams poem he'd written down for me after our first meeting, because my own words didn't suffice. I wrote him his own personal poem the night after the funeral, when sleep evaded me and all I could do to calm myself was look at the stars.

And then, everything was done. His sister had to go back home and I found myself alone. Doing the washing up.

I'd put the radio on to distract myself from thinking about him – about the haunting knowledge that his body had been there in the box in the church where we were all sitting. That inside that box he was lying, cold, as though he were sleeping. The radio was playing a pop song. So I sang. I sang along with a song I hadn't even realized I knew the words to. And when the images of his coffin being lowered into the ground swam into my vision, I sang louder. When the sight of his sister crying and throwing her fistful of dirt into the open grave came into my mind, I sang louder still. And then I was no longer at the funeral but in the care home, in The Field. And I had his face in my hands, and he was looking up at me.

I'd kissed him.

And then he'd said ...

A plate I'd just balanced on top of a saucepan on the drying rack slipped out of its spot and shattered on the floor.

And I found myself on the floor beside the plate, because I knew then, in my bones, that the last time I saw Humphrey James he hadn't forgotten me. He'd been pretending.

He'd kissed me back. He'd smiled. 'It's a once-in-a-lifetime astral event,' he'd said. A once-in-a-lifetime astral event.

And more than that: when he told me to find my love, he told me to 'find him ... or her', when just the day before he'd asked me about Meena, though we hadn't spoken of her in years.

That terrible, wonderful man had pretended not to know me so that he could say goodbye while he still knew who I was. He'd saved me from those visits, and in his own way he had set me free. And, no doubt, he was able to check if I really would keep my promise.

I laughed for about twenty minutes because the idea of Humphrey pretending not to know me was so infuriating and silly and so very him. And then I cried.

Light ... Dawn ... Day

MY FATHER IS standing at the end of my bed.

Or he isn't.

(I haven't been well.)

He looks smaller than I remember.

I go to talk and become aware of a mask on my face. My words echo back at me. I pull the mask off, and recall a conversation I had with a nurse. It's to help me sleep, or to keep me awake. To help me live, or to help me die. One of those.

He says something in Swedish. The verbs don't agree and neither do I.

'Hi, pickle,' he says, holding my hand and rubbing his thumb over the cannula where it burrows in. Back and forth, like a rhythm. It hurts, but I can't remember the words in either language to get him to stop.

You would think after all this time there would be a lot to say, that I would be bursting with stories of my adventures and he would be bursting with his. But nobody says anything. Maybe it is a dream, after all, and my brain is struggling to generate his voice. What was it like? High? Low?

'Lenni,' I tell him, and then immediately wonder why, but I've said it now and I have to watch his face crumple in confusion. My father grabs the arm of a passing blur and asks me to repeat what I've said, but I don't remember.

'Is it about my mother? She's eighty-three. We're almost one hundred.'

'The anaesthetic can cause some confusion,' the blur says to him, and he sits down.

'Did you go to Poland?' I think I ask.

He nods and shows me a black and grey picture of a bean, I think.

'I had to tell you as soon as we were sure,' he says, 'you're going to be a big sister.'

'It's Arthur,' I say.

'What is?'

I shake my head and then wonder what exactly we both think we're talking about.

'It's *Father* Arthur.'

My father turns to Agnieszka and says with panic, 'She doesn't recognize me.'

'She wears purple for Humphrey,' I say, connecting the thoughts at last. 'Because she's mourning. And it's morning. That's why she always wears purple.'

'Lenni?'

And then Agnieszka is at the end of the bed, but she's different. It's not just her hair that's different, but her face. Has she been standing there this whole time? Did she always look like that? She's slipping, slipping, slipping . . .

'Lenni?' he asks.

I shake my head because it's easier than speaking.

'Lenni, the nurse called,' my father says. And I smile.

'You kept your promise.'

Margot and the Box

'I DON'T WANT to let you down, Lenni.'

I only realized she was there then. I opened my eyes. I had to blink to bring her into focus. At first, there were two Margots leaning towards me from my visitor's chair.

'Let me down?'

'You finished your half of the hundred.'

'My seventeen per cent.'

'Your *half*. And I haven't finished mine,' she said in a small voice.

She shook her head, looked like she was going to say something and then didn't.

'Everyone's helping,' she said at last. 'Else, Walter, Pippa, the others from the Rose Room – they've split into teams to take on each painting. I sketch them out, direct them with colours and then supervise.'

'Wow.'

'The only thing is,' she said, 'while I work with them and boss everybody about, there's nobody to tell the stories to.'

'So you came here?'

'So I came here. To tell you the next story, if you'll let me.'

'Always.'

350

West Midlands, Spring 1999
Margot James is Sixty-Eight Years Old

When he died, I got seasick. It was as though the world had tilted at a strange angle and nothing felt right. What should have been flat was actually an incline, and I found myself holding on to handrails and faltering on steps as I'd never done before. The pain of losing him hadn't subsided like people said it would.

Humphrey's sister had requested some of his books, to donate to the university where they'd both studied and where he'd first begun to explore the skies. She'd provided me with a list of the ones she wanted to donate, and I was packing them up into some boxes the greengrocer had given me. His shelves of books lined both sides of the living room. Most of them hadn't been touched since I first met him but they were all, he had insisted, essential. They'd been there so long that they seemed to be part of the walls rather than objects for use, like additional beams holding up the crumbling stone structure of his little cottage. With each book I took from a shelf, it felt like I was removing a brick from the walls of the house. Without him and his books, surely it would all fall down.

I was doing my best not to pay attention to the feeling that I was giving away something I very much needed to keep. After all, when would I read them? What use were they growing mildewed in the corner of an old widow's cottage?

The *Fifth Annual Astronomy Conference, Calgary, 1972*, a big white book that would slot perfectly into the box that had

351

once held Brazilian bananas, was the last on the list. It slipped its secret onto the floor with such silence that I didn't notice.

It wasn't until I carried the boxes to the car that I saw her. Smiling, about to say something, a cherubic baby Jeremy in her arms, looking up at me from the cold stone floor.

I picked her up and held her in my hand. And I felt that she was so far away that this was the closest I could ever come to holding her again. I hadn't heard from Meena since the previous Christmas. Jeremy would have been nineteen years old by then. I wondered if he had begun to resemble his father – the creaseless professor whom I had disliked all those years ago. When they left, I'd held a hope in my heart that she might not be able to stick it and might come back, but they had moved south and found home in a city named for a certain President Ho Chi Minh. A man who had once, a long time ago, given me some excellent advice.

I surveyed the quiet living room.

I took Humphrey's love for granted sometimes, which is something you can only do when you're really secure in someone's affection. But I know he was happy and I know I was too.

You'll find him . . . or her, Humphrey had said on the occasion of our very last meeting.

So I sat down and wrote her a letter, and then I posted it before I had the chance to change my mind.

a forest has grown between us
in the first silences, little leaves and shoots grew, still so small
that we could crush them if we chose, but we stayed silent, never

walking the space between us, never crunching underfoot the buds and the grass that were growing there

with every month that passed, our untravelled distance became thorny with the beginnings of a tree that blocked my way, and i didn't have the courage to travel that space between us. i felt tired thinking of scratching knees on tall thickets

when the seasons changed and changed and changed and the hedges and brambles thickened, to walk to you would be to take a chainsaw and fight my way through what time had done to the space between us

until one day, the space between us, so solid with life in the middle, so thick with wide trunks and leaves, so green and dense and dark, had closed into a wall and i could no longer see you on the other side

to travel that distance between us now would be to risk my life

and what if i cleared a path, fought my way through that forest only to find on the other side

that you're not there?

m x

Old Friend

'MARGOT?'

    'Yes?'

    'Would it be weird if I said I love you?'

    'Not at all.'

    'It's just, I think you need to know, I love you.'

    'I love you too, Lenni.'

    'What was Vietnam like?'

    'Amazing. It was hot and busy and so alive. I could hardly believe all this life had been going on while I'd been living alone in Humphrey's old farmhouse. And of course, there was Meena.'

    'Did you find her?'

    'I did.'

    'And?'

    'We burned the forest down.'

I followed Margot to the airport sometime in 1999. After a long flight with two stop-overs, we landed at Tân Sơn Nhất Airport. It wasn't the heat but the humidity that hit us as we made the uncertain journey from the plane to the quiet airport terminal. It was night and ours was the last flight arriving before morning. I didn't have any baggage, so I walked freely, following Margot as she juggled papers and phrasebooks and her passport. She was nervous. She'd booked the flight and packed before she'd had time to prepare herself. Which was a blessing and a curse. Time would have calmed her, but it also might have stopped her.

She needn't have worried, though. The almost-stranger half a world away that she'd placed her trust in was waiting for her. He looked like Meena; he had the same face shape and he had her eyes. He was tall, though, and hadn't quite yet grown into himself. He was holding up a hand-drawn sign with Margot's name on it, and Margot, upon the relief of seeing him, ran to him and wrapped him up in a big hug.

I followed them both, listening to them talk, hearing Margot explain that she'd met him when he was no more than a cherub and him telling Margot that he recognized her at once because wherever they had lived, his mother had hung up a picture in a gold frame: a blurred photograph of Meena and Margot at a party. Margot was wearing a green dress and they were dancing, spinning with their arms crossed and held together. It went with them wherever they went, he said.

When they reached his moped in the car park and he said, 'Jump on!' Margot had laughed and then *really* laughed. He handed her a helmet and then, because she's awesome, she climbed onto his moped behind him, her suitcase sandwiched between them. He pulled them into the busy traffic, a thrumming vein of the city made up of scooters and taxis, of people for whom this was just another evening and not something completely extraordinary.

And when they arrived in the narrow leaning alleyway where Meena and Jeremy shared an upper floor flat, I stood beside Jeremy and watched as Meena ran to Margot, crashed into her so hard that they both almost fell over, wrapped her arms around her and cried, careless and free, 'Tao yêu mày!'

Birthday

I THOUGHT IT was my birthday when I saw the candle. I had to sit up before I could work out which was the right way round to look at things. I must have been sleeping because I didn't remember anyone turning off the lights.

They were creeping. Creeping with a candle. Margot, Pippa, Walter and Else (hand in hand), Father Arthur, New Nurse, Paul the Porter. They were all smiling and for a moment I wondered whether I was dead. The candle flickered and lit up their faces, and it was resting on top of the cake that Margot was carrying very slowly and carefully to my bed.

She gingerly placed it on my table and pulled it closer so I could see. In swirling black sugar icing, it said: *Happy 100th Birthday Lenni and Margot.*

'We're a hundred?' I asked. 'We did it?'

Pippa held up a painting I hadn't seen before. It was the best I'd seen. It was of Margot and me, side by side in our pyjamas, and I was laughing, the sky above us filled with stars.

In the bottom corner, it said: *Glasgow Princess Royal Hospital, Margot Macrae is Eighty-Three Years Old.*

'We're your last year?' I asked, not believing Margot had actually captured me in paint. I looked so real.

Margot smiled and patted my hand. 'Of course,' she said.

New Nurse scraped up chairs for everyone and they sat around me. Like pilgrims.

The glowing thing on the cake wasn't actually a candle – it was a plastic Christmas candle with fake wax dribbling down its side and a bright LED bulb which was flickering. It was doing a good job of looking like a candle. 'No open flames,' New Nurse said by way of explanation. Then she lifted the cake and held it in front of us.

'Make a wish,' New Nurse said. Margot and I blew over the cake, and by witchcraft or magic the plastic LED candle went out.

Pippa handed around paper plates and cut thick slices of cake. I couldn't remember the last time I'd had cake. It was delicious. A perfect choice. And now I could honestly say I'd tasted my hundredth birthday cake.

'I never thought I'd see my hundredth birthday,' I said.

'Many happy returns,' Else said with a soft smile.

'Very well deserved,' Father Arthur added.

'It's quite an achievement,' Pippa said, 'and now seems like a good time to tell you that I've been talking to a gallery owner in the city and she wants to display your paintings as an exhibition. That is, if you'd be interested.'

'What do you think?' Margot asked, looking at me.

I nodded.

'One hundred years old. How does it feel?' Arthur asked.

'Weird,' I said. 'It feels like just yesterday I was seventeen.'

'I'm told I don't look a day over eighty-three.' Margot winked at me.

So we ate cake and talked and laughed, and together Margot and I celebrated our one hundred years on the earth. It's been a long life and it's been a short life.

The light they brought with them stayed long after they'd gone.

Margot

WE WERE ONE hundred years and a day old, and a little face appeared at the window of my ward. At first, I thought it was Lenni.

They say you don't notice when you first begin to slow down. They say it starts early – at about fifty – a gradual slowing where you have to be careful on the stairs and getting in and out of the bath, where you don't run but jog, don't jog but walk. But I can forever know that isn't true. I moved faster than I have in months – years, even. I ran. It must have been something to behold, but the halls were quiet. It was barely morning.

Arthur already had her hand in his as he sat beside her. Lenni's nurse, who had run with me, explained in words I heard but didn't hear.

Lenni's face was covered with a mask, and there was a rattle when she breathed. It was jagged. I sat on her other side and took her hand. It was cold and heavy. I didn't let go anyway.

'It might be time to say goodbye,' the nurse said, unable to stop the many tears that were running down her face. She tucked her cherry hair behind her ear and wiped her hand under her eyes. Then she walked over to Lenni and gave her a kiss on the forehead.

'Lenni?' the nurse said. 'Margot's here.'

Lenni's eyes flickered, half opening. She saw me.

'Hello, pet. I'm here,' I said, forcing a smile. She moved her head in an almost nod. I had to blink to clear my vision.

'I love you, Lenni. I always will,' I told her. She squeezed my hand and from behind the mask, she mouthed her reply.

'You're going to be so happy,' I told her. 'You're going to marry a tall man, and he'll have dark hair but light eyes, and he'll sing. He'll sing to you all the time. And you'll get a little flat together and then a house, and you'll send me postcards, and then you'll have a baby or maybe two, and one of them you'll call Arthur and the other you'll call Star, and you'll have a garden with snails but you won't mind them. And you'll be so happy, and you'll remember us all here and think how funny it all seems now. I'll come to visit, and you'll make up the bed with a floral bedspread.' I couldn't stop talking, but she didn't seem to mind.

Then she turned to Father Arthur, pulled at her oxygen mask until it came off, and in a small voice she asked, 'Do you think I'll get into heaven?'

Arthur closed his eyes at the pain of it but then fixed her with a look of complete conviction. 'Of course, Lenni,' he said, 'of course.' He stroked her hand and she closed her eyes.

'And Lenni, when you get to heaven,' he said.

Her eyes opened.

'Give 'em hell.'

It was the first time she had smiled all day.

Margot Again

I THOUGHT I would go first.

How could she slip so gently away? I thought she would go like a firework, with bright lights flashing and alarms ringing and defibrillators being raced around corners. The kind of thing she would have loved. Chaos and commotion, her two closest companions in life, deserted her in her final hours. Her death was hallowed and quiet, and we stayed by her side for as long as they would let us.

And then they took her away. She could have been sleeping, but for the fact that they had unplugged the tubes and wires that had been keeping her alive and coiled them neatly by her hand. No longer needed.

And then there was just a ward. And a place where a bed and a girl used to be. And we were no longer Father Arthur and Margot, we were just a priest and an old woman. Surrogate parents robbed of a real daughter.

I started to panic and Arthur, bless him, held me tight as I wept.

When I was ready, he walked me back to my ward, and we sat on my bed and we cried together.

Precious Little

My mother had two words she always used when she was running out of patience, or when she was tired, or when she was scared. She would turn to me and say something like, 'I don't know, Margot, but there's precious little time left in the day,' or 'There's precious little we can do,' or 'There's precious little left in the cupboard.'

I used to imagine what a Precious Little might look like. A glass trinket perhaps, blue and shining in the light. Something you had to be careful with when you held it in the palm of your hand. It would need wrapping in tissue if you wanted to take it somewhere, but I always wanted to slip it into my pocket. I imagined my mother and my six-year-old self, sitting either side of the kitchen table with the Precious Little between us, deliberating how we ought to split it between us to make a meal.

It feels like there's precious little now. I don't know what to do with myself. All I can think to do is finish my story.

Ho Chi Minh City, January 2000
Margot Macrae is Sixty-Nine Years Old

At the airport, Meena and I clung to each other and I felt tiny – like we were two particles that had accidentally collided in a dust cloud. And I thanked the various gods for letting us collide. We made no promises or vows to see each other again. One year from seventy, I knew better than to make promises about returning to that humid, intense, faraway place. The city had been ours, even if only for a few months. We had entered a new millennium together and that felt like a lot.

'Goodbye, my love,' she said into my hair as she held on tight.

And I felt peace.

Because we had finally answered the question of the gap between our beds.

Glasgow, December 2003
Margot Macrae is Seventy-Two Years Old

We went to Davey's gravestone shortly after the funeral, Johnny and I. I took flowers wrapped with a blue ribbon, and as I placed them at his grave, I looked at my husband and he looked at me and I had this consuming feeling that we were both deep underwater, so far from the surface that we could no longer see the sun. Unable to hear each other's words, as we shouted our mouths filled with water.

Fifty years later, I stood at that same spot carrying a bunch of flowers tied with a yellow ribbon.

Time had turned this little spot in a Glasgow graveyard around the sun fifty times, and yet it looked much the same. Fifty winters had frozen the stone that bore my son's name. Fifty summer suns had shone down where he lay sleeping. And though my feet had travelled far, I had come nowhere near the spot where I now stood.

The graveyard was quiet. The grass was frozen from the bitter night before. I wondered if it was cold down there, deep in the earth. My posy seemed a pitiful apology. I could still picture Davey as clear as day, his forehead scrunched up, his wide eyes exploring every new thing. The hands that were so tiny it made me marvel at his very existence.

I knelt on the cold grass and the dew began to seep into my trousers.

'Hello,' I whispered. Just beyond, on the path, two women in dark blue made their way across the graveyard, one carrying a bag for life with a group of white tulips poking out of the top.

'I'm sorry it's taken me so long,' I told him. 'I hope you can forgive me.' I'd left Vietnam because I had to see my Davey one last time. I couldn't die without saying goodbye. So when I returned from Vietnam, I sold Humphrey's farmhouse and moved home, to Glasgow.

I placed the flowers in front of him. The cellophane around them crinkled.

'I was so afraid of you. Of how much I missed you and how much I loved you and how much I failed you.'

I took in a deep breath. Some of the thoughts were so loud.

'If your father were here, he'd remind me that neither of us could be held responsible for a heart defect. But he's not here. In fact, I don't know where he is.

'But maybe *you* do.'

Beside the flowers I'd placed on the cold grass was a small white candle in a glass holder. I picked it up. On the side of the glass holder were the words *Rest in Peace*. It was relatively clean and relatively new. It had been lit, but had only burned for a short time. There was just a shallow dip in the wax.

Neither of Davey's sleeping neighbours had such a candle, so it wasn't a gift from the church. I couldn't think of many reasons that a stranger might leave a candle at the graveside of a baby who'd passed away more than half a century before. I felt a shiver and I stood, the cold from the wet patches on my knees having seeped into my bones.

I wondered at the power of what I held in my hand. There were so few people who might remember Davey.

Of course, I'd thought about Johnny over the years, but when Meena threw his missing person's report in the bin, she threw away the part of me that felt I had an obligation to find him, whether or not he wanted to be found.

December seemed to suit the graveyard. The sky looked like it was made of the same grey as the headstones.

I replaced the candle and I kissed the stone that bore the name of my Davey. For bearing it so clearly through all those winters, through all those turns of the earth.

Glasgow, July 2006
Margot Macrae is Seventy-Five Years Old

'Good afternoon. May I?'

'Please do.' I made some room on the bench and the vicar sat down. As he sat, he let out a sigh. I caught the scent of fabric conditioner on his clothes. I wondered if he was hot in them. Those black trousers and shirt on a sunny hot day like that must have been warm.

'Have I seen you here before?' he asked.

'I'm here quite often lately,' I told him.

'Visiting someone?' he asked.

'Sort of.'

'It's a beautiful day for it.'

I wondered what 'it' was. Grieving? Waiting for whoever left the candle to return? And was this day truly wonderful for it? I agreed with him anyway. From his bag, he took out his lunch – a sandwich wrapped in plastic and cut into quarters. He held one of the little squares out to me and I found myself taking it.

The vicar took a big bite of his sandwich.

'It gets a lovely light in the afternoons, this part of the churchyard,' he said.

'It does.'

We sat in silence for a while. I watched him chewing on his sandwich and I wondered how someone so nice ended up being the vicar of such a lonely church.

'Right,' he said, standing up, 'I'm afraid I must be off. If I don't get back into the office soon, I think I may melt. The bell ringers are coming at three to petition me about adding a Snow Patrol song to their repertoire.'

'Crikey,' I said.

'My sentiments exactly,' he said. 'See you again, no doubt.'

Although I never did see him again. I stopped waiting for whoever had brought the candle to visit Davey. I had the feeling they were never coming back.

And then the vicar was off across the graveyard, brushing crumbs from his smart black trousers.

As he disappeared inside the church, I took a bite of the sandwich. It was egg and cress.

Moorlands House Care Home, September 2011
Margot Macrae is Eighty Years Old

I got old by accident. Those were Humphrey's words that first time I'd taken him to the doctor's, when his memory had started to fail him. Only on waking in my private care home to be checked by a nurse, and to totter into the day room for breakfast, did I fully appreciate what he meant. The place was faultless – the staff were neat and kind – but there was a miserable inevitability about the place. Sockets where they would need to plug in respiratory machines when I would lose the ability to breathe on my own, panic alarms for when I would be panicking and need someone else to be alarmed. Pulleys on the ceiling for attaching hoists for when I would eventually need help rising up out of bed.

There was a special lunch planned for a resident who was turning seventy. We would be having lasagne. And I found myself at the desk in my room in front of the mirror, feeling a little nervous. I was putting on a lipstick. A light reddish-brown shade from Marks & Spencer that would, I hoped, brighten up my face. I looked at my eyes, my own eyes, the only things on my face that hadn't changed over time, and wondered what Meena was up to at that moment. When I'd sent her my new address, I'd missed off the words 'care home' so she wouldn't know.

The lasagne didn't taste how I remembered lasagne; it had a strange plastic-like quality to it. But I'd fallen into a conversation with two long-term residents, Elaine and Georgina ('Please, call me George'). They were telling me about their childhoods spent in the same seaside town near Plymouth, and how they'd never known one another but had many friends in common. We were talking about the size of the world and then there he was. A few tables over, eating alone. Still thin, but concertinaed a little at the middle from age. His hair wasn't all gone, but what was left was white and fluffy. He was looking out of the window as though he could just sail out of it and keep going. On and on.

Johnny.

Goose bumps shimmered along my arms and I could no longer hear George telling Elaine about her new slipper boot knitting pattern. Because there he was.

He dipped his spoon into his lasagne and ate from it as though he were in a dream.

I considered doubting myself. I'd seen his face in many people before – strangers on London streets, patrons in the Redditch library, even a thin man in Hội An – but this was him. I knew it. I felt it in my bones.

I remembered the court date back in the late 1970s when I'd submitted my request to end my marriage to a man I couldn't find – the evidence to show we had looked, the last known address, the letters not answered by family, the proof that we had lived apart for over twenty years – Humphrey standing patiently by my side. I wondered if Johnny had ever heard I'd divorced him.

I hesitated as I wondered if I was being disrespectful to Humphrey's memory. He'd told me to go and find my love, and I had. Johnny was not my love. Not now, maybe not even then. What would Humphrey think? Should I even go over to Johnny when I had a wedding ring on my left hand? One not borrowed, but truly my own. I asked these questions of myself, but I knew that if Humphrey were with me he would have already been over there, shaking Johnny by the hand and asking him what he thought of Neptune.

My heart belonged then, as it does now, to that funny, starry man who took my pieces of a life and helped me make a whole one. And to the woman who taught me how to set myself free. But my past belonged then, as it does now, to that tall, gangly boy who dropped onto one knee just after my twentieth birthday. To not ask would be unforgivable. A total denial of the mystery of it all – and Humphrey did like a mystery.

My heart hammering, I pushed myself to my feet.

I reached his chair and I let my eyes fall on him and I felt a familiarity so old it was like listening to music. I took him in. Then he looked up, and our eyes met.

I smiled, wondering how my eighty-year-old self compared with my twenty-five-year-old self. How many lives had I lived since I last saw him? How many moments? How many days? Had I known I'd have ended up there, with him, would I have done it all the same?

'Johnny?' I asked.

He squinted at me; his mouth fell slightly open.

'Margot,' he said, and it wasn't a question but an answer. 'How on earth . . . ?'

And then it slowly slid into place, and I must admit it was a feeling not unlike falling.

Johnny's brother couldn't take his eyes off me.

I shook my head, tears forming, the air squeezing out of my lungs.

After a moment of white-hot nothing, I came back. Thomas was still staring at me.

'I'm sorry,' he said, as though it were his fault that he so closely resembled his older brother – it had been the same when he was a fifteen-year-old with bruised bony legs standing on the doorstep of my mother's house, pretending to be Johnny.

'Well' – he smiled – 'I didn't think I'd be seeing you again!'

I had always imagined he would marry young and move to America, train in the air force, learn to fly. But his accent told me otherwise, still thick with Glaswegian charm. The last time I'd seen him might have been Davey's funeral. Or a family dinner not long after. I tried to remember what he had looked like, but there were several memories stitched together and none of them seemed right.

'It was you, then?'

'What was?'

'The candle. Did you visit Davey's grave?'

He nodded. 'Was a while ago, that. It was something Johnny asked, before he went, that I'd keep an eye out, you know?'

'Well, thank you,' I said. 'I didn't get there as often as I should have.'

Thomas waved me away. He wasn't interested in judging me. Which was as true then as it had been when he was barely even a man.

'How ...' Thomas faltered. 'How do I begin?' he asked, and then he laughed at himself. 'Margot, my God. How was it?'

And I imagined, though I might have been wrong, that he was asking how was life? How did the last fifty-eight years treat you? Was life what you thought it would be? Did you live happily, freely, well? But the question was too big, astronomical, and I wasn't sure I had understood it in the first place.

'I'm well,' I said instead. 'How are you?'

He gestured to the surroundings. 'Old!' And then he laughed and I remembered why I had liked Thomas. He was so much lighter than Johnny, so much happier.

'When did Johnny die?'

He nodded, his smile sliding away.

'About two years ago,' he said. 'Though I'm sorry to be the one to tell you. He fell down the stairs, broke his leg. It turned into pneumonia. It was quick.'

'Were you there?'

'No,' he said, 'but he wasn't alone.'

I nodded.

'And yourself?' I asked. 'What became of little Thomas Docherty?'

'After Johnny left, I took over his place at Dutton's. Eventually, it was me and a pal running the place.'

'So no aeroplanes?'

'Aeroplanes?'

'You loved them. I remember you had that red toy one with the rotating propeller.'

He smiled. 'I can't believe you remember that. It's funny how quickly it goes.'

'And did you marry?'

'I did. My wife passed three years or so ago. We had a girl, April. Who's just now pregnant with her third.'

We sat in silence for a moment. Seeing him was so surreal, I couldn't shake the feeling that I was in a dream. Or that I'd ripped through the barriers of time and peeped through into a world I wasn't meant to know about. I was hearing answers to questions I'd carried for so long that I thought I'd never have them answered.

'I looked for Johnny,' I said, 'I followed him to London a few years after he left.'

'You did?'

'I didn't find him though. It would've been a mistake anyway. In fact, I never even knew if he went to London. It was just a guess.'

'You were right,' he said.

'I've always wanted to know what happened to him.'

'He did go to London, for about a month or two, but he couldn't make it work and so he ended up moving to Bristol, working in the shipyards.'

'Was he happy?'

'Yes.'

'Did he have a nice life?'

Thomas leant forward and put his old hand on my old hand. 'Yes,' he said.

I took a breath. That was all I needed to know.

'He stayed in Bristol for most of his life. Moved back here about ten years ago. They say the call home is strong, don't they? In the end?'

'And here we are,' I said.

'Here we are.' He smiled.

Glasgow Princess Royal Hospital, February 2014
Margot Macrae is Eighty-Three Years Old

I woke up in my little room at Moorlands care home with a crackling pain in my chest. I thought I had indigestion, but what happened next was evidence to the contrary.

The panic button that had so intuitively foretold the day I'd need it was right. I would need it. And I'd be panicking and hoping that someone else would know or care, or come into my room and panic with me.

And then a face I couldn't place but I knew I *knew* appeared. It's a blur after that. I remember them taking off my top in A&E to stick on the pads for the ECG, and I remember wishing heartily that I'd been wearing a bra.

The next thing I knew, it was the morning. And I was in recovery from an exploratory surgery which left some open-ended questions. The doctor, whose dress beneath her stethoscope was covered in white flowers, said it would probably be weeks before I'd be strong enough for the next surgery stage. The very posh woman in the bed beside mine tutted loudly at that.

'Weeks!' she said.

I noticed her red dressing gown was monogrammed with the initials W. S., and I wondered what life a person must lead in order for them to need to identify their dressing gown from others with such regularity that monogramming would seem a wise choice.

The doctor pulled the curtain around my bed and came closer. Her perfume was a sweet vanilla. 'You're not to worry,' she said. 'Just rest. You'll be strong again soon.'

I lived out my days happily in the little curtained-off area. A week or so into my stay, the monogrammed lady lent me a book and gave me two pears from her personal fruit bowl on her bedside table. She told me that she was a gynaecological surgeon for thirty years and, in her own words, 'loathed what she'd become'. Her ex-husband was managing her estate until she was released, but she'd been bouncing between infections and various treatments for weeks. Had she been her own doctor, she would have disliked herself for taking up a bed space for so long.

'Try a pear,' she said, 'they're Conference.'

A few days later, a letter arrived for me.

Perhaps not an incredible thing in and of itself.

But it was incredible to me.

How can it be that paper is still flown around the world, in the era of email and text?

And then it went into my postbox at Moorlands Care Home. And then it was cleared out and given to Emily, one of the assistants at the care home whose task it was to bring me a suitcase with some more of my pyjamas and essentials.

'This came for you,' she said, as she slid my suitcase under my bed.

The envelope had a stamp with a man I didn't recognize. And the return address was Ho Chi Minh City.

I could barely hear sweet Emily for a moment because all I wanted was to open the letter. But she wanted to tell me about Johnny's brother Thomas, about how his daughter April had invited him to live with her family, just in time for the birth of his third grandchild. Emily stayed and we talked for a while, and then the nurse came to give me my DVT jab, and then dinner arrived.

I woke up to my great surprise. Mostly because I had no idea I'd fallen asleep. My dinner tray had been cleared away, as had yesterday's newspaper. And something else too. What was it?

I was out of my bed like a flash. I pulled the suitcase from under my bed. I rifled through the pyjamas and cardigans, all the while knowing it wasn't in there. I pulled my bed covers off and lifted up both pillows. I put on my slippers, pulled my curtain back and slippered over to the monogrammed lady.

'Have the bin men been?'

'I'm sorry?' She pulled her glasses from her nose and squinted at me.

'The cleaner. Have they, has he, taken away the rubbish?'

'Yes.'

'When?'

'I'd say . . .' I wanted to shake her to hurry her up. 'About . . . a good while ago, certainly.'

I'm not sure I even thanked her. It was my first unsupervised walk in the hospital. I felt like a fugitive. A slow one, though. I tried to think like a porter. I remembered him now; he had a series of tattoos that, were they mine, would annoy me endlessly for being so crooked.

I wandered out of elderly care towards maternity, but they had a video link at the door so I turned back. Then I made my way down a long corridor that sloped just slightly, but in such a way that I felt like Alice in Wonderland shrinking down to fit through the keyhole. I tried to picture the envelope – the writing in black, several ink stamps from customs and air mail. The stamp itself, with a man on a green background. I faced a number of crossroads, and made my decision based only on the feeling that if I were the tattooed porter, this would be the route I'd take. His big bin was one of those on wheels that has four separate bins – medical, recycling, food and general waste. With any luck, my letter would have made it into recycling.

And then there it was. Waiting patiently, completely un-attended. I crept up to it. I got onto tiptoes to see if my letter was in amongst the rubbish, but I couldn't see. The porter with the bad tattoos was behind the closed door of the nurses' office, so I climbed up onto the side of the bin cart. I stuck my hand in and tried to shake the tissues loose. I could see a pointed corner. There it was. Just a little further out of my reach ...

I heard a noise behind me and I turned. On the other side of the corridor, a girl of about sixteen or seventeen with bright blonde hair and pink pyjamas was watching me. Then the door to the nurses' office opened and I froze. I was most cer-tainly going to get caught, but the girl started to speak. The tattooed porter and the grim-faced nurse turned their atten-tion to her.

Just underneath a clump of white tissue was my letter. I leant over once again and I stuck my hand out. My fingers brushed the letter and I finally got it free.

Fully expecting to turn around and see the porter and the grim nurse staring at me, I turned to see that they were gone – heading into the May Ward. Only the girl with the pink pyjamas was still there. She smiled.

Clutching my letter from Meena, I headed back to my bed.

When I wrote my reply, I told her, *I'd put my hand in a hos-pital bin to find a letter from you. That's love.*

And my answer to the question she'd asked me, of course, was 'yes'.

~

Father Arthur popped in to see me yesterday. He visits a lot. And mostly we talk about you, Lenni, which I think you would enjoy.

I showed him the letter from Meena and I told him how you helped me save it from the bin. And I showed him your name – written in permanent ink on the little whiteboard that used to hang on the wall above your bed. Rescued by your nurse and now hanging next to mine.

And then I took a breath and I asked Father Arthur what he thought of the prospect of me and my rattling old bones and my damaged heart flying to Vietnam, to answer the question a soulmate of mine had asked with an emphatic 'yes'. To let her put her handmade ring on the fourth finger of my left hand. Though, since Meena made it herself, I am fairly sure it will be made of copper and will turn my finger green.

He smiled sadly, looked about himself for some paper, and then pulled a receipt out of his pocket and wrote: *Ecclesiastes 9:9*.

And then he picked up his scarf, gave me a wave and headed home.

I asked a nurse to find me a Bible – they're everywhere in hospitals so it wasn't difficult. An American lady in the ward across the corridor lent me hers.

As I carefully turned the skin-thin pages, I steeled myself for what it might say.

Something about stoning and eternal punishment, I imagined. The horror of my love for her. Something so damning that Arthur had felt unable to say it to my face. I imagined that would be one of the harder parts of being a priest. The times when you have to remind the sinners of their fates.

I turned the page and read Ecclesiastes 9:9.

Enjoy life with the woman whom you love
all the days of your fleeting life

Glasgow Princess Royal Hospital, March 2014

I had just woken up from a nap when a woman appeared at the end of my bed. She was wearing a thick woollen jumper covered in dog hair and she had green paint splatters on the hem of her polka dot dress. She told me there was a new art therapy room for patients of all ages and she invited me to come along to a class. She handed me a leaflet and smiled.

She smiled again when I turned up at the class designated for patients aged eighty and over. I found myself a seat near the window, and I wondered if at any point we'd get to paint the stars. The lesson actually was on stars, or something else, I can't really remember now because it has been replaced with my memory of Lenni. Into a room full of octogenarians she came, with a confidence beyond her years. She was fierce, thin, with that bright blonde hair of Nordic children. She had a face full of mischief and a pair of pink pyjamas.

She walked up to my table, introduced herself and then proceeded to change my life, immeasurably, for the better.

Margot's Goodnight

IT'S SO UNFAIR, Lenni. That I got to get old and you didn't. That I continue to be old and getting older when you aren't even here at all.

If I could take my years and give them to you, I would.

Nobody could quite tell me how you'd managed to arrange your burial in the very same graveyard where my Davey sleeps.

I'll miss your truth and I'll miss your laugh, but it's your magic I'll miss most of all.

There are one hundred paintings lying in an art room because of you. One day soon they will go on display in a large white gallery in the city to raise money for the Rose Room. Perhaps I will visit alone, or perhaps we will visit together in spirit – to walk hand in hand among our hundred years.

My big operation will take place next Monday morning. When your lovely nurse came to my ward with Benni the beanbag pig, and told me you wanted me to have him in surgery so I wouldn't be scared, I couldn't help but cry. I thought you might want him down there in the cold earth with you to keep you company, but then I realized you're not down there in the earth, you're somewhere else now. Beautiful and painless and free. I promise I will take good care of him. I've been tapping his nose on mine to say hello while we get to know each other, and I will carry him with me until the end of my days.

380

I've packed a bag, Lenni. And I think you'd approve. It's underneath my bed, waiting. I also have something else. It's a piece of paper. Which doesn't seem enough to constitute a boarding pass, but apparently it is. Father Arthur printed it off for me on his computer. If the surgery goes well, I'll be catching a plane. To see Meena once more. To see if the ring she made me fits. To finally say 'yes'.

If I don't wake up, I'll be boarding a plane to find you. Either would be the greatest adventure.

I see that you've written something on the very last page of this book, and so since you've left your last words I don't want to leave any. I will simply bid you goodnight.

Lenni, wherever you are. Whatever wonderful world you find yourself in now. Wherever that fiery heart is, that quick wit, that disabling charm. Know that I love you. For the brief lifetime that we knew each other, I loved you like you were my very own daughter.

You found an old woman worthy of your immense friendship and for that I am forever in your debt.

So I have to say thank you.

Thank you, sweet Lenni. You made dying much more fun than it should be.

Lenni's Last Page

WHEN PEOPLE SAY 'terminal', I think of the airport.

I've checked in now. Most definitely.

I still have my hand luggage but the bulk of it – the hold stuff – it's gone now.

I will miss Margot with my whole heart, but she isn't ready to leave the terminal. She still has things left to do. Buy a giant Toblerone, finish telling our story, live another hundred years, all of it.

It's quiet here, and the sun is reflecting off the shiny floor so that the whole place is alive with light. I'm standing amongst the other passengers in the departure lounge, staring out of the great glass window at the plane, and thinking, *That's it? That's the thing I've been afraid of this whole time?*

And it's okay.

It doesn't look so big from close up.

Acknowledgements

Lenni came to visit me one night in January 2014. I was supposed to be working on an essay for my Master's degree, but I was feeling distracted. So, like any good student, I immediately abandoned my work and started writing. And for the last seven years, Lenni and Margot's world has been my home. I'm so excited to finally send their story out into the world.

The biggest yellow-rose-filled bouquet of thanks to my agent Sue Armstrong at C&W. From the moment Lenni and Margot landed in her inbox, she's given me her support and her guidance. Lenni and Margot wouldn't be where they are today without her. I'm also grateful to the incredible team at C&W – especially Alexander, Jake, Kate, Matilda and Meredith – for championing my book around the world with such energy and enthusiasm.

A huge thank-you to Jane Lawson, my editor at Transworld, who has shared her wisdom, humour and patience with me and who has supported me throughout the editing process. I knew Lenni and Margot were in the right hands the moment we met. And thank you to the whole team at Transworld for believing in Lenni and Margot and working so hard to share their story.

I'm grateful to all of my family who cheered me on, let me ramble at them about word counts and read early drafts and had only nice things to say. And to the friends I've assembled from various places: from the baffling, terrifying years spent at Catholic comprehensive school, from university, from hours spent laughing at improv, and from all the places in between. The excitement we've shared about this journey has been so much fun. And, let's be honest, these people inspired some of the themes of the book: friends who had teenage parties in weird places with me; my dear departed grandparents, who met on a train; a friend who shook my hand when it was time to say goodbye.

I'm very grateful that I married someone who has loved Lenni and Margot from the beginning. Someone who read my rejection emails when I was too scared to open my inbox, who came home crying after reading the end of the book and nicknamed me 'word witch', who jumped about the kitchen with me when my first book deal came in. Thank you for believing, Goose.

But most of all, I am grateful to Lenni for visiting me that January night. She arrived a fully formed voice in my head and this story belongs to her. She kept me company when I was lonely, she reflected my fears when problems were found with my heart and 'sudden cardiac death' was being mentioned with alarming regularity. She taught me patience and persistence. She brought all of this magic into my life.

An interview with Marianne Cronin

First things first – where and when do you write?

The One Hundred Years of Lenni and Margot took just over six years to write – which sounds like such a long time now. The first words of Lenni's that I wrote (which are more or less intact in the opening paragraphs) were written sitting at my desk in my bedroom in January 2014. I'm a total night owl. I'm always trying to change this, because it's not very convenient in a world made for larks, but I love to write at night. It feels like there are fewer distractions. Everything's quieter. I usually work at home, and usually when I'm alone. I get really embarrassed if anyone looks over my shoulder when I'm writing. It's like letting someone peek at the inside of my mind.

The first draft didn't take long – only around three or four months – and I wrote almost all of it at night. Then came the task of shaping it into something that made sense. This is the part that took a long time – by then I was working full-time on a research degree and lecturing, so I edited in stolen moments in the evenings and at weekends. Although there were definitely days when I'd be in my office working on Lenni and Margot instead of on my thesis.

What is your favourite book or books and why?

One of my favourite books (and the book I recommend the most to other people) is *Homegoing* by Yaa Gyasi. I love a good ending and I think it's one of the most beautiful endings to a book I've ever read. I also loved *We Need New Names* by NoViolet Bulawayo – the boldness of Darling's voice really stayed with me. *A Tale for the Time Being* by Ruth Ozeki is another book that's really stayed with me. I loved its oddness.

When I was writing *Lenni and Margot*, *The Hundred-Year-Old Man Who Climbed Out the Window and Disappeared* by Jonas Jonasson and *The Unlikely Pilgrimage of Harold Fry* by Rachel Joyce were early sources of inspiration. The idea of an ordinary person trying to do something extraordinary really resonated with me. In their own way, they both ask, 'What is a life made of?' and that's something I was thinking about when I was working on my book.

Finally, I'll always be glad I read *This Lullaby* by Sarah Dessen when I was fourteen. The protagonist's mother is a writer who leaves notes for characters and stories everywhere. I thought everybody did that. Reading that was the moment when I thought, *Maybe I'm writing ideas all over the place because they belong in a story*. What resulted was a YA ghost love story that lives in a box under my bed. But as much as I cringe at it now, once I had written something of book length, I knew I could do it again. They say the first pancake is always a test.

What is your favourite film and/or TV show?

I'm a bit embarrassed to admit that my favourite film is a children's film. It's the adaptation of Oliver Jeffers' *Lost and Found*. It's simple, but beautiful. Ultimately, it's about friendship and how friendships can save. I don't think I've ever watched it without crying! I also love TV. It's not very high-brow to say, but I love it! My favourite TV shows have all had an influence on how I write dialogue, especially *30 Rock, Unbreakable Kimmy Schmidt, Archer, Green Wing, Peep Show, Fresh Meat, Friday Night Dinner* and *Grace and Frankie*.

What is the last book that made you cry?

There are so many great books that have made me cry. The most recent was *Expectation* by Anna Hope, which explores female friendships and the hopes women have for their lives at different points of adulthood. I don't want to give any spoilers, but there's a scene towards the end that took me by surprise and made me cry.

What is the last book that made you laugh?

I had Tina Fey's *Bossypants* on my 'to read' list for years, and when I finally got around to reading it I adored it. There are so many great lines in it – I kept stopping to read out lines to whoever was near me at the time. I don't think I've ever laughed so much at a single book – with the exception of a book I wrote aged five that my mum recently fished out of the attic. It's called *Lucky Lump* and is about a sentient lump who wears a hat made of flowers and is very unlucky. She gets rained on through an open bus window, which it seemed to my five-year-old mind was one of the worst things that can happen to a sentient lump.

What makes a good story? What do you think is an essential ingredient in your writing?

I think all good stories have a truth to them, even if they're fiction. For me, writing *The One Hundred Years of Lenni and Margot* started with my own fear of dying. There were two things that really got me thinking about death. (I'm so fun!) The first was at a routine medical appointment when a doctor found (to her alarm) that my resting heart rate was around two hundred beats per minute. I had scans and tests (including one where I had to run on a treadmill stripped down to my bra while connected to an ECG machine – not my finest hour), and while I was at the hospital for these appointments, I found myself thinking about how scared I am of dying. Around the same time, a fellow student passed away. I didn't know her well, but she had spent years living in the face of death and her courage was another thing that led me to think about what it might be like to know you were going to die.

In my own writing, I'm drawn to characters who are missing something, and I'm especially drawn to loneliness. When we meet Lenni, she's very lonely – she's not only without her parents, but she's without any true friends. And it's not necessarily a reflection of her, it's just the way things worked out. I think Lenni's journey out of loneliness shows who she is as a person – she assembles a 'found family' in Margot, Arthur and New Nurse. When she dies, she's surrounded by love, and it's love she's found for herself.

Lenni and Margot resist convention in every way. Where did the inspiration for these wonderful personalities come from?

I love unconventional people. A lot of the books, films and TV programmes I love feature unusual, quirky characters, and in real life I definitely gravitate towards people who are eccentric in some way or other. It was only when I started talking about Lenni and Margot during the editing process that I realized how many of my characters have little quirks or personality traits that I've seen in other people or myself.

When I started writing, it really felt as if Lenni had come to visit me in my head. I feel like I should be wrapped in scarves and holding a crystal skull to say that. But honestly, her voice was so clear in my mind. I knew how she'd react to things, how she'd push people's buttons, how she would respond to kindness and to indifference. I mentioned earlier that the first words I wrote are more or less intact in Lenni's opening chapter. Throughout the editing process, so much of the book has changed, but that first scene with Lenni has stayed the same. It makes me happy that the reader's first meeting with Lenni was also my first meeting with Lenni.

Meena is a fascinating character. Where did she come from? Do you know anyone like her in real life?

In the early stages of writing, Meena was inspired by a person I knew briefly in real life. What was magical about this person was that she just didn't care what people thought about her. She was very free. I'm the opposite. I'm very self-conscious and I want everyone to like me. If a stranger is rude to me, I'll think about it for days. From that starting point, Meena evolved into her own person, but that unselfconscious spirit and energy is where I began. I also didn't want Meena to be too idealized – she can be selfish and undependable, but Margot sees those things in her and loves her anyway. One of my favourite parts of the book is when Meena is finally able to tell Margot how she feels (in Vietnamese, of course, because Meena has never done things in conventional ways). If Lenni had been able to grow up, I think she would have been a bit like Meena as an adult – very free, unapologetic.

You are a very visual writer, there are so many colours and images scattered through your book. Do you have a background or any special interest in visual arts?

Whoever marked my GCSE art 'portfolio' would tell you I have no business being an artist, but I love colour and art. There are a lot of people in my life, past and present, who I associate with certain colours or items or images. When I had the idea of Lenni and Margot's friendship growing from an art-therapy class, I went to some painting-while-drinking-wine classes and they gave me a sense of how it might feel to be in an art class. (Lenni's frustration at not being able to paint what she can see in her head came from my own feelings!) I also collected online pictures of amateur art, to get a feel for the kind of things Lenni and Margot might have made.

You get into the heads of two characters who are at opposite ends of the age spectrum. Are you interested in cross-generational friendships? What appeals to you about the potential of such a relationship?

I love the idea of two people becoming friends despite being at completely different points in their lives. I think inter-generational friendships offer so much opportunity for sharing. It's not just the case that Lenni is learning from Margot, but Margot is learning from Lenni. I remember years ago someone telling me that they felt the same inside at forty as they had at eighteen – their body was ageing, but who they were essentially as a person remained the same. I thought that was really interesting. Although Lenni and Margot have sixty-six years separating them, who they are fundamentally is unchanging and their personalities are inherently compatible. Each is exactly what the other needs in a friend. The same is true of Arthur and Lenni. There is a big age gap between them and they have completely different world views, but they become friends without even trying. It's a natural reaction.

Your book is full of delicious humour. Do friends know you as funny, or do you reserve that for your writing?

Oh gosh, I think you'd have to ask them! One of the things that surprised me when *The One Hundred Years of Lenni and Margot* was being read by people outside my immediate family was that they kept mentioning it being funny. I didn't intentionally set out to write a funny book. Sometimes Lenni would come out with something that would make me smile (usually when talking to Arthur), but finding that people have found it funny has been a really nice surprise.

I'm blessed to be surrounded by entertaining friends and family, and I'm lucky to spend time around funny people through the improv scene in the West Midlands. Doing improv is like writing a story on a piece of paper that's already on fire. By the time you've finished, the whole thing is gone for ever and you can never step back and see it as a whole. That felt almost wasteful at first, at first, but it's taught me to jump into 'without overthinking them so much'.

Marianne Cronin was born in 1990. She studied English and Creative Writing at Lancaster University, before earning a PhD in Applied Linguistics from the University of Birmingham. She now spends most of her time writing, with her newly adopted rescue cat sleeping under her desk. When she's not writing, Marianne can be found performing improv in the West Midlands, where she lives. Her debut novel *The One Hundred Years of Lenni and Margot* is to be published around the world and is being adapted into a feature film by a major Hollywood studio.